To Dorothy

— with lots of love

Nov/9

Grey Sunshine

Grey Sunshine

STORIES FROM TEACH FOR INDIA

SANDEEP RAI

ALEPH

ALEPH

ALEPH BOOK COMPANY
An independent publishing firm
promoted by *Rupa Publications India*

First published in India in 2019
by Aleph Book Company
7/16 Ansari Road, Daryaganj
New Delhi 110 002

ISBN: 978-93-88292-79-5

1 3 5 7 9 10 8 6 4 2

For sale in the Indian subcontinent only.

Printed at Parksons Graphics Pvt. Ltd, Mumbai

To the thousands of men and women
Fellows, Staff, Alumni and Students
who are fighting for a better tomorrow

CONTENTS

INTRODUCTION
UNMERITED GRACE

I'll never forget the day I became a teacher.

It was the middle of July in Washington DC. I stood in the summer heat outside a three-storey brown-brick school building where I had my final interview with the principal. Wanting to make a good impression, I had put on my best—and only—suit, a grey one, accompanied by a blue tie and a slightly wrinkled white shirt.

As I pulled open the metal door, I was greeted by an elderly security guard. He wore a look of curiosity and concern.

'Can I help you?' the gentleman asked.

I cleared my throat before muttering a response. 'Yes, sir. I'm looking for Mr Lipscomb. I'm here to interview for the eighth-grade science teacher position.'

'Where you coming from?'

'Teach For America, sir. They told me to come here at 3.30 p.m. sharp.'

He had a scratchy, slightly shrivelled-up voice. He furrowed his eyebrows as he said, 'You'll have to walk down the stairs straight ahead. His office is in the basement.'

He chuckled before his final instruction. 'Oh, and you might want to roll them pants up. It's a little wet down there.'

The original building that housed Sousa Middle School, named after John Philip Sousa, the famous twentieth-century American composer, had deteriorated and was now in a decrepit state. Government officials were planning to shut the building down soon and temporarily relocate students to an abandoned primary school nearby.

As I got to the bottom of the stairs, I stood in a dimly lit hallway. I looked across at the puddles of water and reluctantly rolled up my pants. I tiptoed towards the principal's office, which was, unfortunately, located at the very end of the hall.

Dressed in a pair of blue sports shorts, a white T-shirt and a red sports cap, Mr Lipscomb was clearly not expecting me. He swivelled in his chair and stood up as soon as I knocked.

'What can I do for you?'

'Good afternoon, sir. I'm here to interview for the eighth-grade science teacher position. I believe I have a meeting with you today at 3.30.'

'And why do you want to teach here, son?' Mr Lipscomb skipped past formal introductions.

'Well, sir, to be honest, I want to change lives. I know that sounds clichéd, but I *genuinely* do. And I believe that education is the best way to make that happen.'

Unfazed by my naive yet authentic commitment, he pressed on. 'You understand what you're getting into, don't you?'

I was a little startled by the question. 'Well, I think I do. I know I want to be here.'

'This is a rough school, son. Lord knows we've had enough teachers who discovered that the hard way. And we can't have people coming in here and then leaving. So you need to understand what you're getting yourself into.'

'Well, yes, sir, I do understand that.' As I struggled to search for words that would justify my commitment, Mr Lipscomb interrupted me.

'Are you in good health?'

'Excuse me, sir?'

'How's your health, son? Listen, children have a lot of germs. And they can make you sick in a jiffy. When you get sick, you miss days. And when you miss days, the school misses days as well. We can't be spending our mornings searching for substitutes. And that means we can't have you missing days.'

'I think I'm in good health, sir. No major issues... In fact, I would consider myself very healthy. And I guarantee that I won't let you down.' I wasn't sure what else to say.

Mr Lipscomb scanned my résumé for the next few minutes.

'Well, then, we'll just have to see. You won't be working with me though. I'm retiring next month. But I'm sure the kids will be excited to see you. Just make sure you've got tough skin on the first day. They'll say a lot to throw you off. But you've got to deal with it, you hear?'

A few weeks later, I started my first day of school at Sousa. I had spent most of my summer vacation envisioning my classroom ambience, preparing lesson plans and reviewing all of the pedagogical content we had received at Teach For America's five-week training institute. I would soon learn, however, that no amount of training could ever prepare me for what I would encounter that day. Mr Lipscomb's warnings would soon ring louder—and truer—than I ever anticipated.

'I need you all to please take a seat,' I said politely as I looked across a classroom filled with thirty-five eighth-grade boys.

I had decided to wear my suit and tie again, for the first day of class. I had spent more than an hour the night before, taking it to the local dry-cleaners. The stifling heat—and the lack of air conditioning in the temporary building—made me quickly regret the investment. And having dealt with a slew of horrible events all morning—a broken copy machine and three overcrowded classes with more children than desks—I was grateful that my final period had arrived. I was also starving. Having spent the majority of my savings on the move to DC, I was rationing peanut butter and cups of ramen noodles till my first pay cheque came in.

'I need you to please sit down.' I stood firm and attempted to ensure that my voice was assertive yet calm.

The class, however, ignored me. As I looked across the room, I saw a blur of children laughing, playing and throwing literally anything they could find. As cringeworthy as this was, the most traumatic scene was the one taking place at the back of the class.

'Boys at the back, I need you to please sit down as well.'

Daquan and Brandon sat with a small black radio next to them, rolling dice on the floor. Both of them ignored me. The quarters and nickels in front of them left no doubt that they were gambling. Brandon, six-feet-tall and weighing a little more than ninety kilograms, was big for his age. In fact, he was much larger than me.

'Boys, I'm not going to tell you again. I need you to please sit down,' I repeated.

I was admittedly getting nervous yet trying hard not to show it. I could hear Mr Lipscomb's implorations in the back of my head. Brandon looked up for the first time that afternoon— straight at me. Maintaining eye contact, he reached for the radio with his right hand and turned up the volume.

The class erupted in laughter. Brandon smirked, enjoying the moment. I, however, froze at the front of the room. My face, I'm sure, had turned pale.

'Boys, this is the last time I'm going to tell you. I need you to turn that radio off and I need you to please sit down. If you don't, I'll have no choice but to send you to the principal's office.'

'What did you say, Mr Rai?' Brandon stood up, staring directly at me.

He planted his feet firmly on the ground, mimicking an American football charging stance. He kicked his right foot back a few times, building momentum. The other kids, who were silent for the first time that afternoon, looked at him and then back at me. I was still frozen, not knowing how to react. Thirty seconds later, Brandon ran towards me at full speed.

As a young teacher, my reflexes were thankfully quite fast.

Brandon was expelled from school the next morning and sent to the local juvenile detention centre. I would later learn that it was an expulsion for a history of assaulting teachers. Feeling both distraught and guilty for not being able to control the situation, I decided to speak to the principal. I was keen on paying a visit to the boy's house; I thought speaking to his parents might help, though I was not sure of what I would say. A student getting expelled on my first day, regardless of his past, was the last thing I had wanted.

'Mr Rai, do you realize where Brandon comes from?' the new principal asked.

'No, ma'am. I know he lives in the neighbourhood and that's about it.'

'Mr Rai, Brandon's been expelled three times for a reason. Both his mother and father are in prison. They've been in and out of prison for the past five years. And that boy has been shuffled across so many different foster homes, he doesn't even know who or what to call family anymore.'

I walked out of the principal's office consumed with guilt and sadness. It was a feeling that I would never forget. After that day, I never heard of Brandon again.

~

I grew up in Jackson, Mississippi, a part of the United States commonly referred to as the Deep South. My parents emigrated from India in the early seventies, only a few months after they had gotten married. Both of them were born in present-day Pakistan. When India's Independence—and the ensuing Partition—finally happened in 1947, their families spent months walking across the border and living in migration settlements, before they eventually landed in rural India.

Getting out of the country meant beating odds that were seemingly insurmountable. As children of farmers, they had harrowing tales of India's early migration camps, where tens of thousands of families shared tents that were often attacked and pillaged by warring factions. They would talk often of post-Partition violence and of the hardships their families endured as a result of extreme poverty. When they finally made it to the

US, they sought any job that would offer them a glimpse of the American dream—of a promise rooted in better opportunity.

After several years of juggling teaching with a number of jobs in the service industry, they eventually decided to purchase a second-hand grocery store. It was situated in downtown Jackson, one of Mississippi's poorest but most populated urban neighbourhoods. The store was often buzzing with people buying vegetables, paying utility bills and even cashing their monthly cheques.

Because of that store, my parents had the means to send me to one of the city's best private schools. There, I received an education that is largely responsible for the accomplishments and privilege I enjoy today. Every day after school, for fifteen years, I would spend my evenings working with my parents. I loved knowing that I was contributing to their success. From mopping floors and running errands as a five-year-old to managing cash registers and restocking groceries as a teenager, I learned the importance of hard work.

At the same time, though, I found myself face-to-face with the depths of the inequity surrounding us. The store frequently bore witness to many of the issues that invariably accompanied poverty in the United States: issues rooted in marginalization, exclusion, racial discrimination and violence. I have vivid memories of running to the back of the store, when I was eight, to hide from masked gunmen demanding money. That was the first time we were robbed. Over the years, I grew perplexed, confused and oftentimes terrified as I witnessed poverty translate into violent attacks and repeated burglaries.

Like many Indian parents in the US, mine offered me two choices growing up: I could become a doctor or a businessman. Both professions, in their minds, opened doors to a world that would inevitably be better than the one they inherited. My elder siblings—both of who practise medicine—invited me to shadow surgeries and witness autopsies in local morgues. They would read medical literature to me and talk incessantly about the grades needed to attend the country's finest medical colleges. By the time I was seven, I had memorized the names and locations of all 206 bones in the human body. I would also talk openly about reproduction, digestion and a range of other biological processes. These were idiosyncrasies that didn't make me very popular in school, but I didn't care. I was admittedly enthralled by the prospect of working in emergency rooms and performing complex life-saving surgeries one day.

All of those dreams—and the whimsical fantasies that accompanied them—took an unexpected turn when I met a man named Keith Tonkel. I had begrudgingly tagged along with a friend to a Sunday morning service at Wells Methodist Church, where Keith was preaching. Located less than 500 metres from my parents' store, the church was intentionally situated in a low-income community. For three decades of running the church, Keith resisted implorations to move it to a 'better' neighbourhood. He led it through the civil rights movement in the fifties and sixties and other similarly trying times. Throughout, he insisted that the congregation stay close to a community that needed it.

Once I was inside, much to my surprise, I was enthralled by what I saw and heard. Earlier that morning, an African American woman from the neighbourhood had ambled into the church. An hour before the service started, she began sobbing uncontrollably.

'What's wrong? What happened?' Keith asked.

'He left me. He left me,' she was screaming.

'Who left you? Try to tell me what happened. Try to calm down.'

'I can't calm down. You don't understand. He left me. That house was all I had. And, now, I have nothing. I have nothing.'

The woman reeked of alcohol and urine. Her clothes were soiled. She also wasn't making much sense. People stared, mostly in disgust, but they were also curious to see what Keith would do. Any rational person would have easily turned the woman away. She was, after all, drunk and hysterical. Keith, however, not only took her in—he spent the next sixty minutes talking to her, trying to calm her down.

'Let us remember why we have this church here,' he said two hours later in a sermon. 'We are called upon to serve those that need us the most—those that the world has discarded. We are called upon to serve where darkness exists. And regardless of what you or I may rationalize or believe, living in poverty takes you through some pretty dark alleys.' Keith had a voice that reminded me of Louis Armstrong. Listening to him speak made me feel warm and accepted. Even though his message was provocative, he managed to bring his audience gently into the fold.

'As we walk out of these doors, let us remember that our brothers and sisters in need, regardless of what they've done or who they may be, are God's children. It is far too easy to look at those suffering and cast an eye of judgement—to ascribe their condition to lack of hard work or a fate that's in their control. But it's much harder to accept, to remember that we are no more deserving than them.'

Keith paused again and looked out at the audience with an expression that I'll never forget—one that was simultaneously wistful and hopeful.

'Brother and sisters—all of us, including you and me, are in desperate need of grace that is unequivocally unmerited. We would do ourselves a whole lot of good in remembering that we are recipients of that sunshine, every single day.'

I stepped out of the church and stared down the road towards the store I knew all too well; it was a scene I had memorized. I thought about all that I had witnessed growing up, all the violent attacks and accounts of discrimination. This time, though, something felt different. I realized that many of those incidents were merely a result of people desperately searching for a means to survive. Faced with issues deeply rooted in marginalization, exclusion, racial discrimination and violence, they, too, were searching for opportunity.

My relationship with Keith grew over the months and years that followed. I wasn't a particularly religious person. Growing up in a traditional Indian household, I had rarely paid heed to Christian theology. My conversations with Keith, however, managed to transcend all of that. I began spending every Sunday in the pews, listening to sermons that dealt with themes of acceptance, service, poverty and love. Underlying each of these sermons was a message that I found impossible to ignore: our lives are measured by how we treat the least amongst us, by our recognition that we are all recipients of unmerited grace.

Three years after I first stepped into Wells—in my final year of college—I told my parents that I would no longer be pursuing a career in medicine. Instead, I would be joining Teach For America, a programme that recruits college graduates and places them in some of the country's most challenging schools as full-time teachers. While I did not realize it at the time, I would effectively be accepting a calling that would bring me much closer to my motherland.

~

The two years I taught at Sousa Middle School were immensely difficult yet deeply rewarding. In the first few months, my lessons were frequently interrupted by fights and heated arguments. Children arrived at school with a plethora of issues, spanning gang violence to domestic abuse to premature demises of loved ones. Through these struggles, my children taught me the redemptive power of working with poverty. As I began peeling back the facades of toughness and jadedness, I discovered children that were filled with love, but had every reason to wear those impenetrable masks. I met children who were carelessly shuffled between foster homes, teenagers who had witnessed more violence than a war-torn nation and parents who worked tirelessly to put food on the table. They faced challenges that many would deem unbearable. Yet, every morning, they chose to wake up and walk into our school. They chose to fight for a better future—even one that, on most days, seemed distant and out of reach.

I felt connected to my students—and to the communities of DC—because they struck chords that were reminiscent of my childhood. Yet I couldn't escape the reality that my story was, for the vast majority of Indians, an anomaly. While conditions for minorities in America were undeniably severe, they would never compare to the hardships confronting the world's most marginalized. Moving back to India, only two years after joining Sousa, was a decision rooted in the same realization that elicited my first career change. Searching for our brothers and sisters most in need demanded looking beyond our borders.

When I first arrived in Mumbai, I was daunted by the massive cultural and lifestyle changes that faced me. I had left behind friends and siblings who, together, comprised everything I had ever known. I assured my family that I would stay for no more than two years. I was going to help get Teach For India, a model inspired by its American equivalent, off the ground.

What has kept me here, ten years later, is that I have discovered something far graver than all that I left behind. India houses 73 million people who live in extreme poverty—second only to Nigeria in being home to the largest number of poor in the world.[1] Hundreds of millions of Indians live in conditions that are replete with garbage-constructed walls, violent-stricken alleys, and have little, if anything, to eat. More than 60 per cent of India's 320 million children are destined to either never attend school or drop out before they even reach the eleventh standard[2]. Only about 25 per cent of its population will step foot into a college.[3] And for minority Muslim populations—some of the country's most marginalized and discriminated—young girls have a 2 per cent chance of earning a college degree;[4] one of the biggest determinants of success in today's world. Every time I step out of my house I am reminded of this reality. And along with it comes the realization that this reality was once my parents' as well.

When my parents emigrated from Pakistan as small children, they travelled for more than 500 kilometres, finally settling in a small town south of Kota, Rajasthan. Growing up, my mother would often grab a candle and sneak into a small shed to find solace, so that she could study at night. Being the children of farmers, my parents' childhoods were often swayed for the worse by unexpected crop yields, famines and natural disasters.

One summer, I made a trip to Rajasthan where I would spend several days talking to aunts, uncles and cousins whom I had never met before. I paid that long overdue visit primarily because my uncle had just passed away. I wasn't particularly looking forward to the awkward chatter in my broken Hindi. But I was eager to better understand family members who, not having had the opportunity to graduate, still worked fourteen-hour shifts as stone-cutters and farmers.

'You're lucky,' my cousin told me one afternoon.

'What do you mean?' I asked, though I could think of a thousand reasons I was lucky.

'Your parents made it out. Your life is so different now. You are working with the poor. But you don't have to *deal* with all of this.'

His curt yet stark reminder cut deeply. 'Yeah, I guess I am really lucky.'

Sensing that my tone was turning remorseful, he chimed back in: 'Don't be sorry. Life is filled with luck. Sometimes we're lucky. And sometimes we're not.'

I wasn't quite prepared to discover just how contradictory our lives actually are. Perhaps what's kept me here is the recognition that India's poor experience a level of inequity and oppression that is incomparable to anything I've witnessed before. It's a level of suffering that, for hundreds of millions of Indians, blunts any attempt to search for better opportunities. And it's one that underlies my entire existence.

~

This book is about getting closer to inequity. It is an attempt to capture a systemic injustice that underpins the very foundations of India's education system—one that, if left unfixed, will threaten the livelihoods and futures of hundreds of millions of powerless citizens. It is a crisis—arguably, of unprecedented proportions—that threatens the very moral and social fabric of our society.

Over the years, I have met thousands of children and families who have taught me what inequity means. That perpetual process of discovery, rooted in being proximate to our country's poor, has been painful and stirring. Their stories are often harrowing; yet they capture the heart and soul of what makes this country's poverty so evocatively powerful.

They are stories like Nandini's. Growing up in a low-income community in Pune, Nandini Bhandarkar first came to Teach For India when she was thirteen years old. I've had the privilege of watching, mostly from afar, this little girl grow up from a child whose very existence felt threatened to a young woman who has not only overcome the boundaries of her community, but has become a symbol that demonstrates the power of educational opportunity.

In Part One of this book, you'll travel along the journeys of the lives of three of India's children, including Nandini. Through their trials and tribulations, you'll get close to inequity. You'll learn about the injustices that plague India's most impoverished communities. And you'll gain a first-hand glimpse into the conditions that affect hundreds of millions of Indian children. In order to protect the identities of these children, their names and some identifying details (like the names of some of the people in their lives) have been changed.

This book is also about getting closer to hope. It is about recognizing the tremendous opportunity and promise that await us if we can commit to rewriting our nation's social contract, if we can uplift a population that desperately wants to rise up. It's about opening our eyes to witness examples of change and transformation that, today, are proving that a rewritten contract is entirely possible. These examples, we'll soon learn, are deeply ingrained in stories of leadership.

Santosh More, a former engineer at Infosys, left his job to be one of the first Teach For India Fellows in 2009. Hailing from a business family in Bihar, it was hard for his parents to understand and accept his decision. Undeterred, he joined and immersed himself fully in the classroom and community. In the first few weeks, when he discovered that only ten out of the forty-eight students in his class were actually attending school, he rented a cycle for a rupee and rode around the community, going door-to-door and convincing parents to send their kids to school. Today, Santosh's experiences have led him to start an organization of his own, Mantra4Change, where he leads a team of thirty passionate individuals. Together they work with 50 principals and 350 teachers from under-resourced schools in Bengaluru to deliver a high-quality education to 12,000 students.

Jai Mishra, another Teach For India Fellow, applied three times before finally getting accepted into the programme. Having grown up in a small, impoverished village in rural Maharashtra, passing his tenth-standard examination and graduating from college was an uphill battle. With an opportunity to finally earn an income that would change his life forever, Jai recognized that the rarity of his story was, simply put, unjust. After spending two years transforming the lives of thirty children, he's now committed his next ten years to uplifting an entire community in Pune called Vadgaon Budruk. His vision, as he puts it, is to make Vadgaon Budruk an exemplar community that lives and reflects the ideals captured in the Constitution of India.

Merlia Shaukath, a former Teach For India staff member, felt a sense of restlessness ever since she was a young girl. For the longest time she was almost—in her words—'embarrassed' about the many privileges she had: money, access to a high-quality education and an immensely supportive family. Early in life, she resolved to work in the development sector, though she thought that the only way to give back was to become a teacher. Today, she runs Madhi Foundation, which she founded in 2015. Madhi strengthens the foundational learning programme for lower grades. They work directly wih the Government of Tamil Nadu, consulting them on many aspects including curriculum and the use of technology to track learning outcomes. Merlia hopes to create replicable models that can eventually be implemented in other states in India.

In Part Two and Part Three of this book, you'll learn the stories of four young leaders who, like Santosh, Jai and Merlia, took an extraordinary risk. You'll follow their journeys from young adults searching for purpose, to teachers who spent two years in India's most struggling classrooms as Fellows, to alumni of our programme who are today transforming the system. There are thousands more who decided to bet on our country's future and walk this path. Today, they are all doing incredible work. The stories in this book are just a few of a much wider movement.

Through their work—through their stories—our hope is that you learn the story of Teach For India. You'll see the product of a woman who has dedicated more than twenty-five years of service into this work. You'll learn that what underlies this organization of 4,000 leaders—275 staff members, 3,000 alumni, 1,000 current Fellows and 38,000 students are stories—stories of transformation, of leadership and of struggle.

This book, perhaps more than anything, is about getting closer to greyness. It's a journey into stories that, quite honestly, don't always end well. As you read, you'll discover—just as we have—that embedded in every story of hope is a story of truth, a story of struggle and hardship reminding us that, for India's poor, sunshine is always chequered with greyness.

Along the way, our hope is that you are transformed, that you begin to grapple with the reality that while 4,000 people fighting for change is laudable, it's far from what our country needs. My hope, therefore, is that through this book you discover your role in solving India's most urgent and pressing crisis.

PART ONE

ONE

THE ONE-WOMAN ARMY

'He won't let me study. We've all tried to tell him, *but he just won't let me*,' Yasmin shouts. Her cheeks are now the same red hue as her hijab.

'But I know he loves me. He has to love me. I can see it in his eyes. I can hear it in his voice.' Yasmin speaks earnestly of her father, her voice trembling ever so slightly.

We've been talking for more than an hour. Under the intensity of her gaze, I'm also struggling to take in my new surroundings. Yasmin lives in a two-room, 37-square-metre pukka construction along with her family of five. The vibrancy and warmth of their home belie any inadequacies that its limited size presents. I steal a glance at the bustling stove where a plump five-foot-five woman in her mid-forties is confidently stirring a mixture of onions, garlic, tomatoes and chillies. The aroma is surprisingly nostalgic. It reminds me of the kitchen I spent my childhood walking in and out of every morning for fifteen years. Her mother smiles at me coyly. Then, she turns her attention back to the steaming pot.

The wall across us stands behind a mismatched collection of flat mattresses, Indian spices, metal containers and perfectly stacked clothes. It's an eclectic pile that serves many purposes. Squarely in the middle of the room is a line of neatly placed glasses filled with Coca-Cola. Next to the glasses are plastic bowls overflowing with potato chips and biscuits.

'Kuch kha lo (Eat something),' Yasmin's father insists as he invites me to indulge in the snacks for a third time. He's a sprawling, heavy-set man dressed in a white kurta and taqiyah.

Five years ago Yasmin's father experienced an injury that

3

sapped the family's income, making her mother the primary breadwinner. She converted their house into a biryani stand where they take orders from nearby businesses and residents. Her mother cooks and sells biryani for thirteen hours a day, every day of the week. At the end of the month, this venture brings Yasmin's family of five approximately 6,500 rupees. It's meagre, but enough to cover their daily expenses and the cost of rent in Jahangirpuri, home to one of Delhi's largest slum populations.

I've clearly interrupted their plans tonight. They had just finished packing to leave for a five-day trip to Jodhpur, where they'll visit Yasmin's sister and brother-in-law. I'm feeling not only more than a little guilty, but also overwhelmed by their generosity.

Yasmin's parents have been mostly silent. Unable to comprehend English, they're trying intently to follow along the troughs and peaks of Yasmin's pained facial expressions. Yasmin's father is insistent that his youngest daughter drop out at the end of the school year. Being in the eighth standard, she will soon have completed more schooling than any member of her family. It's an accomplishment that isn't lost on her parents.

'She's the smartest in the family, and we know she's doing remarkably well in school,' her mother chimes in with a beaming smile, hoping her words of praise will calm Yasmin down.

'Yes, we are proud of her. But it is now time for Yasmin to move to the madrasa. This school is only getting in the way of that,' her father asserts.

'Why do you want her to study in a madrasa? Why not continue in school?' I ask in slightly broken Hindi. It's been almost ten years since I packed my bags and moved to India from the US, but my Hindi language skills are still wanting. It's times like these that make me wish I had watched more Bollywood movies growing up.

'Look, I just want her to be a good person. In the madrasa, she'll learn the fundamentals of the Islamic faith—morals, principles and traditions. She has learned how to read and write in school. She is good at mathematics too. Now I want her to also learn to live a life of faith. I want her to give back to society. I want her to be better than her brothers and sisters—better than the scoundrels running around Jahangirpuri who are up to no good.'

'But I don't want to go to the madrasa, Abu,' Yasmin implores. 'I want to study in school. I'll wear a burqa. I'll continue to pray and read the Quran. But I also want to continue learning English, math and science. I'll do both deen (religion) and duniya (worldly activities), I promise you. I've worked so hard to come this far. If I leave now how will I grow up to become a teacher? No high school dropout becomes a teacher! I want to help children— *really* help children—children like me.'

'I've seen the quality of the education children get at your school, Yasmin. It's a waste of time. That school is filled with violence, drugs and abuse.'

He turns to me as he adds, 'Sandeep, I agree that Yasmin has had one really good teacher from Teach Of India.' I almost interrupted to correct him: Teach *For* India, before thinking better of it. 'But most of the teachers don't care, you see. And the kids are just spreading bad values. If I leave her in that school, she'll come out the worst possible human being.'

'I know you're afraid of school westernizing me, Abu, but I'll follow Islam. Just let me stay.'

'The biryani is ready. Yasmin, get up. Help me serve the food,' Yasmin's mother announces.

'I just want to study, Abu.' Yasmin reiterates as she stands up. 'This isn't fair.'

As I continue listening to Yasmin's father, I find the conviction with which I entered beginning to wane. The irony of this whole scenario slowly begins to dawn on me. For the majority of the last two hours, this girl has been speaking with me in fluent English, while her father sits behind her, unable to comprehend a word. It is her education, replete with Western littering, that's allowing Yasmin to converse privately and confidently. And in the background is a man shaped not by a stereotypical extremist bent but by his dogmatic belief that Islam—and the accompanying madrasa—offers her the only path to leading a good life. He wants nothing but the best for his daughter, a future that he believes simply isn't achievable through Delhi's public education system. His scepticism arises not from a sense of misguided distrust; instead, it's a product of everything he's witnessed first-hand.

~

Understanding the tussle between Yasmin and her father demands a closer look at the realities of Jahangirpuri, one of Delhi's poorest slums. Yasmin has a only a 2 per cent likelihood of fulfilling her dream. Assuming she needs a bachelor's degree to teach, she'd need to be one of the seven lakh female Muslim students enrolled in higher education. That may seem like a big number, but consider that more than 3.4 crore Indian students attend college.[5] Going strictly by the numbers, it is next to impossible that she will ever become a teacher. And her family's track record mirrors that statistical reality, with none of her older brothers, sisters or parents having made it past eighth standard. It's a reality that will soon put enormous pressure on Yasmin's future.

Jahangirpuri is one of Delhi's many resettlement communities, formed in 1975 during the prime ministership of Indira Gandhi. Her now infamous declaration of Emergency forced millions of Indian families out of their slums and into reconstructed pukka houses spread across the northeastern landscape of Delhi. More than forty years later, the majority of these families and their descendants—comprising more than 200,000 people—still live here. The alleys of Jahangirpuri are bustling with people, stalls and activity that span the full twenty-four-hour cycle of the day.

They're also incredibly cramped. Every house, rarely larger than 46 square metres, often houses multiple generations: siblings, parents, grandparents, uncles, aunts and even cousins.

Jahangirpuri is divided, alphabetically, into twelve blocks. Over the years, an inevitable order of segregation has settled in within these communities—a separation that mirrors the larger divisions of Indian society. D Block, by and large, houses the Hindus. B and C Blocks house the Muslims. EE Block, with a rent that's 10 per cent higher, houses families that are marginally more economically advantaged. Even today, it's largely anathema for people of different religions or castes to loiter into a block that isn't a part of their 'predetermined territory'.

Last but not the least, there are the Bengali refugees. These are people who have steadily trickled into Delhi over the decades and now live on the outskirts of Jahangirpuri. Residents talk about the Bengalis with a tone of fear and disdain. Everyone has a story of running into them. They are stories that usually end in violence.

Yet, between the blocks of segregation and the violence that crosses these contrived boundaries, the community includes several shared public spaces: small gardens, places for the community to gather, restaurants and even a rundown cinema that only twenty years ago was the place to be. The Azadpur Sabzi Mandi, one of the biggest employers in the community, thrives with people and business.

Right in the middle of Jahangirpuri is the government-run Industrial Training Institute (ITI), a vocational centre that offers livelihood skill development courses for youths and adults alike. Established in 1985, it operates with a mandate to give 'technical training to the backward and weaker sections of the society'.[6] Yet, nowhere in Jahangirpuri will residents find access to colleges or any other source of higher education. There are two government-run primary and secondary schools, but nothing beyond the twelfth standard. When I asked a local public official his thoughts on this, his reply was telling: 'Let's be realistic about what's possible with this community, shall we?'

The school, which Yasmin and more than half of Jahangirpuri's children attend, has an ominous feel that envelops the entire building. A big, rusted metal gate greets you at the entrance. Past the gate is an open, barren field surrounded by concrete multistorey buildings on every side. As I walk past the field and into one of the buildings, I immediately hear a shrill scream in the distance, to my right.

A tall, slender man in his early thirties is standing in a corner of the corridor. Dressed in a neatly-pressed, beige button-down shirt, he wields a belt in his hands. A child, no older than thirteen, is next to him, his hands tightly grasping a desk in front of him. The man is raising his hand so high that it seems like he's in a bar fight. With every raise, he brings the metal part of his belt down on the child's bottom. And with every hit, the child wails. I begin to walk towards the man until he sees me and stops.

The man wielding the belt is Manoj Kumar, the headmaster, and he promptly rationalizes his actions. 'I know we're not supposed to hit children. I know it's wrong,' he says sheepishly. 'But I have a weak spot. I just can't tolerate evil.'

'What do you mean evil, sir?' I press him to say more, hoping he'll clarify.

'Some of these kids, they are evil indeed. They are just plain notorious. Look, how old are you?'

'Thirty-two, sir.'

'Hmm. Listen, I've been doing this since you were in diapers. I've worked in schools where kids would bring cans of alcohol and drink out of them first thing in the morning, where girls were fighting, stealing and doing drugs every day.'

You can tell that Headmaster Kumar is used to being taken seriously. His position is a badge of honour he wears with pride.

'Why do you think these schools are in such bad shape?' I ask him.

'The parents just don't care,' he replies, his voice growing louder and sterner. 'They only send their kids here because it's free—because the school gives them free lunch.'

'Hmm... Well, how do we make this school better?' I ask. 'How do we make the state of education better? How do we give these students better futures?'

Headmaster Kumar is clearly not used to being interrogated. Growing slightly agitated with my lengthy questions, he sits down and takes off his glasses before responding. 'You want to know what we should do? We should get rid of everything. Get rid of the benefits. Get rid of the schemes. Get rid of the reservations. Get rid of the RTE. We'll fix this when people realize that the only thing that will save them is hard work.'

Headmaster Kumar brings the same sense of bravado to every interaction. When we're sitting in his office that afternoon, two children walk in because they've been caught loitering in the halls.

'What have you done?' The headmaster's question is directed as much at the boys as at the staff member accompanying them. One of the boys looks down sheepishly and begins to answer.

'I was in the hall—' begins the boy.

Before he can finish, the guard next to him—a tall, sleepy gentleman—interrupts, 'Sir, he threw a rock at a light bulb outside and broke it.'

The headmaster shot me an 'I told you so' look. He looks back at the guard and declares: 'Call his parents. Tell them to bring 300 rupees to the school by this afternoon. They'll pay for the light. If they can't, he can't come to school.'

He looks back at me, feeling fully justified in his agitation. 'Get rid of the free ride. That's how you fix it. There is no free ride.'

The parents of Jahangirpuri hold a similarly bleak view of Yasmin's school. They convey the pain and frustration that's built up over the years. 'It's violent and disgusting,' exclaims a parent during my conversation with him. 'There's just no discipline, so the kids get away with everything. They don't learn. They just run around in that school.'

Perhaps the most hard-hitting are the reflections of a shopkeeper I met while exploring the community. Old, frail and in her sixties, she wears an expression that is both pained and tired. She and her husband have been running a vegetable shop for fifteen years that, occupying about 14 square metres, is smaller than any business I've ever seen. Inside it are trays filled with onions, tomatoes, cabbages, carrots, garlic and an assortment of other vegetables. Hanging above the vegetables are blackened jars half-filled with candy. Between the jars and the vegetables, hordes of flies swarm so voraciously that I find myself hesitating to walk through. Fortunately, she hurries through and leads me upstairs.

We're sitting in the middle of her dimly-lit, single-room home situated on the second floor of a run-down pukka construction. 'You're talking about an excellent education but you just don't understand. This school can't even give us the basics. They can't enforce discipline. They can't keep kids out of fights. They can't ensure that kids learn. Are my kids better off in that school or at home with me?'

I realize I'm apprehensive of my own answer to that question.

She and her friends nevertheless hold Headmaster Kumar in high regard. These parents see him as a disciplinarian that the community and the school need. For them, he is someone with the authority to bring order to an otherwise lawless situation: a brave, glorious lion tamer in a circus of unruly children. They pause every time I mention his name. And all of them echo the shopkeeper, who says, 'I've heard that things are changing because of him. He commands respect. Maybe he can fix this school.'

The parents—like everyone else in Jahangirpuri—are starved for hope, and they have reason to be cynical. Statistically, about four out of every five kids are destined to drop out before they even get to the tenth standard.[7] They will continue living in the cycle of poverty, just like their parents and the many generations before them.

~

Yasmin holds fear and disdain for most men in her life. It arises from a feeling of contempt that spans far beyond her relationships with her father or even Headmaster Kumar. When Yasmin was in the second standard, a man began inviting her to his Jahangirpuri home after school. As an eight-year-old, Yasmin found the invitation harmless. Once there, he would ask Yasmin to remove her clothes—a move she initially found innocuous. For the next eighteen months, this pattern continued.

One day, Yasmin told a close friend about what had been happening. Before that conversation, she hadn't thought much of it. Her friend's reaction though—stemming from shock and dismay—made Yasmin grasp the gravity of her encounter. She grew embarrassed and angry. And she refused to tell anyone. Instead, she tried to find ways to avoid him. She would take different routes home and vary her departure timings. The tactics worked until he eventually caught on. On numerous occasions, he tried to grab her and force her into his house.

Yasmin concluded that leaving D Block would provide her only path to respite. Still insistent on not telling anyone, she spent more than six months coming up with excuses and, eventually, convinced them to move. She told them that she had no friends in D Block, that she hated their current house and that the surrounding community was dangerous. Eventually, they relented. It's been five years since that experience. And she still hasn't told anyone about it.

The incident has left her severely scarred. Her sensitivity and sense of empathy, however, animates her beliefs. She now forcefully argues that the government should be doing much more about the issue.

'I believe that the government needs to open up a department dedicated to fighting sexual harassment and abuse. I never got justice but I want to ensure everyone else does. When I get older, I want to open up an organization that works with women—with the victims of harassment and rape. They shouldn't have to deal with it alone.'

While she's undoubtedly passionate, I soon realize she's also grown hardened and bitter. She believes, more than anything else, that she's living in an isolated world. 'My brothers and sisters have often told me that they hate the colour of my skin and that I'm not a part of the family. They've told me that they found me in a dustbin. And that if I were lighter, they would welcome me with open arms.'

'I've learned that I'm a one-woman army,' Yasmin concludes. 'I don't want anyone's help to solve my problems. I'm strong enough to solve my own. I've stopped caring what the world thinks of me. I don't need their help.'

~

Feelings of resignation and despair permeate Jahangirpuri. Some families have simply lost the will to dream because they've stopped believing that a better life is possible. Others have never known anything else and, as a result, believe that dreams of greater opportunity are nothing more than fairy tales. For some, like fourteen-year-old Arbaaz and his mother, the pain of their current reality is so overwhelming that any effort to change it seems futile.

Arbaaz is a diffident little boy who attends the same school as Yasmin and lives right next door. His voice is excessively soft, to the point of being inaudible, and he rarely makes eye contact.

'What do you want to do after you finish school?' I ask.

'I just want to get a job.'

'What kind of job would you like to do?'

'Any job. I just want to be earning when I get out of school. I *need* to earn.'

'Okay. What do you like to do in your free time?'

Arbaaz stares at me blankly.

'You must have some interests? Do you play any sports?'

'No.'

'Then what do you do after school? School ke baad kya kartein ho?'

'Nothing. I'm just here at home.'

I look at his mother for some kind of explanation.

'I don't let him go outside,' his mother jumps in. 'Three years ago, a local boy pulled a blade out on Arbaaz and threatened to kill him if he ever saw him again. Since then, I refuse to let him out of the house. He walks to school and then comes right back home. Along that 500-metre path, he is to keep his head down and avoid eye contact with anyone.'

'What about your time in school? Do you like it there?'

'Ha!' Arbaaz's mother exclaims, speaking for him again. 'The government isn't interested in D Block, so how do you expect the kids to take an interest in school? The government knows the kids here can't get anywhere. So they send us the worst teachers in town.' Her voice bears no trace of emotion. Instead, she offers an explanation that is both direct and clinical.

'Why do you send your kids to school, especially if you know it's so bad?'

'I send Arbaaz to school because I don't want him to be exploited. I want him to learn. I want him to have a better life than I do. You don't need to tell me that the school is bad. I know that. But what choice do I have? What's the alternative? I'm lucky that Arbaaz is a boy. You know, my sister had to pull her two girls out after the fifth standard. It was too violent. Arbaaz may not talk much, but he can handle the fights. He has to. As long as there's a school, he's going to have to put up with all of this so that he can finish his education.'

Arbaaz's mother talks with a sense of realism and logic that is jarring and depressing. I notice that she looks far older than a woman in her mid-thirties. Over the next few hours, we discuss Arbaaz's battles in Jahangirpuri: the dangers he's faced, his fights with local Bengalis, the simmering tension between Hindus and Muslims and the apparent bleakness of his future. She does most of the talking, and as she speaks, my mind drifts to the afternoon I spent with Headmaster Kumar. I think about his declarations of 'hard work' and his conviction that parents 'just don't care'.

~

Spending my days and evenings with the families and children of Jahangirpuri forced me to acknowledge, in ways that I hadn't before, the deeply damaging effect of hopelessness on the very essence of the human spirit. Every family, child and public official had recounted incidents that were harrowing and alarming. Underlying their words was a starvation of hope that carried a permanent aura of darkness. It made me confront the pervasive power of despair to break the human will. If the 200,000 residents of Jahangirpuri are largely without hope, and the people intended to serve them are similarly despondent, can they even begin to believe in change and redemption?

On the rare instances when I've heard families daring to dream of a better life, they talk of neighbouring wealthy communities, like Adarsh Nagar and Shalimar Bagh. They speak of worlds with functional schools. They speak of alleys with no violence. They speak of cleaner streets. They speak, quite honestly, of the fundamental rights that any human being should be afforded.

Yet, very few of them have visited any of these surrounding communities. They've rarely left Jahangirpuri. They talk wistfully of the 'children who grow up on *that* side of town' and the 'life in Delhi's more "secure" streets'. These places are more the stuff of local myth and folklore—a world of better prospects.

After spending hours chatting with parents and children, I meander back to the local community centre where I am staying the night. Before I go to bed, I take advantage of the extraordinary view this three-storey building offers. From my open window, I can see the thousands of pukka constructions that have now become permanent homes for more than 200,000 citizens. I look at the river to the east and the waste dump to the north. The famous cinema that so many residents had vividly described is also visible. I try imagining it in its former glory, buzzing with action and energy.

As I gaze across Jahangirpuri, I think of my conversations with Yasmin and of the many memories that the families had so graciously shared with me. I think of the hundreds of families I had talked to over the course of my career; they had echoed sentiments that were eerily similar. And I thought of the thousands of children we had served but I had never actually *listened* to—whose struggles I had never fully understood.

And, yet, I thought most of the promise of hope.

That's the thing about folklore. However dreamy or far-fetched it may seem, it fuels hope and ultimately becomes a lighthouse for the children of Jahangirpuri to aspire towards. The truth, however, is that we need *real* stories of success to sustain their aspirations—to fuel their desire to hope.

Betting on hope, for most people, amounts to nothing more than betting on a segment of your imagination. It isn't strategy; it isn't concrete. And it's excruciatingly tough when you don't have tangible evidence that tells you success is achievable.

Therein lies the ultimate dilemma. To eventually see success—to see a life with greater opportunity—perhaps what we need *first* is hope. Václav Havel, writer, political dissident and former president of Czechoslovakia, argues that during the era of Soviet domination the only thing that impoverished citizens of Eastern Europe needed was hope. They may have wanted many things such as more money and more diplomatic pressure from the West, but the only thing they actually *needed* was hope. According to Havel, hope is more than a mere preference for optimism. It is an 'orientation of the spirit' that allows people to live in hopeless places, to deal with hopeless schools and still believe that a better future is within reach. When faced with the absurdity that conditions like those in Jahangirpuri force on the human spirit, it might be good to remember, as Havel posits, that 'life is too precious a thing to permit its devaluation by living without hope'.[8]

Perhaps what the people of Jahangirpuri, and even little Yasmin, need the most is that very 'orientation of the spirit'. They need more reasons to believe that betting on hope is worth their time.

TWO

EVERYTHING RUNS ON MONEY

'I love design. I love to paint. And most of all, I love lines. There's something fascinating about them. A line starts as a zigzag. But if you let it play out for long enough, it has the potential to turn into something stunning.'

Asif and I have been walking all afternoon through the narrow streets of Govandi. We had just passed a run-down municipal Marathi school before abruptly stopping to absorb the magnificence of the sight—and the smell—in front of us.

'That's where it all comes. Every single day, they just dump more and more,' Asif says in his signature high-pitched voice.

We're staring at the Deonar Landfill, which accumulates more than 4,000 tonnes of garbage every day from towns and districts across Mumbai. It is India's oldest and Asia's largest dumping ground.[9] To put this in perspective, it is a whopping 92 times the size of Lord's, the famous cricket stadium in London. It's also less than 200 metres away from Asif's low-income private school, where he's spent the last ten years studying.

All that separates us from this massive dump is a thinly wired, partly broken fence. We watch as dozens of residents toting garbage bags and gloves climb over it and jump to the other side. Some of them are ragpickers. Others are teenagers looking for a private spot to get away from the unfathomably crowded streets of Govandi. Because of the combustible methane the garbage releases, residents are subjected to raging fires every few weeks.

'One February, the fire was so large that even authorities couldn't contain it for thirty days,' Asif tells me. 'The burning got so bad and lasted for so long, it covered all of Row Eight in ashes. It was kind of disgusting to think that those ashes were essentially the waste of the city disintegrating right at my doorstep.'

Asif has impeccable manners—the kind that would make any mother proud. He insists on opening doors. He's careful to always walk behind you. The few times I try to insist on a reversal, he politely interjects, 'Please, you're my guest and you're in my community.' These are social graces that are not only hard to find, but also make it impossible not to like him.

After a few awestruck minutes at the landfill, we continue walking towards Asif's house. 'That's where my best friend was born, sixteen years ago,' he says, pointing to the left. In the middle of a barren patch of land is a building surrounded by piles of run-down automobile parts.

'Your friend was born in a junkyard?'

Asif laughs. 'Sandeep bhaiya, this is the local clinic.'

I must have still look confused, because Asif feels the need to reiterate.

'You don't believe me. I can see it on your face. But this is a hospital. Trust me. Let's keep walking.'

Sure enough, less than a hundred metres ahead, we pass the medical sign.

Asif aspires to become a fashion designer when he is older. It's a dream that fuels his fascination with art. He talks, quite passionately, about working at companies like Vogue and Prada. He can name famous artists and designers, most of whom I've never heard of before. And while he dreams of attending the country's best design colleges, he often worries about his chances of getting accepted.

Every day after school, Asif travels to a nearby coaching centre for a computer programming course. It's a compromise he's recently made with his father, who frets that Asif's design dreams will lead nowhere.

'When I told my father that I wanted to become a fashion designer, he slapped me. If I fail my tenth-standard exams next month or can't follow my dream, I guess I can open up my own internet café or try to work with a local computer shop.'

'What does your father do again?'

'He works as a carpenter. He has his own shop too. They make jewellery boxes. You know—it's funny. Now that I think about it, I'm sure I get my love for art from my father. I used to spend hours as a kid in his shop, watching him carve these beautiful designs into wood.'

'How much does he earn as a carpenter?'

'Maybe 6,000 rupees a month? He used to make 8,000 a few years ago, but then he quit his job because he wanted to start this jewellery business. I won't tell him, but it wasn't the smartest decision.'

Asif was born and raised in Govandi. After dropping out of school in the sixth standard, his father left his Nepali village and migrated to Bihar where he would meet his wife and, shortly after, settle in Govandi less than two decades ago.

'What's he like, your father?'

'My father cares about values more than anything else in the world. But he also might be the angriest man I've ever met. Actually, he *is* the angriest man I've ever met,' Asif quickly corrects himself. 'I once disrespected a neighbour by talking out of turn. My father beat me that night. And I never made that mistake again.'

'So, you get both your love for art and your excellent manners from your father, huh?'

'I guess,' he smiles.

We finally arrive at Asif's one-bedroom house and are immediately greeted by his mother who is waiting at the doorstep. Having never met me and likely wondering why a strange man is entering her house, she looks at me suspiciously for a moment. Then she politely smiles and retreats to the kitchen.

'Forgive her.' Asif says, clearly sensing my discomfort. 'My mother is calm on the outside, but broken on the inside. And that's because of my father and brother. She's almost given up on this life. She just looks to her afterlife, to what Islam will bring her.

'I don't really get along with either of my parents, you see,' he continues. 'They're always fighting with each other. We're just different people. And they don't understand me.'

The 'differences' that Asif alludes to concern his sexual orientation. Less than two years ago, he concluded that he was gay. After a local non-profit conducted a community class on sexuality and gender, the realization that he liked boys more than girls struck him the hardest.

'It was like a gigantic light bulb suddenly went off. I spoke to the facilitator after the workshop and he even offered to give me counselling. He said he could help me come to terms with it. I thought about it for a few days, but then I said no.'

'Why didn't you take it?' I asked.

'I had my exams coming up in less than three months. If I failed those, I'd lose any chance I have at design school. I can't let anything come in the way of that.'

Asif's homosexuality, combined with his eccentric love for fashion design, has invited more discrimination than what an average child experiences every day.

'When I was in the eighth standard my teacher started calling me a girl in front of the class. She refused to let me participate in any sports. She said they were reserved for "true boys".'

'I'm sorry to hear that. What did you do about it?' Though horrified by the teacher's actions, I was trying hard not to show it.

'I shouted and yelled at her in front of everyone. I'm not proud of it. *But how could she say something like that? How could she do something like that?* Two years have passed since the incident, but it still gets him visibly angry and shaking.

'When my brother found out–' he swallows before he continues, 'he began grabbing my butt and trying to kiss me. I resisted, but he would respond sarcastically, "You should like this. It's what you want, isn't it?" Since then, I stay in school as late as I can. I don't want to see my family.'

Perhaps most troubling for Asif are his struggles with Islam. Over the years, his parents, siblings and uncles have all invoked religion to nudge him towards a more traditional career path. Their behaviour has not only damaged their relationship, it's also reduced his once unshakeable faith to feelings of disgust and rage.

'Islam basically says that I can't be myself. I can't be gay. I can't be a fashion designer.' Asif's voice fills with emotion. 'Why should I believe in religion? It only tells me what I can't do.'

Despite years of harassment and ostracization, the most fascinating thing about Asif is that he still attempts to search for strength and motivation. 'People in my community tease me a lot. They find my weaknesses and they exploit them. It's because they don't understand the differences between genders. I want to change that. I want to be an inspiration for kids who can't be themselves.'

~

Shivaji Nagar, where Asif has grown up, sits at the heart of Mumbai's Govandi district. Today, Shivaji Nagar houses more than 600,000 people in a densely populated area of 32.5 square kilometres. That's about 2 square metres of space per person—less than the size of a double-door fridge. The residents are migrants from Uttar Pradesh, Gujarat, Bengal and rural Maharashtra. They come to Shivaji Nagar in search of a 'better' life. Some of them live in slums. Others are housed in the area's resettlement high-rises, a product of the government's many efforts to 'clean up' large swathes of the city. As a result, migrant communities— many of who carry conflicting ideologies and beliefs—are now packed into small blocks and shared alleys.

The M-East Ward, where Shivaji Nagar sits, is one of Mumbai's twenty-four wards. It ranks twenty-fourth—dead last—on the Human Development Index,[10] which is a universally accepted measurement of social and economic development created by the United Nations. The data behind that poor ranking is startling. The infant mortality rate is 60 per cent higher than the rest of the country and almost double the mortality rate for Mumbai. (66 children die per 1000 births compared to 34.57 in the rest of the city and 41 in the rest of the country). Fifty-seven per cent of the children in Govandi are classified as 'severely malnourished',[11] a rate that is comparable to levels observed in parts of sub-Saharan Africa. Perhaps most alarming, the life expectancy in Govandi is thirty-nine years of age—little more than half the lifespan for the rest of India (which is sixty-seven years).[12] It is a statistic that most residents and workers attribute to abysmally poor health and economic conditions: while the National Urban Health Mission (NUHM) recommends fifty-four dispensaries for the population in Govandi, there exist only nine in the area.[13] Exacerbating these are the innumerable environmental and health complications that come with the country's largest landfill being located only a few hundred metres from the doorsteps of the ward.

Taken together, the environmental, economic, health and safety challenges pose numerous risks and concerns for the children of Govandi. An abundance of research points to the links between these challenges and social outcomes like educational attainment. Having persisted for decades, social activists argue that Govandi's seemingly intractable problems have caused the government to simply *expect less*.[14] And that reality couldn't be more pronounced for the children of the community: more than 50 per cent of the population is under the age of twenty, but no free secondary school exists to serve them.[15]

Adding to the litany of Govandi's challenges are harrowing accounts of violence and discrimination that seem to spare no resident. Underlying Asif's impeccable manners are a series of incidents that have left him fearful of the community he calls home.

'When I was eight years old, I was out playing with some

friends one evening. It was just after sunset, I remember clearly because the azan had just finished. My friends and I watched this young man pull out a knife to threaten a girl. He then dragged her into the bathroom and raped her. For a few minutes, I simply stood outside, hearing her screams and cries. Then my friends and I ran to get help. But when we returned, the boy had disappeared. I still hear cases of little boys getting raped all the time in the same public bathrooms.'

Despite the surrounding violence that has now become a part of the town's folklore, Asif and his family largely feel safe in their current house. They attribute that to the local ward officer, Zafar, who has overseen the area for the past seven years. According to multiple residents, Zafar has a long history of illicit activities. These allegedly include drug dealing, murders and extortion. Nevertheless, people argue that he has brought down the level of violence in the ward, particularly on the street where both he and Asif's family live.

'He's a gangster for sure. But he keeps us safe,' says Asif.

'Hmm.' It's all I can manage to say, as I process everything Asif tells me. After a few minutes of silence, I decide to prod further.' Asif, imagine this. Imagine you have a powerful ticket that would take you back in time. You could move to any community in the city. Where would you go?'

'Bandra,' he replies instantly.

Bandra is a high-income and relatively posh neighbourhood more than 20 kilometres away from us. It's home to many famous Bollywood, cricket and even political personalities. More importantly, it is a place where the challenges and statistics of Govandi seem remote and unreal.

'There's no violence in Bandra. It's a good place. My father has told me that I need to get my education, grow up, earn money and figure out how to move the family to Bandra. I'm going to get us out of here.'

~

Within Govandi, the sentiment of powerlessness gets worse for children who are the most impoverished and, as a result, the most beset with struggle. Nevertheless, some persist with an unqualified sense of optimism, such as Asif's sixteen-year-old classmate, Malini. Malini is a favourite amongst her teachers, primarily because of her hard work and the positive spirit she brings to class. She loves to watch cartoons. She loves reading books; her favourites are *The Boy in the Striped Pyjamas* and anything from the Harry Potter series. She has respect and adulation for her school, despite its many shortcomings. The novelty of her disposition is something I only begin to understand much later.

When Asif and I enter Malini's one-room abode, we find her mother sitting on the floor. Situated on the edge of the community, their home is one of Govandi's cheapest available accommodations. The tin walls are taped with water bottles and pieces of cardboard to prevent rainwater from entering. White sheets overlay the cold concrete floors, serving as beds where Malini, her brother and her parents sleep every night. Malini's mother works for a local packaging company where she assembles boxes for twelve hours a day. Her father works as a temporary day labourer in the Deonar Landfill next door.

'Aap kitna paisa kamaatein hai ek month mein (How much do you earn every month)?'

'3,000.'

'Aur aapke husband (And your husband)?'

'Wohi toh. Hum dono ka mila kar 3,000 hota hai (That's just it. Our combined income is 3,000 rupees).'

We're both quiet for a few seconds before Malini's mother fills the silence.

'Yes, my life is hard. But look—I believe that we have to accept whatever we've been given as God's blessings to us. I say that I'm lucky to even be in Govandi. I'm lucky to be alive today.'

Her mother grows animated and begins talking much faster.

'Look, this is the third community I've lived in. I've seen a lot in life and I understood pretty early on that my life is in my hands. I control my happiness. I control my family's happiness. I make sure I'm providing my daughter with everything I can. Beyond that, she —actually all of us —must be *grateful* to God and pray to God that He gives us more of His blessings.'

Then, she slows down to a whisper.

'We have no choice but to accept this life day after day. Every morning, when we wake up, we just have to pray for a blessing. And then, whatever God gives us, we must accept it.'

Once we leave Malini's home, Asif and I wander silently through the alleys of Govandi. Sensing that I am contemplative and still digesting the conversation with Malini's mother, he grows quiet as well. For the next twenty minutes, we walk through the narrow lanes, rocky sidewalks and chaotically lined sheds that form the path out of her home.

More than anything, I battle with my own ambivalence this afternoon. On the one hand, I find myself struck by the spirit of gratitude and optimism with which this mother approached her struggle—a struggle far greater than I could ever begin to imagine. Despite the uncertainty and hardship Malini's mother endures every single day, she chooses to focus on her individual locus of control. I immediately begin reflecting on how much I personally value the concept of gratitude—the ability to recognize that we are all recipients of grace that is unequivocally unmerited. We are recipients of opportunities, experiences and affection that we probably don't deserve.

At the same time, though, I find myself troubled by the underlying sense of resignation that her mother's gratitude was masking. While deeply touching, her optimism was the result of multiple decades of continued hardship that, over time, has probably forced her to conclude that a better life is out of reach. It is a plight that has turned her inwards and ultimately pushed her to discard any notion of a social contract, any notion of a better community.

If Malini's mother *believed* that she could expect more help and support from her school, community and government, would she be as accepting of her current circumstances? If she was hopeful that others believed in—and some were even responsible for—helping her find a better life, would she be more inclined to fight for a greater collective good?

~

The next morning, I'm sitting with Pankaj on the fifth floor of his building. Observing the Govandi community and the rivers that surround it below, I'm still pondering over Malini's mother's helpless acceptance, while savouring some poha and chai for breakfast.

Pankaj lives less than a kilometre away from Asif. He stays in one of the area's many resettlement high-rises. Ten years ago, the government forcefully shifted Pankaj and his family from the slums under Mumbai's Chhatrapati Shivaji Terminus (CST) railway station. Along with thousands of others with similar fates, they now live in a series of tall, white buildings, stacked neatly in a row. The high-rises were intended to offer a better alternative to the flimsy tin sheds of their earlier lives. But they come with their own share of challenges. Residents get running water for only thirty minutes a day. The proximity of these buildings to one another—likely designed to pack more people into a smaller space—ensures poor ventilation. They also fail to offer access to any of the basic amenities that the rest of Mumbai's high-rise residents enjoy.

'I liked our lives in CST. Problems were there too. We lived in sheds that were made out of garbage. And we often had to sleep outside on the streets. But we were *free*. Here we're suffocated. We're also no longer connected. They've put together an island of buildings, but they haven't put any thought into education, health, employment or social inclusion.'

Pankaj speaks in a tone that is both eloquent and convincing. He has a strong command of English, something he attributes to attending a local after-school centre run by the Akanksha Foundation. He recently graduated from college and, for his first job, joined an international call centre. While he doesn't enjoy his work, he recognizes that his degree and salary place him above the vast majority of the area's residents.

After breakfast, we go on a walk through the dimly lit passageways between the many buildings. We see a group of kids, no older than seventeen, rolling dice and holding bottles of beer. They're passing around a joint that's emanating a strong smell of marijuana. It is eleven in the morning.

A few moments later, two police officers on a motorcycle pull up to the lot with batons in hand. The kids immediately run off.

The encounter makes me think about the vast difference between Pankaj's existence and those of his neighbours. He now has an opportunity to live a life of greater potential—something most would deem impossible, given his background. I wonder if he thinks about how to change the lives of those around him, of how to give back to his community. Or does he hold a predisposition similar to Malini, her mother and most of Govandi?

'We all want to change things,' Pankaj says. 'But it's harder than it looks.'

'Tell me more.'

'One day, I tried to break up a fight between two guys. They were cursing and hitting each other. After telling them to calm down several times, I found myself at the receiving end of their threats. And over the next few weeks, they harassed me daily.'

'Even though we want to make things better, over time the daily grind of life wears us down,' he says regretfully. 'It becomes about surviving. And the issues around make us numb. We're all scared that if we go off script, we'll get dragged down. So eventually, we start to think that the best thing we can do for ourselves is to do well and get out of here. It's a cycle that, honestly, can't be stopped.'

Pankaj and I continue walking. I start thinking about the dark truth embedded in what he's saying, a truth that was echoed not only in the stories of Govandi and Jahangirpuri, but in the stories of the hundreds of children and families I've met over the years. For most Indian citizens living in impoverished conditions, it is a fight to *simply stay alive*. They worry about their day-to-day survival, not about something as long-term and lofty as systemic change. The harshness of today's reality impedes any ability to think of the future. *Escaping* their current realities is what these citizens of India can hope for, at best. *Changing* that reality for the greater good of the collective, however, seems like a fairy tale.

People may debate the role that adults from these communities have played in shaping their own situation. But it's hard to argue that the children growing up in these circumstances[16]—have had *any* power in shaping their destinies. It's difficult to argue that they haven't been forced a terrible hand at life, to not see that they've essentially received none of the basic protections that a country should offer its most vulnerable citizens. They've been handed a broken social contract.

History tells us a parallel and unfortunate reality: change can only happen when people begin to mobilize. Unless they foster a collective voice that can demand their most basic rights, they'll never see change that is sustainable. They won't have a shot at changing a system that was never designed to serve them. A spirit of hard work *alone* may help a few individuals rise—and may result in a small sprinkle of success stories—but it won't be enough unless supplemented by a rewritten social contract.

Their voices are essentially inconsequential in today's world. Most people with power, intentionally or otherwise, tend to give less weight to oppressed voices. For the few underprivileged individuals that manage to get a seat at the table, their lack of exposure and financial prowess ultimately render them vulnerable. Their bad fortunes are either rationalized or ignored. Without the ability to come together and raise their voices collectively, they'll continue to be powerless.

Pankaj echoes this sentiment as he speaks about the differences between his community and his more affluent counterparts—the folks that live in Bandra.

'People in Bandra have a voice. They speak up whenever their expectations aren't met. They demand cleanliness. They demand good schools. They demand a government that works. And people listen, because they have both money and power. With our citizens, we get excited when a politician visits our community. We see *that* as privilege. We get trash, literally, from all over Mumbai dumped right at our front doors. We don't speak up. And as long as we don't speak up, we won't solve anything.'

~

If individual struggle takes precedence over the mobilization of the community, the immense struggle *between* individuals adds a layer of breakdown that is heart-wrenching.

Asif's older brother, Hanif, just turned twenty-five. He is currently wanted for charges of extortion and murder. Since he was a teenager, he has been in and out of trouble with the law. At the age of thirteen, he began experimenting with hard drugs, a habit he funded with money that he would borrow (and sometimes steal) from his parents. A few years later, when Asif's brother was twenty-one, he began illegally supplying electricity to local residents. Using easily accessible tools and equipment, he acquired the knowledge and capabilities to harness electrical connections by rerouting existing setups. It was an illicit business that soon sparked intense competition among the older teenagers of Govandi.

Shortly after Independence Day in 2015, Asif's brother got

into a heated argument with another teenager. The two began fighting over territory and the profits from electricity supplied to a large residence. Before going their separate ways, they hurled a number of expletives and violent threats at each other. Later that evening, in a fit of rage, Asif's brother found a knife and murdered the teenager. After discarding the dead boy's phone in a nearby sewer and running away, he called his mother to explain what he had done. He was instantly remorseful but also terrified.

The police arrived at Asif's house the next morning. They intensely interrogated both of his parents, whom they then detained for three days in jail. Adding to their misery, gang members close to the dead teenager in the community began violently harassing the family. A few days later, when no one was home, some gang members looted their house, doused it in petrol and set it on fire. The incident forced Asif to move in with his aunt for several months and, eventually, left the family with no option but to flee to another part of Govandi.

Asif talks about the incident with tremendous angst. He speaks of the challenging relationship he shared with his brother. He laments his brother's early drug use and heavy partying. But Asif also talks about the life and opportunity his brother never received. He talks about his brother's education—about what might have been possible if things were different.

'If my brother had gotten a better education, if someone had channelled his skills and strengths, he might have been in a different place right now. In fact, I'm certain he would be. Clearly, he was a really smart person. I mean, he ran his own business as a teenager! Yes, it was an illegal business, but I don't know any other teenagers in Govandi that can do what he did. He would be in college right now, that's for sure. But his teachers in school were terrible. He hated them, in fact.

'Many of my friends are in the same place. They never learned in the classroom. They didn't know the basics. Still, the school kept passing them from one grade to another, even though they weren't mastering the concepts. It's like the school had already decided they couldn't do it. By the time they got to the ninth grade, they dropped out. None of them could get any further. Now they do odd jobs or waste their time doing nothing.'

While Asif might not realize it, he is essentially providing a commentary on a countrywide crisis. For decades, our national focus has remained insulated to the relentless chase for access—getting as many children enrolled in schools as possible. The Right to Education Act (RTE), 2009, hailed as one of the biggest legislative victories in the last decade, made schooling mandatory for children between the ages of six and fourteen. It has resulted in almost universal primary education (92 per cent of children today are enrolled in primary school[17]). The strategy has strong merits: getting children into the classroom has to be the first step. However, it has unearthed a much bigger problem: the quality of education students receive in the classroom.

According to the 2016 Annual Status for Education Report (ASER), a bi-annual publication that has become a national report card on today's educational system, only 25 per cent of India's third-standard students can read a second-standard level text and only 27 per cent of them can do two-digit subtractions.[18] That means barely a quarter of our third-standard students can perform at grade level. Children like Asif's elder brother may be showing up every morning but they are, by and large, failing to receive a quality education that will set them up for success.

As students grow older, the learning gaps only get worse. Once India's students get to the fifth standard, the same study finds that half of them are more than three years behind grade level. For the vast majority of students who remain far behind, school simply stops adding value to their lives as they get older. Many of them—like Asif's brother—turn their attention to more engaging, but also more damaging, activities: drugs, alcohol, gang violence and illicit businesses. For these children—and the hundreds of millions of children who experience that reality every day—dropping out of school becomes inevitable.

And when they do, they drop out in droves. According to the national enrolment data, nine out of ten Indian children enter primary school, which is a strong start. However, by the time they reach the ninth standard, seven out of ten remain.[19] A few years later, only five collect their bona fide certificates.[20] And finally, only two out of ten actually make it to college.[21]

Asif often suggests that his brother, if only he had stayed in school, would now be in college. But the statistics clearly show that only 25 per cent of Indians actually make it to a higher education institution. For the poorest in our country, like Asif, that number drops precipitously to 5 per cent.[22]

'If you all lived in Bandra, none of this would have ever happened, huh?' I ask Asif, without thinking.

'Yeah, that's true,' Asif replies.

'Why do you think the education is so much better in Bandra?' I am genuinely curious to understand how he processes the differences.

His reply is stunning.

'If a child at my school went and paid the principal 5,000 rupees a month, when everyone else is paying 200 rupees, the principal would naturally treat that child a lot better. Similarly, those kids are able to pay a lot of money—much more than we're able to pay. So they get treated better. That's a fact of India. Everything runs on money, including education.'

THREE
I DESERVE TO DREAM TOO

'Why do I deserve an education that millions of children will never get?'

Nandini and I have just boarded a flight to Delhi. We're in the air for only twenty minutes before she launches her usual array of questions that I struggle mightily to answer. They're questions that carry a tremendous amount of depth, especially when coming from a sixteen-year-old.

As I attempt to gather my thoughts, our plane starts to shake and the seatbelt sign above us illuminates.

'What's that?' Nandini asks, startled. She is flying for the first time and is no longer attempting to hide her fear.

'That's turbulence. It's normal. We'll be out of it in no time, don't worry.'

Growing uneasy, she quickly grabs both armrests and shuts her eyes tightly.

'I think I'm going to be sick,' she says.

I instantly regret having booked the last two seats at the back of this aircraft, a position that allows us to feel every single bump and shake—not a good idea for a child flying for the first time. I try to reassure myself that the two-hour journey ahead of us will soon be over. I try searching for questions—anything—to distract her.

My desperate tactic works and we're both relieved when the plane finally lands. We hop into a cab and head to Delhi's InspirED conference, where more than 300 students, educators, academics and government officials gather to discuss the state of Indian education.

Conscious of being more than ten minutes late, I nervously

enter the dimly lit auditorium, walking past the many rows of seated audience. I glance over at Nandini, who seems much calmer than I am.

A panel on stage, consisting of two high-ranking ministers, a professor and a school principal, are fielding a barrage of questions from the audience.

'Students should always think of improving themselves. Self-confidence comes by putting ourselves in challenging circumstances and working hard to rise above them. In addition to the right knowledge and skills, what a student needs is self-confidence,' says one panellist.

'So do you want me to take a class for your parents today?' another panellist chimes in. The students in the room burst into applause and laughter.' Firstly, we must not doubt the intentions of our parents,' he asserts. 'Parents always want the best for their children. That being said, parents who focus only on academics are not doing the right thing. Everything must have balance. Children need to go out and play, they need to build their emotional IQ as well.'

The back and forth between the panellists and audience members continues for the next thirty minutes. I, for one, am jaded by the tired truisms disguised as legitimate solutions. As the moderator calls for the next question, I realize he's walking towards us. Sitting next to me, Nandini grabs the mic confidently and stands up with a sheepish smile.

'We're talking about problems in education,' she says. 'We have distinguished ministers and educators on this panel. But with all due respect, we're missing a key perspective. Let me ask you this: who is the ultimate beneficiary of education?' Nandini pauses only momentarily after her rhetorical question. 'It's the student. So where is the student voice on this panel? Why are we not asking children what they need? I have noticed this not just at this conference, but every day in how we run our schools. We are not listening to what children want. We're not thinking about what children need. No one asks us what we would like to learn, how we like to be taught, how much homework is helpful and how much is too much. We're just thinking about adults. But the problem is we're not educating *adults*, are we? We're educating *children*.'

Dressed in a white kurta and jeans, Nandini puts an extra emphasis on her last sentence: 'We're educating *children*.'

The audience is captivated as they silently process every word, unable to take their eyes off her. Moments later, they erupt into thundering applause. They are surprised, as am I, by the profoundness with which this five-foot-three-inch girl from the slums of Pune speaks.

~

Currently attending the prestigious Franklin & Marshall College in Lancaster, Philadelphia, Nandini is cognizant that her life story is, at best, rooted in unlikely odds. Raised by a single mother, she spent the vast majority of her childhood shuffling from one caretaker to the other. Her mother was ambitious. Employed by a legal typist, she wanted to secure a better life and advance her career. It was a pursuit that often found itself at odds with the weight and responsibility of raising a child almost single-handedly. At first, she tried leaving one-month-old Nandini at home—alone—while she went to work at the Pune courts. The dismay of her neighbours, who would hear Nandini crying unstoppably, forced her to eventually find a local orphanage that agreed to provide daycare.

'I found the orphanage really tough. They were always forcing me to talk and interact with others,' Nandini told me on the plane ride. 'As a child, I was really shy. So I would rebel and get angry a lot. And they, in turn, would beat me. When I got to the second standard, I kept telling my mother that I could take care of myself at home. But she wouldn't listen.'

Though initially resistant, Nandini's aunt and uncle

eventually agreed to supervise her in the evenings. The exposure she received, and the relationships she cultivated with her two older cousins, provided Nandini a source of stability that had been deeply lacking in her life. But it also brought with it a wave of unanticipated chaos.

'My aunt and uncle would get into fights every single day, swearing and cursing at each other. I hated it. One day, my uncle got so angry that he began beating my aunt. And I just sat there, helplessly watching it unfold.'

Nandini's mother's struggles with finding a balance between work and her daughter became a source of resentment between the two.

'My mother was extremely hard-working and determined, but she was also really selfish. She often used to tell me that she wanted me to get married at a really young age because I was a burden on her. She would say that she should have aborted me. When you hear that enough number of times, you eventually begin to believe it.'

The lack of affection and frequent shuffling around ensured that Nandini's childhood was marked by feelings of estrangement and loneliness. Her family struggled to understand her perceived reticence and inability to dutifully complete household chores. They chided her, often sardonically, calling her both 'retarded' and 'slow'.

'"Go be a whore if you want to help us. Go sell yourself in the red light district. We'll have money then," they told me every single day.'

Over time, Nandini began to find solace and comfort in being alone.

'As a child, I used to watch a lot of television, particularly shows about scientists and forensics. I would often end up copying their experiments and, at times, make up imaginary characters. They became my friends. They actually became my family.'

Nandini's relationship with her father was the most complicated. When he was a young man, at the age of nineteen, he and his friends got into a heated argument with their landlord. After a testy exchange of insults, the group of teenagers eventually beat the landlord to death. Later that evening, the police arrested them, charged each with murder and transferred them to Pune prisons where they would serve their sentences.

As per Indian law, prisons regularly offer incentives for inmates who display good behaviour. Nandini's father, over time, earned four days at the end of the year away from prison. Once granted a temporary release, he disappeared and changed his identity. He would spend the next ten years evading the police. It was during his release that he met Nandini's mother and, ultimately, conceived their only child.

'I never knew why I had to keep it a secret. But I had three rotating stories to tell people: he was in the US, he was driving a rickshaw or he was back in our village,' Nandini says, describing their clandestine relationship.

Before eventually being recaptured, her father would split his time between Nandini's mother and another woman, whom he later married. Unsure why her relationship with her father was so secretive, Nandini grew up feeling deeply conflicted. On the one hand, she found his affectionate nature a direct contrast to that of her mother, who was aloof and often angry. She appreciated, and perhaps needed, the love and care he would sporadically give her. On the other hand, she struggled to grapple with his frequent periods of absence and, over time, began to resent his constant need to assert his dominance. He would see Nandini for less than two days a week, during which he could grow both violent and temperamental.

One day, on a regular visit to the prison, Nandini told her father about an extracurricular theatre programme she was excited to attend. They were sitting across each other, separated by grey metal bars. Nandini spoke passionately into the receiver as her father watched and listened on the other side until she finished.

'Are you crazy? The school is trying to brainwash you. Why do you need to do all of this? Just focus on your studies, or else leave the school. Anyway, what use is any of this going forward? Take a look at your mother for proof,' he shouted.

His outburst took Nandini by surprise. It sparked a rare flash of rage in her.

'Who are you to tell my mother or me anything? Take a look at where we're sitting. You're in jail!' she replied angrily.

'AYYYY!' he yelled at the top of his voice as he slammed his free hand on the platform in front of them. Nandini jumped up in response and her handset fell to the floor. She was thankful for the bars that separated the two of them. Other prisoners and their visitors turned to stare at them. He, on the other hand, was unperturbed. He gestured to her to pick up the handset. Slowly, she held it to her ears.

'Don't forget that I have the power and the ability to kill you and your mother,' he whispered.

Nandini said nothing, placed the phone on the receiver and walked out of the room with a brave face. As soon as she was outside, her eyes welled up with tears. It was the last time she visited him.

Nandini's father is due to be released in 2021, the same year that she's expecting to graduate college.

'He'll either kill us or he'll leave us alone.'

~

Nandini grew up in Luhianagar, Guruwar Peth, a small locality at the heart of Pune's old city. It houses many of India's traditional industries. The streets are lined with shops catering to carpentry, textiles, manufacturing and metal production. Those streets bear the weight of disparities found across the city. While Pune has witnessed unparalleled growth and migration over the past three decades owing to the large upswing in technology and manufacturing firms, the subsequent economic gains have failed to reach most of its inhabitants—particularly residents of the old city.

As a result, Pune has largely adopted two competing identities. The first is that of a massive and growing business community that includes new migrants as well as wealthy residents, most of whom have stuck around to watch the city grow and flourish. Residents enjoy Pune's burgeoning development, which includes access to high-end stores, excellent medical care and a rising quality of life. This part of the city closely identifies with Pune's nickname, the Oxford of the East, which it holds due to a large concentration of higher education institutions.

Its second identity, however, is associated with much of the old city that's largely been left behind in the rapid development race. It is an identity that comprises 11.5 lakh people—a third of Pune's population—who live in a state of perpetual poverty.[23] Together, those 477 slum pockets occupy less than 3 per cent of the city's land[24] and make Pune the third largest slum-dwelling city in India.[25]

No place exemplifies this dichotomy better than Parvati Hill, home to Nandini and her classmates. The climb up Parvati Hill is much like the rest of the city—a solid stretch of grey cement. Initially, because of the incline, you can see nothing but the hilltop and a glimpse of the golden neighbourhood temple. As you ride further up, the horizon expands into a majestic landscape. House upon house stands proudly one behind the other. As you get closer, though, you realize they're not so 'proud'. They are dilapidated and run-down. They resemble the pukka constructions in Jahangirpuri and Govandi. The ones standing proud are the neighbouring high-rises behind them—they belong to the city's new identity.

We walk past similar examples of inequity every day—each one of us—thinking nothing of it. We see them on our way to work or school. We see them on our way to a restaurant for Sunday lunch with the family. We see—and yet don't really *see*.

Nandini, on the other hand, like most children of the city, has repeatedly watched that dichotomy bear the weight of human faces and failed futures.

One September evening, Nandini was walking home from school when she saw a young teenage girl run past her. No more than fifteen years old—the same age as Nandini at the time—the girl paused in front of her. Her face was dishevelled and filled with fear. Her clothes were slightly torn.

'I couldn't even muster the courage to say anything. They just started beating her. Sticks and bricks—anything they could find. And I just cowered.'

Fifteen years later, Nandini experiences more success now than she ever thought was possible. It leaves her hopeful, but it also fills her with unabated guilt.

'When I look across Luhianagar, I know people have been through so much worse,' she says. 'You walk through the community and you know there's a big problem here—actually, multiple big problems. But you don't quite know what will solve them.' Nandini winces for a moment before continuing. 'You know that the community lacks something. You can feel it. And rationally, you can see that education and good teaching will solve a part of the problem. But you can also sense that it's going to take more than that. The crazy thing, right now though, is that we're not really talking about it.'

As Nandini is speaking, I think about Govandi again. I think about Malini's mother, about the themes of gratitude and acceptance that left me so ambivalent because of the oppressive forces they appeared to mask.

'Most people will argue that you—and the people in Luhianagar—should be grateful for the opportunities you do have.'

'If you're only thinking about what you're grateful for, then you're accepting your fate,' she quickly retorts. 'You're blinding yourself from pushing the limits, from wanting more. For me, that means I'll be just like my mother. I'll end up working as a typist and I won't get more. Don't I deserve to dream too?'

I almost answer her rhetorical question with a faint 'Yes' but she quickly interjects.

'I *definitely* deserve to dream.'

~

Nishi and I are sitting on the grey concrete floor of her house in Vadgaon Budruk, a neighbourhood less than five kilometres away from Nandini's. I'm working hard to glean every word of Nishi's barely audible voice. It's a task that isn't made any easier by the blaring television or the loud clanging of kitchen vessels.

Nishi wants to one day become a doctor. She hopes to fulfil a dream her father, now a local tile labourer who emigrated from Bihar, never could. More than two decades after dropping out of school, his house still holds all of his old science textbooks and class notes, as well as his half-broken lab equipment.

'My father's reaction every time he sees those notes is just incredible,' Nishi says. 'You look at his face and you can just see the passion. It's sad. He never got his dream. I have to get it for both of us now.'

Nishi is acutely aware that an almost identical set of barriers and limitations will soon confront her as well. Her father earns less than 6,000 rupees a month, which allows them just enough to cover their expenses. Faced with exorbitant tuition costs, Nishi will have to perform extraordinarily well to ensure she gets the scholarship needed to attend medical school. Like many of the children in her neighbourhood, her dreams are directly at odds with the statistical reality of Vadgaon Budruk.

'Children from my community simply can't afford a high-quality education. They just pay for whatever they can find—and that's often really poor.' Nishi's voice grows louder with emotion as she continues, 'Ironically, because we're all poor, it means we have to do really, *really* well to follow our dreams—because we have to get scholarships.'

'What do you hope to do once you become a doctor?' I ask.

'Every day, I see people in my community who need care. But they just can't afford it. And so they suffer, even if they're in pain.' she says. 'I know it's not that simple. I know that medicines and healthcare are expensive. And I don't know, right now, what my solution will be. But if I become a doctor, I will make it my mission to serve these people.'

I'm a bit puzzled by the conviction and passion with which this child describes her ambition. When I was thirteen, I too had dreamt of becoming a doctor. It was also a pursuit fuelled by my father. I envisioned a future filled with high-risk surgeries, life-saving operations and late nights with patients in the emergency room. Aside from my whimsical daydreams, though, I never held or displayed a fraction of the energy or commitment I'm witnessing this afternoon.

'Here's the truth about Vadgaon Budruk,' Nishi goes on, now taking charge of the conversation. 'Five years down the road, most of my friends won't be studying. They also won't be working in jobs they love. Instead, they'll be drowning in social and financial problems, much like the generations before them. They'll be wandering aimlessly through life, and even if they are passionate about something, they'll have no chance of pursuing it.'

'Some people say that your friends create their own problems. They argue that a lack of hard work, combined with a penchant for crime, is the real culprit. What would you say to that?' I ask.

'When a child is born, they get a clean slate. We're equal. But when children grow up in communities like Vadgaon Budruk, they don't learn the difference between right and wrong. And so, often, they will see someone doing something wrong—littering, eve-teasing, taking drugs and even being violent—and they'll think it's acceptable.'

Nishi pauses again. It's a tactic she uses often, and I wonder if she can sense that it makes me slightly anxious.

'And that's the second truth of Vadgaon Budruk. When there are no role models, destructive forces soon become the way of life.'

In that moment, Nishi's dream of becoming a doctor took on an entirely new perspective. Yes, she wanted to fulfil her father's dream. But more than that, she realized how powerful her example could be for her community.

'Everyone looks down on low-income people. They think we're lazy,' Nishi says. 'But that's not true. The world doesn't even see us as people. They stay away from us. And that perception, whether we like it or not, limits our potential.'

Her comments, while startling, force me to confront a much larger problem. It's a theme of forced resignation that's shared, in ways both big and small, by the stories of children across our communities. It was repeated most resoundingly through my conversations with Nandini.

'There are these narratives that society quickly forms, you see,' Nandini explains. 'And these narratives eventually lead to more arbitrary expectations. And then everyone expects you to fit into that narrative. If you're a young boy from my community, you're expected to curse and fight. And if you don't fit that mould, all of a sudden, society begins to look at you strangely.

'These expectations are most pronounced from people outside the community, from those looking in. I hang out with this friend from a high-income community. And I've never admitted it publicly, but I feel really inferior around her. She knows so much more about the world than I do. But, honestly, that doesn't bother me as much as her low expectations of me. She's not even surprised when I don't know something. It's like she has no expectations because she knows I'm poor.

'The truth is that people just expect us to perform poorly. And so if someone makes it out of the community and is able to engage with the world, everyone is surprised. As a result, people rarely end up making it. They *know* the world expects us not to.'

Nandini and Nishi are alluding to a phenomenon that social scientists have meticulously studied for decades: the self-fulfilling prophecy of low expectations. Dozens of studies have shown that expectations play a crucial role in the development of children.[26] Those who are held to higher standards, regardless of background or ability, almost always perform better than their counterparts.

Yet, we regularly lower our expectations for children from low-income backgrounds and we consistently raise them for their affluent peers. Children from high-income backgrounds are expected to attend good colleges and secure well-paying jobs. These are outcomes that are never doubted or questioned for people like you or me. On the other side of the spectrum, we find ourselves surprised at the rare instance when a child who grew up in poverty succeeds. Simply put, we expect them to accomplish less.

Our state of shock can be rationalized to an extent. Both media and cultural folklore have taught us to believe that low-income children will inevitably lag behind. But over time, our expectations form a narrative that becomes defining and limiting: the belief that poverty must dictate destiny.

FOUR

OUR SECOND TRYST WITH DESTINY

Nandini, Asif and Yasmin bear the forces of inequity and oppression that have plagued their communities for generations. Their journeys may be thought-provoking and surreal, their stories undoubtedly unique. But their experiences also provide a window into a reality that is more pervasive than their individual lives and neighbourhoods.

Nandini, Asif and Yasmin are far from anomalies.

They are children of India.

Their struggles offer a glimpse into the hundreds of millions of Indian lives plagued by poverty and hopelessness. Immersing ourselves in their daily lives—however briefly—forces us to confront the uncomfortable realities that accompany their predicaments. Their challenges compel us to grapple with our very definition of what it means to be poor in India today.

In a country with 130 crore people, roughly 20 per cent of Indians live under the international poverty line.[27] That translates to more than 27 crore people earning a little over 100 rupees (or $2) per day. While you may think these numbers are startling— and they certainly are—let's recognize that they're probably conservative. Being poor in India goes well beyond a definition of monetary wealth. It includes many hundreds of millions more who simply lack the basics. Fifty-three per cent of Indians have no access to latrine facilities. More than 40 per cent don't have bathing amenities.[28] Eighty-two per cent have no access to the internet[29] and more than 30 per cent live in houses made of garbage, plastic or mud.[30]

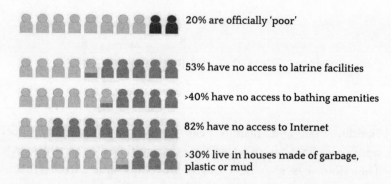

	20% are officially 'poor'
	53% have no access to latrine facilities
	>40% have no access to bathing amenities
	82% have no access to Internet
	>30% live in houses made of garbage, plastic or mud

Exploring what it means to be poor in India

We see these statistics come to life through the stories of Nandini, Asif and Yasmin. By the international definition, none of these three children are officially 'poor'; they are, in fact, above the poverty line. Yet, Yasmin and the residents of Jahangirpuri face a seemingly never-ending battle with violence, religious conflict and the worst cases of discrimination. In Govandi, Asif and his neighbours live in an environment with alarming rates of infant mortality and abysmally low life expectancy. They wake up every morning to the stench and debris of unmanaged landfills. And less than 200 kilometres away, Nandini and her Luhianagar neighbours are navigating the labyrinth of anachronistic social norms, coupled with poor sanitation and substandard housing.

It would be a tough sell to argue that children living in these communities are poised to face futures filled with promise and security. It would be hard to argue that their lives today are capitalizing on even the most basic aspects of India's potential. And it would be *impossible* to argue that these children—the future of our country—will receive the opportunities and choices needed to create a better society.

When we're faced with socioe-conomic issues that are complex and vexing, it's frightening to think of the right place to start. Underlying India's stories of inequity is the realization that changing their narratives won't be easy. It will be laborious and exhausting.

Within these stories of struggle are also the deeply embedded implications of an education foregone. They echo in the stark differences in opportunities that await both Nandini and Yasmin—children who share similar backgrounds but are on decidedly different trajectories owing to their antithetical school experiences. They're heard as Asif and Yasmin recount what an education similar to theirs could have done for their older siblings. Finally, they're seen in the tenacious ambition that persists from one generation to the next, waiting for a chance at an education that will transform dreams into realities—like Nishi's commitment to fulfilling her father's dream.

Let's be abundantly clear: education is no panacea for all the social and economic ills that plague India's impoverished citizenry.

But it might be our best shot at changing the future.

This is the reason why families go through painstaking efforts to ensure their children receive an education—any education they can find. They have no illusions about the steep uphill battle awaiting their children's futures; they're reminded of it every single day. Despite that, they choose to put their faith in the potential of what an excellent education can offer—often risking their lives to do so. They understand, perhaps all too well, that no amount of economic reform or government assistance will succeed if it's not coupled with an education that leaves their children more empowered. They recognize that the only path out of poverty is one that goes through the walls of a stronger school.

Being empowered in today's India means a whole host of things. On the one hand, it means that families are able to economically cope—that they're able to climb their way out of poverty. At the same time, though, it demands that children be fully capable of changing the current realities permeating their communities. They must be equipped to chart a different future not just for themselves but also for their neighbours, even when they discover that this is incredibly difficult. It means putting our hopes for change in the hands of people—specifically, in the hands of children.

Gautam John is a social activist who devotes most of his time to building agency among marginalized entities. He makes a bold but rational claim: 'I believe that at the root of all of our problems is a power imbalance. That is not to say that there are no technical challenges in each domain. But they are all solvable if we enable the voices of those who are most affected.'

In education, that means empowering our poorest students and families.

So, what leads to empowerment?

Perhaps underlying it is the *mere opportunity to choose*, coupled with the belief that those choices can indeed result in a fundamentally different life outcome. Inherent to the right to choose is an education that equips children with the knowledge, skills, values and mindset to not only make the *right* choices but to also believe in the transforming power of a reimagined future. This kind of an education creates safe spaces for students to process and reflect, gives them the ability to question the status quo and ultimately teaches them to hold all of us accountable to building a better nation. For our most vulnerable children, numbering over hundreds of lakhs across the country, it demands that we start believing that they too can be empowered citizens—that they deserve an education that will give them the same opportunities as anyone else.

~

The recognition that better prospects are inextricably linked to an equitable education is not a novel idea. India's hard-fought Independence movement—an effort won more than seventy years ago—was predicated on the belief that a fully empowered republic was the country's best shot at a promising future. That belief was reinforced in Gandhi's proclamations of self-reliance and equality. It was alluded to in India's Purna Swaraj declaration that demanded 'full opportunities of growth' as an inalienable right for all citizens.

Our ability to one day realize that vision, however, depends on our capacity to acknowledge and confront our current reality—no matter how painful it may be.

Over the past seventy years, we have made progress that is undeniable. Our poverty levels have dropped by more than 50 per cent in the last three decades.[31] We have ensured nearly universal primary school access—at 92 per cent—for children living in both urban and rural India.[32] Our female literacy rates have seen substantial rises.[33] Taken together, this means that we have an unprecedented number of children accessing a basic education. These gains lay the foundation for the vision behind our original declaration of independence and they should be hailed as progress that is unquestionably good.

At the same time, though, we must acknowledge the truth. The data—punctuated by the stories we've witnessed in Jahangirpuri, Govandi and Luhianagar—tells us that we are woefully far from realizing a vision in which India is a *fully* empowered republic.

Whatever our national trends may be, they can't be looked at in isolation.We live in an increasingly globalized world, where today's young generation must collaborate and even compete with peers from around the globe. Perhaps the most accurate depiction of our educational system, then, is how well we're able to stack up against other countries.

In 2009, India participated in the internationally acclaimed PISA exam. PISA is a math, science and reading test administered to fifteen-year-olds. It is meant to be indicative of a country's educational attainment. With the ability to choose which cities and districts would participate, we sent students from Himachal Pradesh and Tamil Nadu, two states known for having some of the highest literacy rates in the nation. And yet, India ranked second to last, seventy-second among seventy-three countries. Students from our most notable counterpart, China, ranked first.[34]

India's learning levels are even more abysmal for our most marginalized and impoverished citizens. According to the World Economic Forum, India's poor receive approximately nine years less schooling than their more affluent peers. That gap is greater than most countries with similar income levels—Thailand, Vietnam, Philippines and Indonesia.[35]

If only our most privileged people—accounting for less than 25 per cent of our total population—can compete globally, what happens to the remaining 100 crore Indians?

~

Staring into the depths of our current reality often leads to finger-pointing and premature hypotheses to try and explain the mess we're in. While it's important to acknowledge that we are far from being an empowered republic, it is also necessary to recognize that this isn't because of a lack of effort. For decades, policymakers, government officials and practitioners have been working relentlessly to improve our country's state of education. Many of these efforts may have fallen short or been misguided, but they have mostly been well-intentioned.

So, if it's not a lack of intent or effort that lies at the heart of our current problems, then what is it? That is a difficult question with no straightforward answer. Plenty of academics, practitioners and policymakers have wrestled with it at length. When you peel back the layers, as they have, you'll inevitably end up with compelling conclusions that are hard to overlook.

For decades, our national strategy has placed an almost *singular* focus on increasing input. Policies, including the RTE, 2009, have targeted inputs ranging from infrastructure improvements (such as classroom benches, paintings, bathroom renovations) and student-teacher ratio reductions to textbook designing and science lab development. At first glance, these strategies seem rooted in common sense: they're much needed given the decrepit state of many Indian schools. When viewed in relation to student outcomes, however, they can easily go awry.

Data collected in recent years suggest that the vast majority of input-driven initiatives have led to little or no improvements in students' abilities to learn. Learning levels since the original implementation of the much-hailed RTE—passed in 2009 as a means to dramatically improve inputs—have remained stagnant, or worse, have declined. The ASER 2017 report most notably underscores this. In 2005, 72 per cent of eighth-standard students surveyed could do simple division, a third grade skill. Ten years later, that bad statistic got worse: the number dropped to 44 per cent.[36] Given the poor conditions of Indian schools, investments in infrastructure are undoubtedly needed. But, when taken alone, they can only do so much to improve student outcomes

If our children aren't learning, what's the point of improving the building? What's the point of even putting more students in school?

In response, parents have begun pulling their children out of government schools and enrolling them in the burgeoning—yet highly unregulated—affordable private school market. Desperately searching for the high-quality education their children deserve, they're losing faith in the abilities of our public institutions to deliver. Sadly, quality can vary significantly from one private school to another. Many private schools prey on impoverished populations with low tuition fees, but performance in these schools is no better than their government counterparts.

'It's all about marketing,' says Anil Swarup. A high-ranking official at the Ministry of Human Resource Development, he is responsible for overseeing the development of school education and literacy across the country. 'These schools capitalize on a

perceived notion parents hold that private schools are better—
that paying for their child's education guarantees a better
outcome than a free one. As a result, private school enrolment
has increased much faster than government enrolment in many
states.'

Ashish Dhawan, a respected private equity investor-turned-
educator, offers a different point of view. 'Yes, there are some
low-income private schools that are hoodwinking parents,
but they can do that for one year, two years at most? The real
conversation should be centred around a recognition that these
schools have proliferated because our government schools are
failing their students. Private schools are simply capitalizing on
a demand in the market for alternatives to public education.
They are playing a critical role in providing parents a choice on
where to enrol their kids. They're putting "market pressure" on
government schools to perform better.'

Regardless of where you stand on the private versus public
schools debate, with declining enrolment rates and stagnating
learning levels, it's easy to wonder why the government hasn't
been more nimble at changing strategies. And while shifting
from the input-based approach at the heart of policies like the
RTE to an outcome-driven strategy is necessary, this is hardly
easy.

Ashish Dhawan himself follows up his criticism with a
profound explanation. 'In a company, there is a clear definition
of success: the top and the bottom lines. In education, we're still
debating what the right outcomes are. Is it test scores like PISA
and the board exams? Is it the percentage of graduates who are
able to secure jobs? Or is it rather a reduction in unemployment
and crime accompanied by a narrowing of the achievement gap
between the rich and the poor, and if so, how do we connect these
broader societal indicators back to educational investments?
Without an agreed-upon definition of the goal of education, how
do we track student outcomes?'

Regardless of the measures we choose, shifting from an input-based approach to a system rooted in student outcomes is paramount. Getting there, however, is going to demand massive and even radical shifts in an outdated system. We are living in a century that is defined by the internet, yet our classrooms are still focused on memorization and rote-learning. Outside the classroom, students access unlimited information from thousands of sources. They require skills to parse through it all. Inside the classroom, however, the vast majority of our students are dependent on a single source of information—the teacher. Our workplaces are rapidly transitioning from being characterized by rigid authority structures and defined career paths to ones that value teamwork, bottom-up ideation and entrepreneurship. Yet, within our schools, we teach children to strictly adhere to predictable structures and shy away from higher-order skills.

Why should we accept that our institutions of learning, where we spend almost a quarter of their lives,[37] fail to provide these essential skills and experiences, especially when employers are asking for the same? In surveys of employers, more than 75 per cent believe that Indian graduates are entering the workforce ill-prepared.[38] They aren't demanding domain expertise (only 19 per cent say that's important); instead, they want young adults who can thrive in a rapidly changing world.

The lack of evolution is abundantly evident in our policies and not just in our classrooms. The Right to Education, for example, only mandates a government-provided education until the eighth standard. After that, parents in most states face difficult choices on how much they're willing to pay for a private school. Fifty years ago, many employers may have found an eighth standard education to be sufficient. Today, in a world that is built on high-skilled employment and higher education degrees, it is effectively meaningless.

This is not news to most of us. We've all, in fact, likely

lamented the obsolete nature of the schools we've attended. But, we have also had the safety net of privilege, equipping us with the exposure and opportunities our schools failed to provide. For the majority of our country's children—the country's one billion—there is no such alternative. Gautam John refers to this, with a sense of dark foreboding, as 'a broken promise that we are making to the youth of our nation'.

'We have built the expectation that if you go to college, you'll find a job and you'll emerge out of poverty,' John says. 'In reality, the path through school and college is inundated with obstacles and when they graduate—*if* they graduate—they're underprepared and under-skilled for the market. These individuals, who have mortgaged their futures to be a part of this promised land, will emerge from our education system frustrated and disappointed. They will be in a place where they are more educated, but no better off.'

We could likely create a long litany of reasons—ranging from curriculum and technology to accountability and spending to assessments and a whole host of other factors—that explain India's current educational crisis. Choosing which of those levers is most likely to fix a broken system, though, is a bit of guesswork. And, more notably, it's masking the fact that a *combination* of these levers is required. As Shashi Nair, a renowned former professor at Azim Premji University, puts it: 'Those levers are, for better or worse, intricately interlocked. Working to fix one element alone—such as teacher training—is doomed to failure, unless it takes into account the many factors that accompany it. Ensuring our children receive an education—one that promises opportunity—will not be solved through a few silver bullets. We would have fixed it by now if that were the case.'

So how do we change a complex system so that it leads to results that are sustainable?

Well, we look deeper.

We look deeper at what underlies each of these levers—at

making shifts that are primed to deliver foundational change.

We look deeper and we find *people*.

Fundamental to each of these factors are the *people* that are driving them. While blaming individuals for the current mess is a futile exercise, it is obvious that our educational system today suffers from a massive dearth of human capital. Due to a shortage of educators, there are more than 100,000 single-teacher schools in the country where all classes (and effectively the entire school) are run by one person.[39] Many states face major shortages of teachers, such as Uttar Pradesh, where 50 per cent of secondary teaching posts were vacant in 2018.[40] That's *half* of the positions going unfilled.

This is heavily compounded by the fact that India's most outstanding young people, by and large, choose every career path but education. That scarcity of high-quality talent is evident in the 25 per cent of Indian primary school teachers who are absent on any given day.[41] It is evident in the mediocre standards of our teacher training institutes and in the less than 6 per cent of teachers who pass teacher eligibility tests.[42] Comparatively, in a country like Singapore, which incidentally scored among the top five on the 2009 PISA assessment, all possible steps are taken to recruit top talent that delivers on one promise: teaching their children. Prospective teachers are selected from the top third of a high school graduating class, and only one out of eight applicants is eventually accepted. Of accepted applicants, 80 per cent have already completed a bachelor's degree in the subject they will teach. Since compensation often plays a pivotal role in attracting the best and brightest, the Singaporean Ministry of Education aggressively monitors teacher salaries to ensure they're competitive.[43]

In India, capacity and competency gaps only widen as we move up the ranks. There are only a handful of institutes focused on school leader preparation or on-the-job professional development for principals and headmasters. Moreover, school leaders in the country are mostly chosen based on seniority, not aptitude. The same trends apply in appointments of administrative staff, state and local officials, policymakers, as well as many other critical positions. Continuing our comparison with Singapore, after three years on the job Singaporean teachers must actively choose between three career tracks: teaching, leadership or specialization. Each track has thirteen levels that ensure they are adequately equipped with the knowledge, skills and mindset required for their roles. For instance, all Singaporean principals are teachers who have taught for at least three years, have chosen the 'leadership' track and have then served in two administrative roles before advancing to school leadership.

Policies and processes aside, international comparisons reveal that there is a lot we can learn from the cultural outlook of other countries as well. Teaching in India is considered a 'pseudo-profession'—almost akin to social work. Indian parents, including yours and mine in all likelihood, encourage their children to become engineers, doctors, lawyers—seldom educators. In China (again one of the countries that ranked high on the 2009 PISA assessment), educators enjoy the same social status as doctors. Fifty per cent of Chinese parents say they would definitely encourage their children to become educators—a stark contrast to how India's most talented view teaching.[44]

If we're not able to enrol our most outstanding and capable citizens to address our country's most vexing and pressing issue, do we even stand a chance?

~

Over the years, I've run into dozens of well-intentioned people who've wondered aloud if our current state of education really demands a sense of urgency. For decades, despite our shoddy state of affairs, India has grown both economically and socially— we have reduced the number of poor and literacy rates have increased. So why should we care?

Consider this: India is projected to be the country with the world's youngest population by 2030.[45] The median age of our citizens will be thirty-two years—ten years younger than most other nations. Our youth has the potential to give us a massive economic advantage in the decades to come—only if we're able to fully prepare them for it. We have the opportunity to supply the world with a talented and competitive workforce. But that potential is largely untapped if only 25 per cent are able to attend college and the rest—the Yasmins, Asifs and Nishis of the country—have to overcome insurmountable odds to get there. Meeting the world's human resource demands and realizing the potential of our economic growth will require a reimagining of our current educational system. The links between quality schooling and economic growth are clearly backed by research. Dramatically improving our schools, according to one report, could lead to a GDP that is thirteen times higher than what it is today.[46] The imperative for quality couldn't be more apparent; it is why virtually all experts agree that this potential can only be unlocked if we correct the dismal state of education that plagues us today. Failing to do so could have massive implications: namely, a country that is economically depressed.

While frightening in its own right, the implications of our current state go well beyond economics. We are indeed at risk of raising a generation of children—the largest share of young people the world has ever seen—who are disenfranchised and altogether unable to contribute in any significant way. For children like Asif's brother, their ability to positively participate in society is significantly hampered, if not already a lost cause. Perhaps most concerning is that we risk raising a generation that is simply incapable of solving the country's—and the world's— most intractable problems like climate change, food and water security and corruption.

The community issues seen in Jahangirpuri, Govandi and Luhianagar are exacerbated by a long list of challenges confronting the whole of India today. These challenges will demand scores of our best thinkers and most capable citizens. But will we have enough of them?

A bittersweet reality undercuts our current state of affairs: we know what it takes to deliver an excellent education. We see our most privileged students receiving one at some of our country's most prestigious institutions. If we can do it for a few, then isn't it our moral responsibility to do it for all?

Our country's founders—visionaries like Nehru and Gandhi—undoubtedly wanted education to be attained by *all* of India's citizens. They believed that our success as an independent nation should be predicated on the empowerment of our entire population. Radically reforming our education system, and thereby ensuring the vision of India's founders comes to life, may be the greatest and most urgent task ahead of us.

Nehru referred to the dawn of our Independence as our 'tryst' with destiny. That tryst was rooted in building a new social contract with India's people. Today we stand at another crossroads. This may be our *second* tryst with destiny. It may even be our modern day freedom struggle.

The rooftops of Luhianagar, where Nandini lived with her mother.

Ladders in a maze, an aerial view of the homes in Jahangirpuri.

Inside out, daily activities spill outside the home into alleyways.

Inside out, a glimpse into a home in the community.

Outside in, trash from all over Mumbai ends up in Govandi.

Child's play: children playing with kites in the community.

Top and bottom left: Children playing cricket.

Bottom right: Two boys in traditional clothes.

The human faces behind the statistics: two boys riding on a broken bicycle.

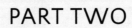

PART TWO

FIVE

GOD FLIPPED A COIN

The belief that India's future is inextricably linked to the state of its education was the driving force that led Shaheen Mistri, the founder of Teach For India, to dedicate a lifetime working for impoverished children. Once she arrived at the realization, she found herself at a crossroads that would quickly prove to be life-changing.

'What are your names?' All three girls were staring at her blankly with their hands wide open. She stole a glance at the seemingly unchanging traffic light.

'Ramya,' one of them shyly responded. She couldn't have been older than seven. Lifting her left finger from the tear of her purple kurta, Ramya held out her hand.

'Hi Ramya. Where's your mother?' Knowing her question likely didn't have an easy answer, Shaheen watched as the little girl looked down. For the next thirty seconds, she would remain transfixed, eyes locked, with Ramya and her younger sisters.

The light turned green. The black and yellow taxi sped off. Ramya's blank stare was quickly replaced with window displays of South Mumbai's high-end shops.

Shaheen spent her childhood trotting between countries. Her father's role as a Citibank executive took the family to Lebanon, Indonesia, Greece and America. Visiting India each summer—regardless of where they lived—had grown into a much-anticipated ritual. Her time in Mumbai brought her face-to-face with children who spent their days and evenings loitering at traffic signals and street corners. It was a stark contrast to the world she'd grown accustomed to, one replete with swimming pools, executive mansions and tennis classes.

'They're not going to make it,' she said to herself, quietly.

She knew the thought was morose. It wasn't the first time she had encountered Mumbai's entrenched poverty. But the image of Ramya and her sisters—coupled with the growing realization that their lives would continue to be bleak, at best—gnawed at her conscience all afternoon. Three days before, her family had boarded a flight to the US. In her second year of college at Massachusetts's Tufts University, she was expected to follow suit and start the new semester. Returning to college, however, no longer felt right.

'Do I really belong in America?' she asked herself. The question—and her eventual decision to remain in India—was irrational and almost whimsical to those around her. Like many of Shaheen's decisions, it was guided more by instinct than by logic.

'I don't know how to explain this, Dad,' Shaheen said later that night. She had dreaded the phone call all evening.

'You know this is ultimately your decision. But you're not making any sense, Shai. Tufts is a great school. Why would you want to leave that?'

'It's nothing about Tufts. It's just that—'

'It's what?'

'It's that I feel something here I haven't felt before, Dad. I feel something larger.'

'And why can't you follow that feeling back to America? You have everything here. This is your future we're talking about.'

'I know it's my future. And I know I have everything. That's the problem, Dad. I am the one who has everything.'

'And why is that a problem all of a sudden? I'm really trying to understand you, but you're not helping me, Shaheen.'

'The problem is that I don't deserve to have everything, Dad. But I do.'

Shaheen paused for a minute. She knew he was coming from a place of concern and logic. It's what he was great at. 'Well, maybe life isn't fair, Dad. And maybe life needs to change. I'll tell you what separates us, Dad. Luck. That's it. It's like God just flipped a coin one day. And I got lucky. But those kids didn't. And maybe I can change that.'

They eventually found a compromise. Shaheen could stay in Mumbai, but only with a commitment to continue her undergraduate studies at St Xavier's, one of the city's finest colleges. In exchange, she would get to follow her intuition. She soon found herself ambling into Mumbai's slum-dwelling communities, talking, in her very broken Hindi, to any child she could find.

The tiny houses in rows, constructed from garbage and scrap aluminium, enveloped her so tightly she could feel the breath of its inhabitants. The wind that day carried a nauseating stench from Cuff Parade's fishing community nearby.

'Well, who is this pretty little girl?' Shaheen asked, with her characteristic energy and effervescence. Dressed in a pair of tight shorts and a white t-shirt, the child was playing with a big red bow on her long black hair. For the next few minutes, she would continue staring at Shaheen through the dark kajal that covered her brown, sparkly eyes. After a few uneasy seconds, though, her stare gave way to a wide smile.

'Don't you have a name?' Shaheen asked again. 'Your eyes. They're stunning.' She couldn't stop looking at the soulful gaze of the six-year-old child.

'Her name is Pinky,' said the older girl sitting next to her.

'Pinky. That's a beautiful name.'

'She's my sister. And she loves that bow. It's more important to her than food.' The girl laughed and scurried away with Pinky into their home.

Over the next several days, completely uninvited, Shaheen continued visiting Pinky and her family. Talking mostly in sign language, they would share biscuits, chai, poha and other food, trying to mitigate the apparent lack of communication by eating together. As her relationship—and attachment—with Pinky grew, the unlikely pair began walking the alleys of Cuff Parade together. With every child they encountered, Shaheen would unwittingly pause and look into their eyes, wondering aloud about their dreams and fantasies.

'I bet you want to be a scientist. I wonder if we could make you India's next Einstein.' Anjali's quizzical expressions reminded Shaheen of the German scientist.

'And you want to be a cricketer. Look at how strong you are. Maybe you're our next Tendulkar.'

'And maybe you'll be our next Gandhi.'

She knew her musings were slightly crazy. Their eyes— and the immense potential that she could sense—drew her in, nevertheless. On the one hand, she began to deeply understand the richness and depth that accompanied the children of Mumbai's slums. Her pitiful first impressions, seeing these families and communities as starved and bereft of life, were wrong. Instead, they were resilient, joyful and compassionate. At the same time, though, she knew their many assets—no matter how rich—wouldn't come close to guaranteeing a better future. Pinky and the others, she quickly concluded, lacked the opportunities that Shaheen had always enjoyed.

'What is opportunity?' I asked her, as we sat in a café in 2009—a decade ago—when she first told me this story. I was curious to understand how she defined it.

'Opportunity is everything. Getting to attend one of America's best schools is opportunity. Growing up and travelling the world is opportunity,' she replied.

'Isn't that all luxury?' I asked, somewhat amused.

'Yes. It is. But the freedom to choose that is inherent in those experiences is much more than luxury. It's a human right.'

'Don't India's children have the freedom to choose their lives? To choose their dreams? Don't parents have that choice?' I asked.

'No, they really don't. Our kids can't access good schools—

that's a fact. They accept whatever money will give them. They don't have access to healthcare, to tutors, to mentors. Access is opportunity. Without it, they won't get anywhere.'

That realization prompted Shaheen to eventually start the Akanksha Foundation, an organization committed to serving India's neediest urban children. Over the next seventeen years, she would grow the foundation into an organization serving 4,000 children through sixty after-school centres and an emerging school model. The impact she witnessed there—seeing impoverished children transform into successful social workers, teachers, marketers and scientists—cemented her belief in the revolutionary power of education. It also left her feeling restless to do more.

The Akanksha Foundation, from its inception, was designed to be a model rooted in depth—they wanted to ensure they were dramatically changing the lives of every student they served. Their seemingly conservative growth was grounded in the belief that quality superseded quantity. Serving 4,000 children was quite a feat, but eventually it only fuelled Shaheen's realization that India's children simply needed more.

Bus rides to communities to pick up students, which had previously been a beloved part of her morning rituals, were now painful. Overshadowing the smiling faces of children climbing aboard were the cries of dozens more who couldn't enter. Her Cuff Parade visits no longer reminded her of the thousands of Pinkys they were now serving. Instead, she could only see the tens of thousands they weren't—the brothers, sisters, nieces and nephews of those she served.

'We have to be able to do more.' The gnawing thought wouldn't stop growing. The stories of change were no longer sufficient; she knew that hundreds of millions of children were still waiting.

'There has to be a faster way. There has to be.'

A few months later, Shaheen discovered the Teach For

America model. Teach For America's 'Fellowship' hinges on placing bright, highly-qualified individuals from reputed colleges and corporates as full-time teachers in public schools for two years. The premise is that these talented young people will eventually become leaders fighting for educational equity. A series of meetings with Wendy Kopp, Teach For America's founder, ultimately led her to not only replicate the model, but also to arrive at a key conclusion: reaching all of India's children would demand a revolution in leadership.

Shaheen's restless spirit—and the search for purpose that spurs it on—is the driving force behind a movement that's inspired more than 4,000 young Indians to take a similar leap of faith. Together, those leaders are impacting hundreds of thousands of children across India.

SIX

WHAT'S MY TALISMAN?

I will give you a talisman. Whenever you are in doubt,
or when the self becomes too much with you, apply the
following test. Recall the face of the poorest and the
weakest man [or woman] whom you may have seen, and
ask yourself, if the step you contemplate is going to be of
any use to him [or her]. Will he [or she] gain anything by
it? Will it restore him [or her] to a control over his [or her]
own life and destiny? In other words, will it lead to swaraj
[freedom] for the hungry and spiritually starving millions?
Then you will find your doubts and your self melt away.

Mahatma Gandhi, 1948

Tarun Cherukuri

Tarun stepped off the train and onto the crowded platform.
Surrounded by hundreds of swarming commuters, he was now
far away from his hometown in Vijayawada. Using both hands,
he lifted his overstuffed suitcase and gently placed it on his head.
He was beginning to regret the mounds of clothes and books
he had eagerly brought along, not to mention the days' worth of
food his mother had insisted on packing.

Tarun and his father walked briskly through the streets of
Hyderabad, searching for a rickshaw.

'It's just two years. It's just two years,' he whispered under
his breath. With every bump and turn, the ride quickly turned
unsettling.

'Son, good luck. And do well. I'll see you in the evening,' his
father said before he rode back to his friend's house, where he
and Tarun were to put up for the night.

Tarun stared at the giant billboard above the three-storey

building in front of him: 'Mega Circle: Cracking IIT-JEE at India's #1 Ranked Coaching Centre'. He walked past the tall iron gates and through the rusted wooden front door. An elderly gentleman sat quietly at the reception, his head buried in the day's *Deccan Chronicle*.

'Name, age and address?' he asked Tarun, curtly.

'Tarun Cherukuri. Fifteen years old. Vijayawada.'

'Breakfast is at 4 a.m. Classes start at five in Section G. That's in one hour. Don't be late,' he added, before settling back into his reading.

Tarun walked into Section G. The unadorned walls and dusty chalkboard were far from inviting. The chipped paint, mouldy corners and sporadic stains on the walls made the room feel more like an abandoned institution than a place he could call *his school*. But, he knew that this well-reputed coaching centre— which cost his father a fourth of his yearly income—was all they could afford.

'It's just two years. I have to make this work for just two years,' he whispered to himself.

Tarun knew how much the coaching classes meant to his parents, and to *his* future. His father didn't want him to endure the twenty-five years of monotonous labour he had toiled through as a government insurance agent. His mother wanted him to be a role model—a symbol of economic liberation for his siblings. And he wanted, more than anything else, to prove that he could do it all, that he could live up to the lofty expectations they had thrust upon him.

His confidence, however, was precarious. At the tender age of twelve, he had quickly risen to state-level stardom as a badminton player. He ranked first in doubles and third in singles. But three months ago, he had lost the most important competition of all—the nationals. He was knocked out embarrassingly early in the second round, and the wounds from the recent tournament loss were still fresh. Not knowing then how to process this failure, he decided to give up the sport and bet his future on his solid academic reputation. It was all he had left.

Section G was packed with seventy students, crammed into eighteen benches. Tarun had recently overheard one of his uncles referring to coaching centres as a 'conveyor belt system'. He was only beginning to understand what that meant.

Less than two minutes after he sat down, Mr Sridhar walked in. A middle-aged man with a greyish beard, he glared at the class and cleared his throat.

'The next two years, for each of you, will define your next fifty. You don't need me to tell you that less than 2 per cent of students get selected to the IITs, do you? It is the Harvard of India. Yet it's more competitive. Students spend years preparing, and they still fail.

'Take my advice: you're not here to make friends. You're here for yourselves. You're not going to enjoy every minute of being here, because you're not supposed to. Your parents have paid good money for you to work hard, that's what you need to do— work extremely hard for yourselves and crack India's toughest college entrance exam.'

Tarun began to miss the close-knit community he enjoyed back home. He simply had to give it time, he assured himself. His parents were right when they moved him to V. P. Siddhartha, one of the best private schools in Vijayawada. They must be right about this too.

'We'll start at five every morning,' Mr Sridhar continued. 'And we'll end at seven every evening. You will receive three hours of instruction from 5 a.m. to 8 a.m. in chemistry, math and physics. Thereafter, you will spend the rest of the day solving 100 practice problems in each subject. Every weekend, you'll be given mock assessments to test how far you've come. We won't waste a single second. You want to be a graduate of the country's greatest engineering institution? Well, this is what it takes. Now, any questions?'

Mr Sridhar was confident and blunt. He had, after all, coached more than ten batches of students successfully through the IIT-JEE.

A few days later, Tarun and a friend found a rented apartment less than two blocks from the school. It was his first week of living without his parents—meals, laundry and travel were foreign concepts and only added to the gruelling study schedule.

Every day, Tarun and his peers would wake up, attend classes and then spend the day methodically solving problems modelled after the questions on the entrance exam. And every weekend, they would take a practice test only to learn that they still had miles of content to cover.

Tarun continued the regimen for twelve gruelling months. He was now ten kilos heavier. He wasn't exercising. He wasn't even moving. He was just solving problems. But he got better and faster. By the end of the year, he was at the top of his class and ranked third in Andhra Pradesh.

'Just one more year. After that IIT and then Harvard. And then my life will be set,' Tarun said to himself.

'Crack the IIT-JEE' became his mantra. He repeated it to himself, every morning.

Until he became the one who cracked.

Maybe it was the double case of malaria and typhoid. Maybe it was the chickenpox he developed a couple of months later. Or perhaps it was just the product of more than fourteen months of solving problems and not seeing the purpose of any of it. He woke up one morning and decided he had had enough.

'I give up. Not another year. Not another day. Not another *minute.*'

He walked to the railway station and hopped on the first train to Vijayawada. For the next six hours, he obsessed over what he would tell his parents, running through every possible scenario. He would tell them he was too sick. He would tell them he had lost his sense of purpose. If neither of those worked, he would assure them that he could get into IIT himself. He didn't need the coaching classes.

But when the train finally reached Vijayawada, Tarun couldn't muster the courage to get off. 'What am I going to tell them? They'll never understand. They'll just be disappointed.'

And so, he kept riding for five straight hours until he reached Tirupati. It was the last stop and he had no choice but to disembark. Known for its pristine landscape and its revered temples, Tirupati was bustling with villagers and tourists. To Tarun's left, he could see hills covered with bright green trees. Behind them, he could see the silhouettes of the town's famous temples.

For the next seven days, he wandered through the forests of Tirupati. He visited the city's temples. He spent his afternoons reflecting on life and asking himself the philosophical questions most people save for their mid-life crisis. At night, he slept on empty benches. Having quickly exhausted his money in the first two days, he wasn't eating. His bumps wouldn't stop itching; his chickenpox was only getting worse. There was no shortage of suspicious people around him—strangers who tried to hurt him, rob him and even molest him.

Despite the unending barrage of struggles, he knew one thing for sure: he wasn't going to attend another one of Mr Sridhar's classes. The only thing scarier than going back to the coaching centre, though, was the thought of facing his parents. So he lingered in Tirupati for eight days, growing hungrier, more confused and more desperate—until a moment of serendipity.

'Ammoru vadaledu, nee onti nunchi (Hey kid, you don't look good).'

Tarun opened his eyes to see a woman standing in front of him. He could barely see her, with her bright yellow sari illuminated by the rising sunlight. It took him a few seconds to orient himself. He had passed out on the forest floor the previous night.

'Ollu antha ba ledu abba (You *really* don't look good),' she repeated. 'Maatho ra (Come with us).'

As she extended her arm to help, Tarun couldn't help but notice her hands. Her skin was wrinkled and yellowed by jaundice. There were deep cracks and cuts—each filled with dirt—extending across her hands, wrists and even her feet. The sun no longer illuminating her, he saw the holes spread across her worn-out sari. It was the kind of wear and tear that could have only been born from countless hours of manual labour, from not having the most basic sanitary equipment or water to wash up.

Putting his fears aside, Tarun followed her to her hut. Her two children stared curiously at the stranger. After all, they rarely had guests. Despite the intensity of their gaze, Tarun's fears were forgotten when the woman placed a bowl of groundnut powder and rice in front of him. He hadn't eaten in five days. Without saying a word, he hurriedly devoured it all.

As Tarun ate his last morsel, he was overcome with emotion. He couldn't stop thinking about the irony of his circumstances. This family seemingly had nothing. He, coming from a middle-class family, seemingly had everything—a good house, parents who loved him, money to buy food and clothes and an opportunity to get the best college education in the country. Yet *they* were the ones feeding *him*. He was running away from his life of abundance—from the many blessings he enjoyed—all because of a stupid exam. That's when the guilt was too much to take; he began to weep uncontrollably.

That act of generosity not only helped Tarun muster the courage to go back home, but remained ingrained in his mind forever.

It became his first talisman.

~

Tarun never got into IIT and, instead, settled for his second-best option at BITS Pilani, Hyderabad. For his friends and family, it was hardly a compromise. As a college student, Tarun worked incredibly hard; he was still determined to make his Harvard dream come true. After four successful years at BITS, he secured a job at Hindustan Unilever Limited (HUL), a prestigious multinational company. At HUL, Tarun was placed in an eighteen-month-long leadership programme. It gave prospective managers the opportunity to learn different aspects of the company from the bottom-up. He would spend three-month cycles rotating across various functions: shadowing salesmen, observing experiments in research and development labs, executing marketing campaigns in retail stores and even working the factory floors. For a twenty-two-year-old, it was a privileged and exciting opportunity. Tarun was intrigued by the notion of making products that served two-thirds of the Indian population: soaps, ice creams, jams and other commodities that would ultimately enhance the lives of India's laymen. The work at HUL fit his vision of giving back to the country he loved.

Eight months into the programme, he was placed as a production manager at an ice cream factory overseeing 500 people. Assigned the night shift, he worked the assembly line and chatted with factory workers. That experience, initially insignificant and potentially unworthy of his time, would ultimately make him crack—again.

Every night at the factory, Tarun filled ice cream cones through an oversized steel machine. He was a mere cog in a much larger assembly. Once he filled a cone, the next man's responsibility was to pack them. Except that, every night without fail, Tarun would catch the man falling asleep. This shirking of work initially annoyed Tarun, who dutifully filled his cones. But without being packed immediately, the cones would eventually go to waste.

'We have a job to do. Why can't you get this right?' Tarun confronted the gentleman. Frustrated and confused, Tarun left his post that evening. He found a table behind the plant and used his scheduled break to blow off steam. Much to his surprise, the gentleman followed.

'Sir, I'm sorry,' the man began to explain. 'Every morning, when my shift ends, I travel more than 15 kilometres back to my village. And every day, when I get home, I help my wife with the chores and tend to our kids. Before I know it, it's time to report back. Amongst everything I have to do at home, I don't have time to get proper sleep.'

As he spoke, Tarun realized it was his first time actually seeing the man's face. His dark circles, baggy eyes, dishevelled beard and coarse grey hair all made him look, well, old. Donning a dirty pair of navy blue trousers and a white shirt, the man looked as old as Tarun's father. As he continued to speak though, Tarun couldn't help but notice how different the two men were. The job at HUL, Tarun soon learned, was the only work he could find. Married by fifteen and a father at the age of seventeen, he had to take the first job available. Being a fifth-standard dropout didn't afford him many job opportunities.

Tarun was shocked at his own naivety—at the realization of his own privilege: he not only attended college but had a family that was invested in his education. As he began chatting with other workers, he discovered that their stories were troublingly similar to the old man's. They were filled with hardship—long distances to travel, chores to manage, children to raise and little time and money to do it all. Each of them was struggling to make ends meet. With long shifts at the plant, they had no time to sleep. Instead, they were getting pulled up by managers who would yell, scream and curse to get them to work. On multiple occasions, Tarun would cringe as he helplessly watched these encounters unfold. Unable to contain himself any longer, he impulsively decided to write to the company's senior leadership about the factory's malpractices.

'We have a value dissonance at Hindustan Unilever,' Tarun wrote. 'The values we espoused in our induction are not in sync with the reality at this plant. Both in terms of how trainees, including myself, are treated and how floor workers are handled. This is not the HUL I signed up to work for and am passionate about. This is not the HUL I dream of growing in.'

Taken aback by his email, HUL executives immediately transferred Tarun to a more functional plant. But his letter left a mark on them. They were impressed by his audacity. At the end of the leadership programme, he was the only management trainee promoted to the Head Office. He was made responsible for introducing new and innovative products under the Kwality Wall's brand of ice creams in India.

The promotion excited Tarun. It vindicated his relentless work ethic and commitment. The opportunity enabled him to travel across the country, liaise with executives and top officials and work on strategy as well as execution.

He was grateful. But his talisman—the image of the Tirupati family—wouldn't disappear. In fact, the further along he moved in his career, the stronger it became.

'I'm making ice cream. Really, how is that helping the family in Tirupati? How is it helping these factory workers?' He couldn't escape the nagging stream of self-inflicted questions.

A few weeks later, Tarun boarded a routine flight to Delhi. He couldn't find his usual read, the *Economic Times*. So, he picked up a copy of the *Times of India*, stuffed neatly in his seat pocket. Plastered across the front page was an ad, a ticket to reunite with his talisman.

YOU COULD SETTLE. FOR THE DESIGNATION. THE NEAT PAYCHECK. THE LONG, LONG INTERNSHIP. THE SAFETY OF THE HERD. A BOSS. A SCHEDULE. YOUR DAD'S PROFESSION. YOUR MOM'S APPROVAL. A COMPROMISE OF DREAMS. A KNOWN TOMORROW. A HUNDRED KNOWN TOMORROWS. FOR A NAME, PRINTED ON A CARD. **OR YOU COULD FIGHT. FOR THAT DREAM YOU'VE ALWAYS HAD.** FOR CHANGE. FOR A CHANGED NATION. FOR A HUNDRED KIDS YOU DON'T EVEN KNOW. FOR THEIR FREEDOM. AND YOUR FREEDOM. FOR THE LEADERS THEY COULD BECOME. AND THE LEADER YOU KNOW YOU CAN BE. **FOR A NAME, CARVED IN HISTORY.**

TEACHFORINDIA

NEEDS LEADERS AND VISIONARIES.
TO BUILD THE NATION AND THEIR CAREER.

find out more at www.teachforindia.org

Anurag Kundu

'Wow! I've always wanted to use one of these.'

The NIT Kurukshetra librarian was amused at Anurag's reaction. Hundreds of students walked into the library every day and none of them were as fascinated by the computer kiosk used to find books as this young chap was.

'Yeah. It's pretty neat. Just type the name of a book,' the librarian suggested. 'And it will tell you exactly where to find it— which shelf, which section, which aisle. It's all in there.'

Anurag had never seen a library so big. There must have been 100,000 books here. He had already spent an hour roaming the aisles of the library, the antithesis of the tiny and highly regulated bookstore in his rural hometown in the outskirts of Delhi.

While the selection of books there was poor, the experience of choosing one made worse by the austere librarian. 'Study guides and dictionaries only. Your schoolwork comes first,' she would say. Anurag often tried to fabricate creative and compelling reasons to get his hands on the books he actually wanted to read. 'But our Hindi teacher asked us to write a two-page summary of Kiran Bedi's *Galti Kiski*,' he pleaded. Needless to say, the plan didn't work and, eventually, he quit trying. Instead, he resorted to relying on the kindness of a few teachers, who every once in a while, would borrow books in their names and secretly pass them on to him.

Anurag spent most of his afternoons watching his father till the land and harvest the next crop of rice, wheat and vegetables. Though embedded in his lineage, farming hadn't been easy on his father. His body was frail and the physical toll caused him to age much faster than expected.

The opportunity to attend college couldn't have been more important to Anurag's family. For the first decade of his life, his family lived on limited means. In 2000, his father hit a jackpot when their tomatoes were sold for a generous profit. The money enabled them to make humble changes to their lifestyle. They built a toilet at home. They could afford to move Anurag from a public to a low-cost private school. As it turned out, Anurag was academically gifted. And so naturally, over time, they hoped he would be the first to graduate among them and the first to earn a degree. Those expectations didn't fall short on Anurag. He wanted all of that too.

When it came to selecting his course and career, the choice was automatically made for him. All the smart kids took science. It guaranteed that Anurag could propel his family to the next step on the socioe-conomic ladder.

The first week of college was a plethora of discoveries. His first trip to the post office. His first bank transaction. And, of course, his first introduction to a real library that morning.

'Is this it?' the grey-haired librarian asked, impassively.

Anurag had picked up an eclectic set of books—Abdul Kalam's *Wings of Fire*, J. K. Rowling's *Harry Potter and the Philosopher's Stone* and Mahatma Gandhi's *The Story of My Experiments with Truth*. He was excited, but he was also convinced the librarian would deny his request. As he walked sheepishly towards the front desk, he rehearsed his explanations.

'It's all for coursework. We have several big papers due next week. You know how Professor Joshi is.'

Just as he began to nervously fumble over his words, the librarian swiftly grabbed the books and interrupted.

'Return them in two weeks. Enjoy reading.'

'That's it?' Anurag was half shocked, half outraged. No questions. No interrogation. Does he not know how to do his job? he thought to himself.

'Excuse me?' the librarian was confused.

'Umm. I mean. Don't you have to write this down somewhere? That I'm taking these books?'

'I scanned them. That's what the scanner is for. It records which books are checked out and tells me which ones are on the shelves.'

'You mean you can see which books are in the library using the computer?'

'Yes. See. I type the name of a book, and it tells me exactly how many copies are out, how many are in the library, and where to find those.' Anurag was amazed. He had theoretically studied computers growing up, but he had never actually used one.

'Sir, just one more question. What are the timings for the computer lab next door?'

'It's open twenty-four hours.'

'And what am I allowed to use?'

'You are allowed to do anything and you have access to the *whole* computer,' the librarian replied, smiling at Anurag's questions.

Anurag experienced many culture shocks during his first year in college. He wasn't used to the access or the freedom. From evening parties and the nightlife of Delhi to libraries, museums and classes that were all optional to attend—it was all a bit much. Over time, though, the shock gave way to something much more powerful.

It was the access to endless information that was perhaps the most disorienting. Anurag would spend his days glued to the computer, often skipping classes to explore the many facets of the internet. He would read wiki after wiki, following the links wherever they took him: India's freedom struggle. Nobel Prize winners. Apartheid. Ambedkar's writings. Gandhi's letters. Nehru's letters. Democracy. The French Revolution. When he wasn't in the computer lab, he was in the library poring through piles of newly borrowed books, newspapers op-eds and magazine articles. Desperately trying to make up for years of starvation, his appetite for knowledge was voracious.

Anurag found himself drawn to topics like politics, applied history and government. He was fascinated by the epochal moments underpinning Indian Independence. Gandhi's reflections on gender and labour challenged him. They forced him to debate why society valued a CEO more than a toilet cleaner. Kalam's writings on values and character forced him to question and envision a better India. Perhaps most defining of all were Ambedkar's exhortations to his countrymen in his speech delivered the night before the Constitution was adopted and Independence formally claimed. His warnings, which ring true more than fifty years later, caught Anurag's eye:

> We must make our political democracy a social democracy as well. Political democracy cannot last unless there lies at the base of it social democracy. What does social democracy mean? It means a way of life which recognizes liberty, equality and fraternity as the principles of life.

We must begin by acknowledging the fact that there is complete absence of two things in Indian Society. One of these is equality. On the social plane, we have in India a society based on the principle of graded inequality which means elevation for some and degradation for others. On the economic plane, we have a society in which there are some who have immense wealth as against many who live in abject poverty. On the 26th of January 1950, we are going to enter into a life of contradictions. How long shall we continue to live this life of contradictions?

—B. R. Ambedkar, Constituent Assembly Speech, 1949

A semester into college, Anurag realized he was changing. He was starting to grapple with notions of inequity and social injustice, quickly losing interest in his engineering coursework. His upbringing now made sense not as random individual struggles inflicted out of chance, but as legitimate, systemic issues that needed to be solved. His lack of access to computers and toilets growing up was no longer circumstantial; it was a symptom of the deep-rooted problems in Indian society. More importantly, he understood that this wasn't limited to *his* family or even his hometown. These were pervasive issues that affected an entire country.

The state of the poor in our country is unimaginable. Why is nobody talking about it? Why isn't *this* on the front page of every newspaper? Why aren't people up in arms? he thought.

He considered dropping out of college, no longer sure of his plan to become an engineer. But he was afraid of the shame it would bring to his father, to his family. So he continued, doing the bare minimum to pass his engineering exams and spending all his free time cooped up in the library. The vastness of politics, applied history and government fascinated him. The only challenge was figuring out what to do with this newfound knowledge.

Nalika Breganza

'I hate this damn curfew,' Nalika grumbled as she looked at her watch.

She had ninety minutes to be downstairs, walk to Amarsons Garden, go on her daily run, play with Mamta and return before her college hostel's 8 p.m. curfew. This was the last day of classes before the break, so she didn't want to miss her cherished routine.

'We live in the poshest part of Mumbai. I don't know why we even need a stupid curfew.' As Nalika hurriedly tied her shoelaces, her roommate half-heartedly listened to a rant she had heard too many times before.

She pushed open the bright orange door and sprinted down the three floors of her dormitory stairs. While intent on finishing her daily 5-kilometre run, she also knew Mamta would be waiting for her. And the journey to Amarsons Garden was one she hated to rush.

The walk from Sophia College to Amarsons Garden was Nalika's favourite part of the day. It was a routine that started with the back entrance of the regal college, which was once home to the Maharaja of Indore. The pinkish-orange neoclassical architecture, adorned with flowers and surrounded by neatly groomed plants, offered a feeling of tranquility. The roads outside Sophia College captivated her just as intensely. Her path started on Pedder Road and took her by Antilia, the majestic twenty-seven-floor residence of the Ambani family that's rumoured to have more than 600 staff members. In the streets that followed were Tommy Hilfiger, Lacoste, Raymond and a wide array of high-end imported brand-stores. Every day, as Nalika made that walk, she would peer into the windows of South Mumbai's most impressive bungalows, her mind drifting to the lives of their occupants—lives filled with riches and extravagances.

Only thirty seconds later, those thoughts would be

interrupted by the seemingly incessant line of vegetable merchants, sandwich shops, chaat stalls and corn sellers. Next to the vendors were their children. Most of them couldn't afford the 10 rupees needed to enter the famous park. From across the street, they watched Nalika and others enjoy its beauty.

The deep contrast disturbed Nalika. It was a stark difference to the uniformity she had grown up with in Singapore. The poverty there, while present, wasn't as confrontational. The calmness inside the garden did little to quell her uneasiness.

'You're coming to play today?'

Nalika lit up as soon as she heard Mamta's high-pitched, cracking voice.

'What happened to your kurta?' Nalika asked. She noticed a deep tear that left her lower back fully exposed. Mamta smiled coyly, ignoring her.

Nalika wasn't sure why she was so drawn to Mamta. Perhaps it was the guilt she felt every time she walked into Amarsons Garden, knowing that Mamta couldn't come along. Maybe it was the realization that no other children would play with her. Many of them were quite frightened by her slanted eyes, flat nose, bulging neck and awkward mannerisms. Her atypical body structure, a result of Down syndrome, often made her the subject of terrified stares. It also made her quite lonely.

As Nalika looked down at her watch, she knew she was going to have to choose between her run and playing with Mamta or face the consequences of returning past curfew. She looked back at Mamta, whose fingers were now running down the newly discovered tear.

'Let's go get that sandwich. I'll run tomorrow.' Grilled sandwiches in hand, they peered into the gates of the garden. They watched dozens of children play on the park's swings and run by their mothers, many of whom were heavily engrossed in their phones. A few seconds later, a little boy passed by Mamta, pointed at her and started laughing.

'Look at her neck! And look at her dirty clothes! That girl's retarded,' he shouted to his friends.

'How could they say that? Do these kids not have any manners? Ignore them, Mamta.' As usual, Nalika grew enraged and as always, Mamta was oblivious to it all. She was busy enjoying her sandwich and didn't have a care in the world.

Nalika's mind began moving in a thousand different directions. As she looked down at Mamta, and then back at the park, she thought about the differences between their two lives.

'I wish you could just go in there. I wish all of these kids would accept you. I wish you didn't have to hear these hurtful words so regularly,' Nalika whispered, knowing Mamta wasn't paying attention.

Saying goodbye to Mamta that evening was harder than usual—though she didn't know why. They had stared through that gate at least a hundred times before. They had listened to the random abuses that were always flung Mamta's way. But the unfairness of it all hadn't struck her as painfully as it did that night. As Nalika walked back to Sophia College, the scenic contrasts began to take on a whole new meaning. The fancy shops and the twenty-seven-floor building—and the materialistic promises that they carried with them—all seemed empty now.

She knew Mamta and the other children living outside of Amarsons Garden would never have access to those promises. They would likely not grow up to have access to the regal gates she entered every day, to the caring professors, and to the Shakespeare and Yeats that often left her jumping in excitement. They would never have parents—or anyone really—encouraging them to get their doctorate in English Literature at Oxford.

~

'Nalika! Are you listening? So can I go? I have lots to do,' Ayesha exclaimed. She was clearly in a hurry.

'I am so sorry. I wasn't listening. What did you want me to

do?' Nalika was slightly embarrassed and lost in thought. It was her last year of college; three years had unwittingly flown by. It felt like she suddenly woke up one day and all everyone could talk about was jobs. As a result, she was growing increasingly anxious about her own future. The plan was always to pursue a doctorate in English Literature, but she just wasn't *feeling* up to it.

'I have to miss Drama Club practice today,' Ayesha said.

Nalika, Ayesha and an entire cast and crew were preparing for a production of Vijay Tendulkar's *Silence! The Court is in Session*. Ayesha played a central character in the play. They only had three days left till opening night and there was much to be accomplished. Being the President of the Drama Club and the perfectionist that Nalika was, her usually patient demeanour was replaced by a stressed avatar.

That's when she first noticed Ayesha's T-shirt. It was plain white with the words 'Teach For India' written across the front in bright blue.

'What's "Teach For India"?' Nalika asked, tilting her head slightly.

'That's exactly what I've been trying to explain to you for the last five minutes. Look. I'm a Campus Ambassador for Teach For India. It's an organization that works with underprivileged kids. They place graduates from reputed colleges and corporates— people like you and me—in government schools as full-time teachers for two years. It's a fellowship programme. What's amazing though is you go into it thinking you're going to change the lives of these kids. But, everyone I've spoken to says they've learned more from their kids than the kids have learned from them.

'Ugh. I'm giving you my entire presentation. Look, I have thirty college students waiting for me to talk to them about the fellowship. Since our rehearsal time got rescheduled, it's clashing with this info session. I can't skip it; it's too late to do that now. So I'll be gone for just an hour. Please tell me that's okay? I'll be back before you know it.'

Ayesha Susan Thomas. Teaching? Kids?

Nalika could not imagine Ayesha having anything to do with either of those things. But she was intrigued. Ayesha was one of Nalika's closest friends. Nalika knew her well enough to know that she rarely praised anyone or anything. You could say she had high standards or even that she was a hardcore cynic. Regardless, if *she* couldn't stop talking about Teach For India, Nalika had to find out what this fellowship programme was all about.

'Fine. Go. But I also want to know more the fellowship. So tell me about it as soon you're back?'

'Done. Thank you!' Ayesha sang gleefully as she hugged Nalika and ran towards the door.

Soumya Jain

Soumya was diligently typing away at his desk, his gaze constantly shifting between the two screens directly in front of him. He only took breaks to sip his coffee. He was determined to debug these lines of code and figure out why his software program wasn't working.

Suddenly, the recognizable celebratory music started playing. His colleagues slowly left their desks and joined a core group cheering loudly in the middle of the office. At Lutron Electronics, this was how promotions were announced. As the group made their way across the open office layout, Soumya looked up with a smile. Completely unaware that they were walking towards his desk, he wondered who was being promoted today.

The move to the United States was tough for Soumya. Leaving his entire family in Pune, a city that he had grown to love, was tougher. Getting into Penn State for his master's and securing a job at Lutron was the toughest. And now, in 2012, this was his first promotion. In less than three hours, he would be managing a team of eight and committing to designing an entirely new line of products.

Soumya sat back at his desk after the announcement, feeling immensely satisfied. Throughout the day, engineers, designers and product managers from various teams stopped by and congratulated him on the promotion.

In the months that followed, Soumya's life only grew more exciting. He was successfully managing product launches. His teammates and bosses loved him. He had bought his first car, a second-hand but beautiful Mercedes. And his fiancée was enjoying her work at a local chemical engineering firm just a few miles down the road.

Life in the US, for both of them, was good. Thoughts of Pune seemed far and distant. At twenty-five, they were saving more money than they could have ever imagined. They were convinced that they had found the formula for a successful and happy life.

A month later, Soumya's pay cheque arrived, as usual. A moment that should have unlocked yet another level of happiness and fulfilment for Soumya, couldn't have had a more baffling effect.

'$4,000!' Soumya stared in disbelief at the contents of the envelope. 'What do we even do with this money, Gauri?'

He looked at his fiancée, who was sitting on the couch, unable to comprehend his reaction.

'What do you mean?' she asked, puzzled.

'We have a car. We have an apartment. We've paid off our college loans. We've passed every savings goal we set. Why do we need this money?'

Gauri didn't know quite how to respond. She had never really thought about what they *needed*. Before coming to the US, they had both planned their lives as a series of milestones waiting to be checked off. Everything was going according to plan, and she couldn't understand why he wasn't celebrating.

'I know we can invest it. Sure—it will grow by 15 per cent or whatever. But what's the point? I don't want a bigger house. That's just more area for us to vacuum. I don't want a fancier car. We already have a Mercedes. And we just travelled to Italy and Peru, and have the next two vacations planned out already!'

Gauri was still silent, listening patiently. He sat beside her on their white couch. After a few moments of silent contemplation, he sighed.

'Gauri, what's the larger purpose of my working here? Because it can't be money.'

Soumya knew that he was processing a feeling that had been gnawing him for quite some time. He *should* have been happy. But he couldn't escape a nagging restlessness, something that—he admitted to himself—had been building up for weeks, no, months. It was the same feeling he experienced every time he opened the NDTV app on his iPhone and read Indian news headlines that often carried stories of corruption, violence and poverty. It was the same feeling he experienced every time he talked to friends in Pune, who would spend hours rattling off the many challenges in India, problems which transformed to untapped opportunities in his mind. And it was the same feeling his father once told him would bring him back. After all, he was 12,000 kilometres away from the place he called home.

'Okay, then. What do you want to do? Quit?' Gauri asked, a little peeved.

She couldn't see the point of his ramblings. She picked up the Apple TV remote to put on a show on Netflix. It was their weeknight ritual, their way of unwinding after a long day at work.

'Yes. I want to quit,' Soumya said quietly.

'Have you lost it?' Gauri asked, turning sharply to face him, now giving him her complete attention. 'You love working at Lutron! You just got promoted. You have a clear career path ahead of you. Another two, maybe three, years and you'll be a Senior Design and Development Engineer. And then Project Lead. And finally, a VP role. Did something happen at work today?'

'No, no. Just hear me out,' Soumya insisted. 'What are

we doing here, Gauri, really? We're paying 30 per cent of our income in taxes to one of the wealthiest nations in the world. We're contributing to building a country that is already miles ahead of everyone else, especially our own. I can't escape this feeling that has been growing inside me lately, the feeling that India is where I should be. That's the country we've grown up in, where we studied practically for free for fifteen years, where we learned 90 per cent of what we know today and based on which we're here in the US. Don't we have a responsibility to build that country?'

'But, we've already *built* a life here. And you want us to just throw all of that away?'

Gauri's voice grew more anxious and urgent. For the next thirty minutes, Soumya listened to her list the benefits and the friends and luxuries they had. She preached about the sense of security found only in America. She reminded him of the exciting cutting-edge work they both enjoyed, coupled with an enviable work-life balance. She recounted the life plans they had committed to. Technically, she was right—about all of it. But Soumya knew he wanted more.

'I love the work I do at Lutron, Gauri. That's not the problem. I've loved it for the past three years and I have learned so much. But, I'm tired of designing automated shades for office windows. I'm tired of building products that only 0.1 per cent of the world can access. I want to build something that matters to people.'

'Okay. What's the issue with doing that here? You can do something great right here—in America. Let's talk about ideas. There are endless possibilities.'

'No, Gauri. It's not possible here. We're here on work visas. We're not even allowed to start anything. Hell, we can't even get another job without re-applying. We're tied to our H1Bs. In India, I have a network of hundreds of people—friends and family. I have the ability to take a risk, fail and still have something to fall back on. And if I succeed, I have the satisfaction of positively impacting the very lives that have gone into building my own. Sure, I can stay in the US. The meritocracy is comforting; if I work hard and am reasonably competent, I will live a good life. But to break from good to great as an immigrant in the US is really, *really* hard. Think of all of our friends. They're in good places—Oracle, Apple, Microsoft. But for every Vinod Khosla or Sabeer Bhatia, there are 80,000 engineers who are just writing linear code. They're small cogs in a large machine.'

'And why is that necessarily a bad thing? We're all part of a larger system, Soumya, at the end of the day. We simply choose how we each want to contribute. I, for one, love where I am and am incredibly proud of the work I'm doing.'

'But I don't feel the same way, Gauri. I need something bigger. I need purpose. Every sector in India is exploding right now. It's like the US in the 1900s. Yes, there are enormous challenges, but the flipside of those challenges is incredible opportunity. America may have been the land of opportunity for Europeans in the 1800s and 1900s. But today, I think the land of opportunity for us—and I mean for you as well—is India.'

Gauri was starting to process his words carefully—he was livelier than she had ever seen him before.

'I don't want to build products, dammit. I want to build India.'

My First Recruitment Pitch

I'll never forget my first recruitment presentation for Teach For India. It was also my first visit to an Indian college. Both discouraging and surreal, it was an experience that nevertheless represented the state of higher education in India.

'You're telling me you want young Indians to apply for a two-year fellowship?'

Mr Gangoli, the placement head of a local college at the heart of Pune, was an elderly gentleman who had been running the college's career fair for more than three decades. As we sat in his office that hot afternoon in 2009, he was clearly sceptical.

'Yes, sir, that's correct,' I replied.

'And you want them to teach in government schools? With students from low-income backgrounds?'

'Yes, sir, that's correct. We believe that placing India's top graduates in the country's most struggling schools is one of the best ways of solving the nation's educational crisis. But we believe it's what these leaders do *after* the fellowship that is most important. The fellowship is intended to be a platform to develop a new generation of India's leaders. The intense experience our fellows undergo will, ultimately, transform them in ways that are both powerful and progressive.'

'I see,' he said unconvinced. 'And you want them to teach in those classrooms?'

He had clearly ignored my last sentence. Before I could reply, he jumped in again with his next question.

'Why not just recruit from teacher colleges?'

'Well, we're also recruiting from there. But we believe that we're only going to solve this problem if we're recruiting from India's best institutions. That means going beyond teacher colleges to well-reputed engineering, commerce and humanities institutions as well—that includes yours, of course.'

'And how many people have applied so far?' he asked.

'Not many. Less than a hundred. We've only been running for three months, though.'

'And you actually think they're going to join? You know this isn't America, right?' His last line stung a little. I had guessed from our first introduction that my American accent would be greeted with bemused scepticism. Clearly, I was right.

'Let me tell you something about India, son.' He leaned back in his chair and took off his glasses. I could sense the beginnings of a fatherly lecture and braced myself for it.

'The youth here are different. They don't have the social bent that you Americans have. They're concerned about their careers. I've been watching them for thirty years. There's too much parental pressure. And no parent in India will allow their kids to go teach, let alone in a government school. That's why the government has such bad teachers right now anyway.'

As he continued, I wasn't sure how to respond. I was already a little apprehensive, and struggling to break the ice with him only made me more nervous. So, I just listened.

'This model isn't going to work here. I can tell you that right now. I suggest you either go back to America or you go recruit from the teachers' colleges down the road.' Despite his conviction, he agreed to allow us to meet with their final-year students. I wasn't sure why. Perhaps it was amusement, or perhaps it was just sympathy.

In the ten years that have passed since that initial reckoning, more than 90,000 young Indians have taken the courageous first step of applying for the Teach For India Fellowship. While far fewer have been selected (our candidates say proudly that our acceptance rates are comparable to Harvard), thousands have accepted the call to spend two years fighting for the rights of impoverished children, who currently don't have many.

Some, like Nalika, applied because they were in pursuit of their purpose. They saw a promise in the unparalleled love and undying loyalty children had for their fellows. 'If I could be the person who puts them on a fundamentally different life path— these two years will be worth it. And who knows, I might find a calling,' she recalls thinking at the time. Others wanted to build a better country. Like Soumya, they realized that that pursuit will succeed only if they gave themselves to the cause. No one else was going to build that better country for them. 'It could be Health For India, Run For India or Cook For India. It could be anything. It's the *For India* bit that matters,' Soumya often recounts. And, for many, the fellowship opportunity has spoken to an inner bechaini (disquiet)—a disillusionment with the status quo—that had been brewing for years. They have either closely witnessed—like Tarun—or experienced first-hand—like Anurag—

the injustices that often accompany poverty and inequity.

All of them, regardless of the talismans driving them, believed in the power of ensuring that all Indian children get the opportunities they deserve. Awaiting them were the challenges and stumbling blocks that await any first-time teacher. But, as you'll discover in the pages ahead, it was only through their classrooms that they discovered a calling greater than anything they'd experienced before.

SEVEN
HAPPY HARVARD

Tarun and Aditya struggled to navigate the narrow lanes of Wadgaon Sheri, searching for any signboard they could find.

'Where is this school?' Tarun shouted. He was frustrated. Teach For India staff members had given him explicit directions, which he had followed precisely. They were now searching for a building, a placard—anything. But they only found dilapidated houses, sheds and empty land. 'Excuse me. Yeh National Children's Academy kahaan hai (Where is the National Children's Academy)?' Tarun stepped out of the rickshaw to speak with an elderly woman walking on the street.

'Bas aage, right mein (Just ahead, on the right).' Leaning on her cane with one hand, the woman slowly lifted her other arm and pointed ahead to the empty field.

They walked slowly towards the barren area and through the makeshift, wired gate that formed the entryway. Taped to the side of the gate was a white sheet of paper, folded inwards, with the school's name scrawled across it in a black marker: 'N. C. A.'

'This can't be a school,' Tarun thought out loud.

Still bewildered, Tarun and Aditya continued walking, carefully plotting their steps to avoid broken glass, empty cans and heaps of anthills. Less than 200 metres ahead was a small, six-foot-high brick building (if one could even call it that) sandwiched between two tin sheds of similar height. Moss grew between the bricks and cracks of tin. A faded green door stood in front.

'This is a far cry from a *National* Children's Academy,' Tarun chuckled.

The next moment, his smile disappeared. He remembered

his last day at Hindustan Unilever. Sitting across from him in a well air-conditioned, top-floor office, the general manager's last words to him seemed more like a premonition now: 'You're going to find yourself working in some dilapidated building in the middle of nowhere. And when you do, you're going to wish you were back at HUL.'

His parents hadn't been too encouraging of his decision either. He knew they wouldn't be and, as a result, did not consult them when he quit. Instead, he simply packed his bags and once again found himself on the train home to Vijayawada. This time, though, he had the courage to get off and tell them the truth.

'Have you seen what they're paying you? How many zeroes lost! How could you do this to us?' His mom didn't wait a minute, unleashing her emotions as soon as his spiel ended.

'You teach for two years and then what?' his dad asked incisively.

'What will you do when you have to find a wife? Who will marry you? Please listen to me and don't do this,' his mother pleaded. 'I won't ask you for anything else ever. Please just do this for me.'

As Tarun stared at the school, he knew he had no time to think about all of that now.

If these are the cards I've been dealt, then so be it, he told himself.

Tarun took a deep breath and walked through the faded green door. Inside the school's 'office' sat a middle-aged woman dressed in a blue kurta, wearing a thick pair of glasses with scratches on them. She looked up at her new visitors.

'Yes, welcome!' she said with a wide smile. Her desk was cluttered with large ledgers, old newspapers, dusty textbooks and dozens of unused stamps.

'Ma'am, my name is Tarun Cherukuri. This is Aditya. We're the Teach For India Fellows that have been placed here.'

'That's wonderful. We've been waiting for you. You're both a bit younger that we expected but that's okay. Every teacher has to start somewhere, I suppose. Let's introduce you to some of the other teachers and show you both to your classrooms.'

Tarun paused at the door of his classroom. He took another deep breath as he walked into the tiny space. The wooden benches were turned upside down. The blackboard was covered with dust and old tape. The walls had a yellowish-green tint, a product of years of mould and decay. And the room had a stench of old garbage that was exacerbated by the lack of ventilation in Pune's scorching heat.

It was overwhelming.

But Tarun also knew that he had thirty-three kids arriving in less than twenty-four hours and a classroom that was the least inviting place he had ever seen. He had no choice. He had to get to work.

~

'Class, we're going to be on a mission this year.' Tarun was shouting at the top of his lungs, trying to overcome the yelling, clamouring and sawing noises coming from the construction work that was going on right outside his door.

'We only have two years together. That's not a lot of time. So we're going to set some big goals today!'

He used his hands to make a 'big' gesture as he looked down at the thirty-three third-graders who tightly filled the eight benches in his tin-shed classroom. They stared back at him, their blank expressions telling him something was not right.

He began to speak with more urgency. He grew more animated over the next fifteen minutes, hoping he would gain their attention.

'And every day, we're going to work hard to reach those goals. And reach them we will! Every single one of us! We're going to succeed! Now, who can tell me what is a goal?'

No hands were raised.

'No? Okay, maybe someone can give me an example of a goal.'
The silence continued.

'Okay. Here's an example. My goal is to learn all of your names by the end of this week. Now, can some of you give me an example of your goals?'

The kids began talking amongst themselves and were no longer looking at Tarun. His classroom windows opened right into the streets of the community. Peeping in were a group of slightly older boys. They pointed at Tarun and started laughing.

Before he could continue, a group of students in the back stood up. They began to imitate Tarun's oversized gestures. Pulling their hands above their heads, they stretched their arms to mimic his description of 'big'. The rest of the class looked on for a moment and paused, before erupting in laughter.

'Sir, inko kuch samaj nahi aa raha hain. Subah se kuch bhi nahi (Sir, they can't understand you. They haven't understood a word you've been saying all morning).'

The woman sitting at the back of the room hadn't spoken until now.

'They only speak Urdu or Hindi. Aur tumhara "ek-cent" funny hai. Aap Pune se nahi ho, na (You have a funny accent. You're not from Pune, are you)?'

She had been watching Tarun since the moment he arrived, tapping her nails on the desk, with an expression that was part amusement and part bewilderment.

'Would you like me to translate into Hindi as you speak? Or can you speak in Hindi?'

Before Tarun could respond, the boys peeping from outside interjected.

'Oiii. Iski toh pehle din mein hi wicket gir gayi (He lost a wicket on the first day itself)!'

'Woh bhi duck out (That too, a duck out)!'

'Ab dekh Rajani Ma'am maidan mein aayegi aur sixer maregi (Now watch, Rajani Ma'am will hit a sixer).'

As the boys continued their taunts, Tarun's new class continued to laugh.

Tarun felt defeated. He had led a factory of 500 workers, sat in meetings with big names in business, packed thousands of ice cream cones during late night shifts and even laboured through the IIT coaching centre, but he had *never* faced such humiliation and disappointment—from a group of *children*, no less. Adding to his misery, he had spent hours preparing for today's lesson—carefully scripting his explanations, thinking about what questions he would ask and designing goal-setting worksheets for his kids. He had spent half his evening scouring stores for stickers and colourful post-its to give students. He intended to have individual conversations with them, hoping to learn something new about each one. And now, less than forty-five minutes into his day, he couldn't even get them to listen to a word he was saying. Even if they did listen, they wouldn't understand him.

Tarun wiped the sweat on his brow and cleared his throat.

'Rajani Ma'am, can you take the next class please? I need a break.'

Rajani Ma'am taught the kids for the rest of the day and Tarun went home that Monday evening, filled with despair. Between the tin sheds, the loud construction, the blank faces and a woman who seemed to enjoy every moment of his misery, this was not the grand first day he had envisioned.

'It isn't too late. Please listen to me. There's still a chance. You can still go back to HUL,' his mother said to him on the phone later that evening. He had lost count of the number of times she had tried to reason with him. It's the same call that hundreds of Teach For India Fellows across the country receive, every single day. For Tarun's parents, and for many others, grappling with the notion of a fellowship that brings with it adverse conditions and a humble stipend is tough to accept.

Tarun dismissed his mother's well-intentioned words. He

was preoccupied with one thought: getting his kids to listen. He knew he had to turn things around, and fast.

Before he saw the tin shed reality of N. C. A., Tarun had painted a mental picture of his perfect classroom. It would be colourful and animated, filled with images of his favourite cartoon characters. During this training, he had spent hours conjuring images of Mickey Mouse, Tom and Jerry and Scooby Doo. He thought of the dozens of bright colours that would adorn his walls. His classroom would be a place where kids wanted to stay and learn.

Energized by that mental picture, Tarun pulled out his laptop and a sheet of chart paper. He started searching for cartoon characters. The relics from his childhood days were likely to be no longer relevant. He needed something new, something his kids would understand.

'Atom Ant and Busy Bee. That's it!' The alliteration, which corresponded to the first few letters of the alphabet, would prove useful in teaching his children English.

There, on his first sheet of chart paper, Tarun's classroom was born. Atom Ant, Busy Bee, Crazy Cat and Diamond Dolphin would together become his class mascots. He didn't want to surrender entirely to his children's context. He would leave them with a new thing or two by incorporating Dr Seuss's famous character—Cat in the Hat—into his classroom. Diamond Dolphin was a made-up figure that he and his kids could use to stretch their imaginations and exercise their creative muscles. If he were being honest, he just wanted to hold on to the alliteration and couldn't find a suitable character whose name began with 'D'.

He wanted to move quickly to bring that piece of chart paper to life. The following weekend, he found a painter from the community—the father of one of his students—who agreed to help him for 3,000 rupees. He was thrilled. He didn't think twice about dipping into his savings from HUL. They both spent most of Saturday scrubbing and whitewashing the mouldy walls to remove the yellowish-green tint. Over the next forty-eight hours, using the chart paper blueprint he had created, cans of paint and newly purchased brushes, they created Tarun's new classroom.

On Monday morning at 6.45 a.m., Tarun stood proudly outside his classroom. He couldn't wait for the first student to enter. As they began walking in, they looked at the walls and gasped with excitement. They didn't know where to look first. The painted tree on the front wall of the classroom had names of famous books inscribed on its trunk. Atom Ant was pointing to the class's daily objective template on the blackboard. Replacing the mouldy decay was now a painted canvas of grass, along with bright blue skies and fluffy white clouds. On the back wall, the names of the students were plastered across—he wanted them to know that this was their classroom.

Tarun watched gleefully as his thirty-three third-graders took in their new surroundings. He was even more satisfied when they sat attentively throughout the entire day's lesson. 'I've won their attention and their trust. Now I've got to follow this up with rigour. They have to actually learn something,' Tarun thought to himself.

The next few months held plenty of promise. The copious hours he invested into preparation were beginning to pay off. He learned how to make his classes more creative. Using props, visuals and movies, his lessons ranged from fractions and subtraction to inferences and predictions. His kids were more engaged than anyone had ever seen them. While they still couldn't understand every word of English that he so adamantly used, they began to pick up key words and follow along. Through their broken translations, they were learning new concepts. His relationship with his students also blossomed in the process. He started visiting homes and spending time with parents and siblings, who would remark at his seemingly unorthodox approach to class control.

'You're the first teacher that hasn't hit our children. But you have control of the class,' they exclaimed.

Despite the class's gradual progress though, scepticism was building. During the first parent-teacher meeting of the year—less than three months into his fellowship—that scepticism boiled over.

'Their books are empty! They don't have homework. What do you teach them all day?' One parent was visibly angry. Before she could continue, another child's father stood up and jumped in.

'And they're telling us you're not even following the textbook. Is that true? How do you expect our kids to gain a scholarship? You do realize that's their only shot at getting into a better school in the future, don't you? '

Tarun sat at the front of the class and listened patiently. Every time he tried to offer a rebuttal, another parent would stand up, complaining about the lack of homework or his refusal to adhere to the defined curriculum. He knew their worries were quite rational. In fact, he was reassured to see their passionate involvement in their children's education. Most of his children's parents held odd jobs—some were rickshaw drivers, others were carpenters, while a few were day labourers. Yet, they were spending a large part of their meagre salary every month on tuition. They believed that the affordable private school, despite its decrepit appearance and lack of infrastructure, would ensure their children access to better opportunities.

Tarun, though, didn't know how to tell them that neither the curriculum nor the homework would help their kids, who couldn't comprehend a simple English sentence and instead, were merely copying from textbooks. The school's mandate was to ensure children were learning English; it was also what the parents demanded. After all, proficiency in English was increasingly becoming a requirement for jobs across the country. But Tarun didn't know how to tell them that mastery of the language wouldn't come so easily. Their children were actually years behind where they needed to be at nine years old. When they couldn't comprehend a single word in the textbooks, what was the point of assigning them homework? He had to first teach them the basics.

After twenty agonizing minutes of listening to parents question his credibility, Tarun stood up. He didn't care to react to the combination of complaints and insults hurled at him.

'Listen, I know you have questions but I need you to trust me,' he said in Hindi. He knew that merely telling them wasn't going to suffice, so he did something which he would later deeply regret.

'I'm going to show you something,' Tarun said, as he walked out the door. He came back into the classroom with two of his students, Treza and Akanksha, and handed both grade-level textbooks.

'Treza, I need you to read the first paragraph, please.' Treza nervously looked around the room full of parents. She looked back at Tarun, who offered her a reassuring glance.

'Shivaji was the great k-k-k-ing of Pune. And he climbed many m-mo-moun-mountains.' Treza stuttered as she got out the first two sentences. Despite immediately questioning his rash decision to call the girls in, Tarun let them continue for the next several minutes.

'Treza and Akanksha, that's enough. Can you please explain to us, in Hindi, the meaning of the words you just read?'

The girls looked down at the floor and then up again at Tarun. Treza shook her head vigorously. Akanksha had tears streaming down her face. Their eyes were pleading with him to let them bolt out the door. Tarun felt terrible, but the damage was done.

'Come on kids, tell us what you read?' Treza's father interjected.

The other parents soon began to pile on.

'Tell us, Treza. You know what it means!'

'Akanksha, don't be shy.'

Tarun quickly walked towards the girls and stood in front of them. He stared back at the parents—their expressions ranging from confusion to anger.

'Listen, it was my mistake to call them up here. I shouldn't have done that. But I need you to see that this is where your kids are at. And Treza is one of our class's more advanced students. This isn't just an English problem, though. If we give her—or any of your kids—a Hindi text, you'll see the same thing.'

Listening to the parents gasp, Tarun looked down for a moment before continuing. 'I need you to trust me. Your kids are far behind but we can get them up to speed. We just need time. And we need your support.

'Give me a hundred days. If your kids haven't made progress by then, I'll do this your way. I promise.'

Tarun walked out of the meeting feeling a range of conflicting emotions. He was relieved that he had bought himself three months. But he was also ridden with guilt.

'Why did I call Treza and Akanksha up there? I've gained the parents' trust, but I've lost the kids', Tarun lamented to Aditya later in the day.

'I understand. But don't beat yourself up about it now. What's done is done. Plus, trust me, kids are forgiving. You'll get them back.' Aditya was trying mightily to reassure him.

'I've grown to care for them, really care for them. It's like these are my own kids, man. I can't just get over it. I'm now no better than that ice cream plant manager who'd yell at his staff for falling asleep on the job. It's not their fault that the system let them down!'

Between the guilt and relief, though, he knew he didn't have much time before he would lose the parents' confidence again. A hundred days would fly by faster than anyone could imagine. They would have to make progress, and fast. To do that, his class would have to find their collective next level. He needed his kids to understand why every class mattered so much—they needed to see that it would all add up. Tarun knew that his children were now invested in him, but he needed them to be invested in themselves. He had to reinforce the fact that he believed in them, in their potential.

Lying on his bedroom floor, Tarun looked up at the Harvard University poster plastered over his closet door. He had dreamt of going to the world's best college since he was a teenager. Like most middle-class children, he had heard his father speak reverently of Harvard and he would often daydream, for hours, of walking down the aisle and grabbing his well-earned diploma. That vision had kept him motivated for years; simply thinking about it would leave him inspired and energized. Thinking about the paucity of his current classroom, though, would only leave him drained.

That's it!

We need an aspiration. We need a destination. We need to become the Happy Harvard class.

Tarun knew that none of his children had ever really thought of attending college. In addition to only being in the third standard, they simply didn't know anyone that had. This is a bleak reality that most low-income children battle with. Like Nandini and Nishi, the majority of these children were desperately searching for role models to pave the way for what's possible. A majority of the parents of Tarun's students had dropped out well before the tenth standard, and none had made it to college.

Tarun spent half the night finding videos and pictures of Harvard. He ran to the corner store and printed dozens of images and handouts. When his children walked in the next morning, they were startled to see the blackboard converted into a canvas; they were more confused to see a borrowed projector in front of the classroom.

'Kids, from this day onwards, we're going to be on our biggest mission together.' Tarun told his class. 'Our community—every single one of us—is going to sign the biggest commitment we'll likely ever make: every single one of us will go to college.'

As he looked down at the filled benches, he saw the same blank faces that had greeted him on his first day, an expression that hadn't re-emerged in months. This time though, it didn't unnerve him. He walked calmly to a corner of the classroom, shut the windows and turned on the projector.

'This is Harvard University. It's where the smartest people in the world—the greatest scholars of all time—meet. They're on a mission too—just like us. They're on a mission to pursue the truth. But before we talk about that, who can tell me the meaning of the word "scholar"?'

The kids looked at him in silence.

'A scholar is someone who studies. A student,' Tarun added.

'Does that mean we are all scholars, bhaiya?' Moinuddin asked.

'Yes exactly. You're all scholars and this is the best college in the world for scholars like you. So I want every single one of you to set a goal to attend Harvard.'

'Bhaiya, did you study here?' Sharlina asked.

'No, but it's where I want to study in the future.'

'Then which scholars are you talking about, bhaiya?' Suraj asked, incredulously.

'Presidents, inventors, scientists. Bill Gates, Al Gore, John F. Kennedy!' Tarun had spent the past few months talking about each of them.

'Then, how we go there? Isn't it really hard?' Treza asked, in her broken English.

'It's extremely difficult. But I know every single one of you can if you try. It's going to take a lot of hard work. And it's going to be the toughest thing we do. But I believe in you.'

Tarun spent the next hour inundating his students with pictures of Harvard. He introduced examples of country leaders, industrialists and other notable alumni. Attempting to quell their doubts, he even came prepared with names of Indians who had risen from poverty only to graduate from Harvard—there weren't many. They used the last twenty minutes to make a list of all the benefits they would have by attending college. Each of the thirty-three children wrote a few sentences answering one prompt: 'How will my life change if I graduate from Harvard?'

'Why does it have to be Harvard? Can't I get a good education in India?' Akanksha had been quietly writing in her notebook before she blurted out her question.

'Yes, there are many great colleges right here in India. That is true.'

'So what's the best?'

'I would say it's the Indian School of Business (ISB). The best in the country often go there.'

'So if I'm the best in the full country, I go to the Indian School of Business. And if I'm the best in the full world, I go to Harvard?' Anjali shot back.

'Yes, and that brings me to the biggest surprise. It's my promise to you.' Tarun looked at his class intently. Knowing it would require a lot of funding to deliver on his next promise, he paused.

'If anyone in this class gets a 100 on 100 in their final exams, I will take you to Harvard University this summer. And, given the excellent question from Anjali, if anyone gets between ninety and ninety-nine, I will take you to the Indian School of Business for an entire week.' At this, the class responded with a collective gasp.

He gulped and closed his eyes. He had thought through the implications a hundred times the night before. He knew that raising the money would be tough, but he was committed to making it happen. Dozens of hands shot up; his class was jumping out of their seats. 'Bhaiya, passports kaise banenge (How will our passports get made)?' 'Hum plane mein kabhi baithe nahi hai (We've never sat in a plane).' 'Plane ke tickets ke liye paise kahaan se laaoge (How will you finance the trip)?'

Filled with a combination of excitement and anxiety, Tarun

went home that evening to plan out the year. He had just taken a huge step forward in successfully investing his students in the mission, but he had also committed to an enormously ambitious promise. That duality continued to play out in his conversation with his roommates over dinner who, much like his kids, peppered him with questions.

'Don't you think you're raising their hopes a bit too much?'

'Isn't Harvard unrealistic?'

'What's wrong with being too aspirational?' Tarun replied.

'Couldn't you have at least promised them a university here in India?'

'Yeah, why do you have to sell some vision of a university abroad? It's elitist.'

'Harvard has a lot of smart people, but not everyone who is smart has to go to Harvard. Lots of very smart people never have the opportunity to go to Harvard.'

'I hear you guys, I really do. But why shouldn't I get my kids to dream? Yes, maybe only 1 per cent will make it to Harvard or ISB. But think about what's possible if the other 99 per cent pursue that dream. Maybe—just maybe—that single-minded pursuit will ensure that, one day, *their* children end up fulfilling it. In my eyes, that is a victory.' It's the victory that Nishi from Vadgaon Budruk felt when she committed to fulfilling her father's dreams of being a doctor one day. It's the victory that Nandini from Pune, now in college, feels. And it's the same victory that millions of Indian parents across the country hope their children will one day experience. They hope that their endeavours, even if they fail, will enable their children to—just maybe—be a little better off.

EIGHT
WHO WANTS PITY?

Nalika suddenly felt the weight of thirty-six pairs of eyes fixated on her every move. Bent over in the front of the classroom, she was coughing up blood. She quickly hid her bloodstained hands behind her back. Aghast, her fourth-graders didn't know how to respond.

'Didi, do you need help?' Fahim finally mustered the courage to ask. She had only been teaching this class for two weeks and Fahim—an aspiring palaeontologist—was one of its most outspoken students.

Nalika darted out the door and ran into the school's bathroom, hoping the other teachers wouldn't see her. Meanwhile, her thirty-six fourth-graders continued to sit at their desks, murmuring and exchanging worried glances.

Nalika burst into tears. 'Why did this have to happen today? Why now?' She wanted to scream. Her stomach ulcers hadn't reappeared since her second year of college. More than three years ago, her doctors warned her that a high stress level was the primary culprit. The first few weeks of school were anything but relaxing. Nonetheless, they couldn't have picked a worst day to reappear. Nalika had worked on that lesson for days.

Charlie and the Chocolate Factory, one of her favourite children's books, constituted the next six weeks of class reading. Knowing that the story was slightly advanced, she had prepared an elaborate visual to introduce it and build engagement. The students were captivated by her colourful painting of the 'Chocolate Room'. It had taken her all night to put together. Spread across the canvas was the book's iconic scene of a waterfall carrying melted chocolate amidst sugary grass meadows filled with yellow buttercups. She had spent hours making each of the characters with sheets of corrugated cardboard: Charlie, Grandpa Joe, Augustus Gloop, Veruca Salt, Violet Beauregarde, Mike Teavee and of course the glorious Mr Willy Wonka.

With every paragraph the class read, Nalika would reenact the scene using her canvas and character cutouts. Greedy Augustus had just fallen into the chocolate river, the class giggling at Nalika's rendition of the loud splash. That's when she began to cough.

For the next several months, Nalika only confided about her health to her roommates and a small group of Teach For India staff members. Her parents had reluctantly acquiesced when she told them about signing up for the fellowship. They assumed that teaching children would be fun and easy. If they ever were to find out that her ulcers had returned, they would drive down to Bombay and take her home immediately. Nalika was intent on ensuring that that didn't happen.

She had finally found something that she truly loved— and she was good at it. Her students were fully engrossed in Roald Dahl's famous novel and they were learning quickly. The principal, along with the teachers at school, all praised Nalika for her creativity and resourcefulness—a product of the many hours she would spend each night applying her affinity for the arts to every lesson. Nalika resolved to not let her parents, or stomach ulcers, get in the way of that newfound purpose.

She began carrying a small coffee mug to school, even though she never drank caffeine. Every time she felt an urge to cough, she would simply pause her lesson, step out in the hallway and gently spit into the white mug.

Her students' parents, however, knew that something was awry. Hearing accounts from their children of the harrowing incident, they began to offer her a source of comfort and community. Mahima's mother would walk to school, every day, to bring her lunch. Imran's mother would call her at least three times a week, inviting her home for dinner. Eventually, Imran's audacious actions in class compelled Nalika to visit his home for entirely different reasons.

One day, during the second period, Imran thought it would be hilarious to cut more than two inches of hair from Masira's ponytail. The class was constructing their own cardboard cutouts for Roald Dahl's characters, and both the scissors and Masira's hair pulled back in a ponytail were enticingly within reach.

That afternoon, Masira's screams were heard throughout the school.

Nalika decided that she had no choice but to speak to Imran's mother. She couldn't speak Hindi too well and so she would often take Ajay, one of her students, along as a translator. He, in turn, relished the responsibility.

As Nalika sat across from Imran's mother, the anger on Nalika's face was unmistakable. It made Imran's thirteen-square-metre, single-room home feel uncomfortable and tense.

'Ajay, please tell Imran's mother that he has done something very bad in school today. Tell her that this was the third incident we've had with him in the past month.' Looking down, and then back at Imran, Ajay slowly started to speak in Hindi.

'Aunty, didi keh rahi hai ki is mahiney Imran ne bohut ache se padhai kiya hai. Yeh teesra pariksha hai jismein Imran ne class mein sabse zyaada number laye (Aunty, the teacher is saying that Imran has been a very good student this month. This is the third test where he's scored highest in class),' Ajay said calmly.

'Kya? Aise kaise (Really? How so)?' Imran's mother was baffled.

'Ajay, now tell her that he cut Masira's hair in class today. He picked up a pair of scissors and, while she wasn't looking, cut more than two inches of her hair! Her mother is very angry.' Her arms crossed, Nalika began tapping her fingers impatiently. She needed Imran's mother to share her outrage and promise to scold him.

Ajay looked down again and back at Imran, before reluctantly offering his altered translation.

'Aunty, didi keh rahi hai ki Imran ne Masira se bhi ache number laaye aur woh aapko yeh khud bataana–' (Aunty, the teacher is saying that Imran scored even higher than Masira. And she wanted to tell you–)

Nalika was growing impatient. Before Ajay could finish the next sentence, she interrupted.

'Ajay, now ask her what is she going to do about it. Tell her we need her to step in, before Imran causes any more trouble in class.'

For the third time, Ajay revised the translation and stuck to the plan he and Imran had earlier devised. 'Aunty, didi jaan na chahti hai ki kya aap khush hai Imran ke baare mein sun kar (Aunty, she wants to know if you're happy to see this progress from Imran)?'

Imran's mother looked at Ajay, who was desperately trying to hide his nervousness. Then she looked back at Nalika, whose fingers were still tapping incessantly against her tightly crossed arms. She stared blankly at Nalika's pained facial expression— when suddenly the thought occurred to her.

'Mujhe lagta hai ki aap dono alag baatein kar rahe hai (I don't think the two of you are saying the same thing).'

Imran's mother began laughing uncontrollably. Knowing that Nalika couldn't quite understand her, she tried gesticulating to get her point across. Nalika looked at Ajay's sheepish smile and then at Imran's mother who was struggling to compose herself, her face contorted with trying to hold in her laughter. After a few minutes, Nalika used her basic knowledge of Hindi to replay what she had just heard.

'Ajay, you have to be kidding me!' Nalika shouted in disbelief. 'I need you to tell me exactly what you just told her.'

Nalika grabbed Ajay's hand and stormed out the door. She was visibly embarrassed.

The next morning, Nalika pulled Imran out of class and

stepped into the hallway. The night offered her a few hours to not only calm down, but also appreciate the humour in what had happened. She knew she couldn't let the incident blow over, though; she had to find out what was behind the change in Imran's behaviour.

'Imran, what happened last night was very wrong. It was not in line with our class values.' Kneeling on the ground, Nalika was now at eye level with him.

'I need you to tell me why you did that. Why have you been misbehaving so much lately?'

Imran stared at the floor before he finally uttered his first words. 'I'm sorry, didi.'

Then, it all came gushing out. 'Didi, I know that cutting her hair was wrong. It was just a joke. They dared me to do it.'

'And what about what you and Ajay did at home last night?'

'That was also wrong. I know that. I just got scared, didi. So I told Ajay to tell lies. I'm sorry, didi.'

'You have been misbehaving for the last few weeks now. Why have you changed? What's going on?'

'Didi, what's the point in trying? We all know that you don't like us.'

'What do you mean?'

'Who is us?' Nalika pressed when he didn't respond.

She had always loved Imran. She naturally gravitated towards the kids who struggled. She would play games with them after school. She would sit to eat with them at lunch breaks. In fact, she thought she had formed really strong bonds with them.

'Tell me, Imran. Please,' Nalika urged as she grabbed him by the shoulders.

'Mohtasim, Ram, Sahil, Farid, Nivedita. All of us. We're the naughty kids. We're not the smart ones. So you never ask us any questions. You never make us the team leaders. You only pick kids like Ajay, Priya and Fahim. You even make us sit in a separate group. And the other kids all talk about it. What's the point in trying?'

Imran freed himself from her grip and ran back inside.

Nalika stayed out in the hallway for the next several minutes. She began thinking about all the times that she had ignored that group of six children in the classroom. They were indeed her most struggling students. She started thinking about all the times people had visited her class that year, praising her for her creative lessons. They were enamoured that, despite her high levels of rigour and abstract concepts, the kids were following along so intently. They were impressed by Ajay and Priya, but they never heard from Imran, Nivedita or Danish. She wanted them to leave her class impressed and appreciate her identity as an artist, as a student of literature. In the process, she had quit thinking about what her students actually needed.

'Who have I become? I hate myself,' Nalika said to herself.

That evening, as Nalika walked back to her shared apartment, she started thinking about Mamta. Nalika joined because of Mamta. She liked the kids that were different, that were naughty, that didn't follow the rules. In a way, they reminded her of herself. But today, she realized she was failing them. Something had to change. Her class had to become a place that would make every single child thrive—that would bring out Hussain's interest in guitar, Sahil's obsession with rocks and even Fahim's newfound fascination with picking locks. She wanted them to know—to feel—that they had a place in her classroom. It couldn't be about getting accolades for creative teaching practices. It had to be about that group of thirty-six kids—and only that.

Nalika's first few months were punctuated by similar moments of self-doubt and self-discovery. Often painful because of the emotions they triggered, they, nevertheless, were the moments that led to catalytic growth, both for her and her students. Nothing exemplified that growth more than her conversation with a child from Bombay International School (BIS) a few months into the second year of her fellowship.

BIS is arguably one of the city's most venerated institutions, training some of the country's most influential and wealthiest. The students there, by and large, share backgrounds that are diametrically opposite to the slums that surround Nalika's school. A staff member from Teach For India, having observed Nalika's classroom one day, suggested that she visit a child from a high-income school. It's an experience that I have personally recommended to many of our fellows, knowing that it allows them to see the depth of inequity between low-income communities and their more privileged counterparts. For many of our fellows, complacency often becomes their biggest enemy. It's easy to simply be better than the classroom next door; it's significantly harder to ensure our children are learning at levels that are commensurate with children of privilege.

That Friday evening, Nalika met Vedant at his home in Worli. His parents' apartment—a beautiful four-bedroom condo—was tastefully decorated. The French windows in his living room framed a breathtaking view of the Arabian Sea.

'Sorry, I'll be right back,' Vedant said.

As she sat on the couch, she couldn't help but wonder: how much better can he be than my nine-year-olds? In the last twelve months, Nalika had worked hard to raise the bar for her kids and they had shown significant improvement.

'My mom's asking: would you like some tea or juice?' he asked.

'Oh! Thank you, that's so kind of you. I'm fine for now.'

'Okay.'

'How was school today?'

'Uh, just a normal day. We had yoga in the morning, which I find quite boring. But then we had swimming in the afternoon and I love to swim. I'm pretty good at it, you know.'

'You have a pool in your school?'

'No, but for the kids who want to swim, they take us to a pool nearby. Same goes for karate, they take those kids to a karate coaching centre. Most of the other sports we can play in school.'

'What else do you like apart from swimming?'

'I love to play the piano. It's one of my favorite instruments. I actually think it's one of the most beautiful instruments, especially in an orchestra. I don't like symphonies that don't have a piano part. Sadly, that's most of them.'

'You've seen an orchestra perform live?'

'Yes, many times! Last year, we watched the New York Philharmonic. Did you know it's the oldest orchestra in the US that is still running? It's one of the "Big Five". I begged my mother to take me to watch all five American orchestras. But we only ended up watching two of them. Someday, I'll go back and check them all off my list.'

'Wow, that's pretty incredible. So you must really enjoy playing the piano.'

'Yeah, I love it! I'm currently on the third level in the Trinity exams. I've watched orchestras in London too! Do you play any instruments?'

'Yes, I play the guitar.'

'You said you're a teacher, right?'

'Yes, I teach a group of thirty-six fourth-graders in Abhyudaya Nagar M. P. S. It's a school for kids from low-income communities not too far from here.'

Vedant grew silent for a few minutes.

'Oh. Is that why you're asking about my school? You know, I sometimes think about how unfair it is that I have so much more than those kids do. I was lucky to be born to my parents.'

It was Nalika's turn to grow silent. She was transfixed by Vedant's ability to wrestle with a concept as complex as inequity.

'In my school, I have amazing teachers, clean classrooms, computers, books. Basically, I have a lot, whereas they have so little. They have to work so much harder to achieve their dreams like—'

'Nandini,' whispered Nalika.

'Who?' Vedant asked.

Nandini had just been accepted to the well-reputed United World College in Italy that week. She was the first student from the Teach For India (TFI) community to take that incredible step. Everyone at TFI was excited about her prospects. Nalika was certain that this was just the beginning of Nandini's journey. But Nandini was an anomaly, even within Teach For India. Sitting across from Vedant, she thought wondered what it would take to put her students on a similar life path.

'Sorry, whose example were you about to take?' Nalika continued the conversation.

'Dhirubhai Ambani sir. His story is so inspiring—even to someone like me.'

Nalika and Vedant spent the next two hours talking about everything under the sun. Their conversation, in many ways, wasn't too different from the ones she used to have at Sophia College. They chatted about inequity, politics, cricket and about Vedant's dream of one day becoming a doctor. Nalika told him why she decided to join the Teach For India Fellowship and the fallout with her friends and parents that ensued. He told her about his favourite books from his summer reading list. He named famous titles like *The Blue Umbrella* by Ruskin Bond and *A Wrinkle in Time* by Madeleine L'Engle—books that Nalika would have deemed far too advanced for her eight-year-olds.

As Nalika left Vedant that afternoon, she couldn't stop thinking about the deep disparity between him and her kids. She was both intrigued and depressed. She had spent much of the past year wholly immersed with her thirty-six fourth-graders. As a result, she assumed that their cognitive and learning levels were the standard—that they represented what fourth-graders should be learning.

Vedant doesn't even experience inequity, she thought. Yet he can talk about it. He understands it so much more deeply than any one of my children do. I've been focusing on the basics in reading and math, but I haven't been holding them to a high bar. It's also too limiting. My children need to have access to the world. They need to be exposed to the same opportunities to learn, to think critically and to reflect. Without that they'll never be able to break through the cycle of poverty.

Vedant's reference to Ambani, more than anything else, really disturbed her. Why was it that there were so few examples of kids succeeding from low-income backgrounds? She knew why. She intimately understood the challenges. She had experienced first-hand the pervasive acceptance of the situation that undercut the sincere attempts of her kids and their parents to break through the cycle of poverty. But now, she suddenly was acutely aware of the weight of that hopelessness she and her kids unknowingly carried every day into the classroom—the same weight I felt in Jahangirpuri after spending time with Yasmin and Arbaaz. That evening, she started to question why her kids' parents were so accepting of their fate—a perception she had always seen as unequivocally positive. Now, she wondered if it merely masked hopelessness.

The next morning, Nalika walked back into classroom with a mission to create more examples like Nandini. She wanted her kids to embody the rebellious hope and sense of possibility they needed to succeed in any circumstance. She lit that spark with a carefully plotted presentation. She wanted her kids to see what she saw. Until that day, she assumed her class was simply too young to fully understand the inequity they faced. As children stared at photos of the two schools juxtaposed on the slide—BIS and their own—she debunked her original assumptions.

'Where are these photos from?'

'Didi, the one on the left is our school. The other one is from a movie. And those are kids from the movie,' Fahim responded innocently.

As Nalika moved to the next slide, the kids stared at the inside of Imran's home. Next to it was a picture showing the inside of Vedant's home.

'Didi, Vedant has a lot more things than Imran does,' Ajay noted. The class giggled.

'So why do you think Vedant has more things?' Nalika asked the class, trying to bring her signature intensity and gravity back into the discussion.

'Because his parents are richer. They have more money because they have better jobs. Didi, Imran's father is a rickshaw driver.' As Attiqua spoke, Imran sulked into his chair. Nalika knew it was difficult to have this conversation, but she was determined to keep moving forward.

'Yes, you're right. And because Vedant has more money, what do you think his future will look like?'

'When his parents are gone, he'll get all of that money. And because he goes to such a big school, he'll get a really good education. And he'll live a happy life.' Priya jumped in without raising her hand.

'And do you think that's fair—that he has so much money and gets a great education with so many resources? And you don't?'

'Didi, that's not fair. But that's life, no?'

Fahim's response was disturbing, but it was indicative of the deep pragmatism that permeated these young kids. They spent the next thirty minutes listing the differences between their lives and their more affluent counterparts, like Vedant. They talked about the implications of those differences. They brainstormed possible reasons that had led to their disparities. Most importantly, they talked about what they needed to accomplish, as a class, to get the kind of education that Vedant was receiving, every single day. Perhaps most notably, they concluded that despite their limited means, an excellent education was within reach. It required significantly more effort, but it was possible.

Nalika wasn't finished. She stepped out into the hallway and pulled in her neighbouring teacher, Naida. An Akanksha Foundation alumna, Naida grew up in the same community attending after-school centres run by Akanksha. She later attended college and eventually decided to forego a career in business to come back and teach in her own school.

'Who is Naida more like? Vedant or you?' Nalika asked.

The kids were puzzled. They couldn't tell the difference.

'Where you come from does not have to determine where you will go.' Nalika wrote the sentence on the board, in large letters, for every child to see. We're going to work relentlessly over the next ten months. Not to be like Vedant, but to be the best possible versions of ourselves because every single one of you deserves nothing but the best.'

As Nalika said that last sentence, she realized that she really believed what she was saying. She knew what they were capable of. She simply needed to treat them like they were.

Over the next few weeks, Nalika made a number of big changes to her classroom. She threw out the *Ladybird* books and replaced them with award-winning teenage books and volumes of classics. She became more deliberate about her praise for children, ensuring she only celebrated authentic examples of achievement. She made it a point to begin exposing her kids to the world around them. They studied and discussed major artwork. They learned about the Renaissance period and the World Wars. Interacting with guest lecturers visiting every Friday, they started learning about different career options. They even toured some of the city's best colleges, including Nalika's alma mater.

At Sophia College, Nalika had arranged for her class to see a casting audition of *Final Solutions*. The famous play by Mahesh Dattani explores communal divide and tension between Hindus and Muslims during the post-Partition riots. It exposes and calls into question the religious bigotry many Indians live with by examining the attitudes of a middle-class Gujarati family and two young Muslim boys who seek shelter with them when chased by a mob.

Nalika had brought along a number of older students on the school trip. As the children watched successive college students walk on to the stage and audition, they followed along on their copies of the script They were glued to the storyline. After watching a few people, Saahil, one of the fifth-graders, interrupted.

'Didi, can I try?' He unwittingly spoke loud enough for the entire auditorium to hear. Nalika was embarrassed, but Ayesha—whom Nalika hadn't seen for months—interjected.

'Of course. In fact, why don't several of you come up and audition?' Ayesha was now responsible for the college's annual production.

Over the next thirty minutes, half a dozen of Nalika's students walked on stage. They auditioned for the role of the angry mob (a critical element in the play that serves as a symbol of religious hatred and paranoia), offering Sophia's auditorium a passionate and convincing performance from the youngest artists it had ever seen.

'How dare they?' Priya and Imran yelled.

'For forty years our chariot has moved through their mohallas,' said Suraj as he joined the chorus.

'They broke our rath. They broke our chariot and felled our Gods!'

The kids were seemingly oblivious of the now silent audience as they switched from speaking on behalf of enraged Hindus to outraged Muslims.

'Their chariot fell in our street! Was the chariot built by us?' Attiqua retaliated.

'Blame the builder of those fancy thrones,' Fahim and Danish added.

'A manufacturing defect!' laughed Mohtasim.

'Doesn't their God have a warranty?' Sallauddin demanded.

'We are neither idol makers nor breakers!' they said in unison.

As the audience looked on intently, they could feel the tension in the room. It was as if the kids were no longer acting. Nalika, her mouth agape as she watched intently from the front row, didn't know how to respond. She was as shocked as the rest of them. That's when inspiration struck.

'Nalika—,' Ayesha started to say.

'Yes! I know what you're going to say. And yes, we must make it happen,' Nalika replied promptly.

'I'm thinking they should do the whole thing. This year, we'll have Sophia's annual production performed by your kids.'

'Of course my students can perform this play better than a bunch of college students. This is the story of their lives.'

Nalika's school served two different communities: Zakaria Bunder, a Muslim community and Jijamata Nagar, a Hindu community. Both were ten-minute walks from school in opposite directions. Just like the blocks in Jahangirpuri, the communal tensions here were high and each rarely ventured out of their 'predetermined territory'. Nalika saw an opportunity to create a new narrative, one devoid of violence and hatred. She spent the next hour chatting with Ayesha and the rest of Sophia College's Drama Club members. Her kids, Nalika told them, should be the ones performing that play.

~

The next six months would be both gruelling and invigorating for Nalika and her children. Sophia College, albeit sceptical, agreed to let her class run the entire performance of *Final Solutions* as the college's annual production. The event was guaranteed to attract an audience of hundreds. If her kids were to be ready, it would require countless hours of rehearsals.

Once again in her element, Nalika applied everything she had learned as President of Sophia's Drama Club. She became obsessed. She connected every lesson—no matter the subject or topic—to a different aspect of the play. The children began exploring communal tensions and debating religious issues in class. They learned to name new emotions and practised the subtle nuances between expressions of frustration and anger.

They read passages on post-Partition history. They worked collectively on set designs. The classroom was effectively a full-time production house.

Much to Nalika's surprise, her kids were now picking up concepts faster than they ever had. Issues that she never knew existed began surfacing as well. Until now, she had thought that her class—a heterogeneous mixture of both Hindus and Muslims—was cordial. She had assumed they respected each other's differences. The play's central crisis, though, served as a means to underscore the challenges her children faced every day.

Danish played the role of Javed, a Muslim boy who drops a piece of meat in his Hindu neighbour's backyard. As the characters reacted, so did Nalika's children.

'How could he do that!' Priya yelled out, when they first rehearsed this particular scene.

'That is unjust!' Ajay shouted, as the class's Muslim students looked on. Some were aghast at his anger. Others were embarrassed and reacted much like the Muslim character Bobby in the play, who distanced himself from his religion by changing his name from Babban to Bobby.

Exacerbating the tension was Nalika's insistence that they switch roles and, as a result, religious identities. In the days that followed, Muslim students played the part of Hindu characters, and vice versa. Horrified by their lines and the implications the play had on their long-held beliefs, they would often walk out of class in protest.

'I'm not saying those lines!' Attiqua yelled, as she looked at the class in disgust. She was asked to play a scene in which she had to dress an idol of Krishna and read some verses from the Bhagavad Gita.

Their outrage was initially unsettling. But, it eventually gave way to discussion, which over time transformed into understanding. To Nalika's surprise, the play had done something that no amount of class lectures or norms could ever do. It helped her class grow, as a collective, and develop a deeper sense of empathy and understanding for each other. Their coexistence was no longer just a superficial tolerance but a genuine acceptance of their peers. Whereas earlier they exercised restraint, now they embraced each other with love.

When 15 April—the day of their grand performance—arrived, Nalika was nervous and shaky. In their rehearsals, they had been excellent. Every child knew his or her lines and each delivered them with passion and conviction. But they were expecting an audience of more than 500 people and tensions were running high.

'Tonight is a big night, class,' Nalika said, looking into the eyes of every one of her thirty-six students as she spoke.

'The unfortunate thing is that regardless of how you perform, the 500 people in that audience are going to clap.' Her students looked at her, confused. Instinctively, she knew they could handle what she was about to tell them.

'They're going to tell you you're cute. That you're amazing. That you're better than they ever thought was possible. They're going to do that, not just because you're kids—but because you're poor. You have a choice tonight. You can get their applause out of pity— out of the recognition that you attend some low-income school in the city. Or you can get applause because you're performers, because you're brilliant and mind-blowing performers. You have the ability to be that. But the choice is ultimately yours.'

Over the next ninety minutes, that class of thirty-six performed a spectacular rendition of *Final Solutions*, a play they had spent more than six months rehearsing. They played characters that fundamentally changed their lives, both in and out of school. When they finished, the audience of 500 gave them a standing ovation.

Attiqua, her cheeks red and her forehead dripping with sweat, turned to Nalika to gauge the authenticity of their reaction.

'Didi, are they clapping because we're poor? Or are they clapping because we were mind-blowing?'

Wiping away tears, Nalika smiled.

NINE
LAKHON MEIN EK

'What are the biggest challenges in our community?'

Anurag wrote the question on the blackboard. While the prompt was seemingly far too abstract for his twenty-two fifth graders, he was hopeful it would provoke debate. Much to his chagrin, though, their deadpan expressions didn't bode well. Anurag endured a few moments of pin-drop silence before prodding again.

'Okay, let's do this. List out every problem you can think of.'

He wasn't quite sure about the can of worms he was about to open, but Anurag knew that their community in Seelampur—at the heart of North Delhi's slums—had no shortage of problems. He had been teaching at Bab-ul Uloom, a makeshift school that was part of a local mosque, for the last two months. On one side of the mosque was the madrasa and behind the mosque was the school. Not far from the slums of Jahangirpuri, the school was one of Delhi's most challenging fellowship placements, largely because of the abject poverty that surrounded it. It charged parents only 120 rupees a month. A quarter of the families couldn't even afford that much, so they were enrolled for free.

The school was something of a unicorn. Set in an Islamic backdrop, it stressed religious teaching and traditional customs. Select students were required to attend madrasa classes in the morning where they would memorize and recite verses from the Quran. They'd then be allowed to attend regular school in the afternoon. But the mosque also prioritized educating girls and promoting scientific enquiry, to some extent. They even had a computer lab. The rector running the madrasa would often tell Anurag: 'My intent is that we educate all our girl children in this community—whether they're Hindu or Muslim. Whichever home the girl [gets married and] goes into, she will teach the entire family science and computers.'

Anurag found the challenge of Bab-ul Uloom exciting, particularly because of its strong Muslim identity. As is unfortunately common in our country, Anurag had grown up in an environment riddled with religious divides. His childhood had taught him to be fearful of Islam. He didn't have any Muslim friends. His parents would often tell him tales of historic, violent clashes with Muslims in the months following Independence. Anurag knew intuitively that his understanding of the Muslim community was not rooted in objectivity. Teaching in the madrasa offered him an opportunity to confront his biases. He wanted to break a myth that had governed his actions for far too long.

'Eve-teasing!' Aalia shouted.

'Drugs!' Muskaan now weighed in.

'Eve-teasing and drugs are indeed huge problems in the community. Good. What are others?' Anurag asked.

'Violence—people are killing each other over stupid things,' said Khalid.

'Health!' Rehan's mother had passed away only a few months ago, at the age of thirty-two.

The class was silent for a few moments, until Saad chimed in.

'Garbage. Garbage is our most difficult problem, bhaiya. As soon as you walk out of Bab-ul Uloom, it's just dirty. Our entire community is dirty.'

The rest of the class nodded in unison.

'Okay, so if we all agree that garbage is our biggest issue, here's the question: why do we have such a big problem with garbage?' Anurag prodded.

'Because people don't care about cleanliness. People should be punished for littering,' Muskaan replied.

'I think people care. There's just nowhere to throw anything away. Someone needs to be responsible for keeping the streets clean.' Hifza remarked thoughtfully.

As the discussion meandered on, Anurag began pushing his class to think about the real causes underlying their problems. They traced a lack of accountability to poor performance monitoring, which they eventually linked to no oversight from their elected representative and, eventually, to the very fundamentals of democracy.

'If who we elect matters, then how we elect them also matters. And that means our people in power—the police, the corporator, the chief minister—should all have to face consequences when they can't govern,' Nazreen said.

Anurag watched as his class slowly began making other connections.

Anurag knew he was venturing into a tricky subject. But Anurag loved politics. With Arvind Kejriwal's recent surge in popularity, the city of Delhi was gripped by politics. Anurag's readings on Ambedkar, Gandhi, Nehru, Lincoln and others had left him fascinated with the inner workings—and deep potential—of government institutions. They had pushed him to believe that a high-functioning democracy could actually solve many of India's most pressing problems, and he wanted his kids to believe that too.

'Raise your hand if your parent, aunt or uncle voted in the last election,' he said.

Two hands went up.

'So if people aren't voting, what can we—as a class of twenty-two—do about that?' he asked.

That scorching afternoon in August, Anurag's class agreed to take on their first project: a voter registration drive. For the next two weeks until elections, children committed to knocking on doors across the community. Every day after school, their goal was to ensure that people enrolled and pledged to vote. They set what seemed like an ambitious goal for twenty-two fifth-graders: they would enrol ten new voters and get pledges from twenty-five more.

He used the opportunity to give his kids a lesson in democracy. As preparation, they learned how the Indian voting process works, the structure of Delhi's state government and the government departments responsible for safety, cleanliness, violence and even education. They understood how to fill out an enrolment form so they could teach others to do the same.

This form is frighteningly complicated even for an adult. How am I going to teach it to my fifth-graders? Anurag had initially thought as he planned the day's lesson.

Once the registration drive began, he spent each afternoon venturing into the streets surrounding Bab-ul Uloom. His students faced the same challenges that community mobilizers across the country have been battling for decades. Some slammed their doors before saying hello. Others were sceptical of their party affiliation. Many blatantly refused to take the young children seriously. While these encounters disheartened the kids, causing several to break down into tears, they simply returned to the same streets the very next day.

In the end, fourteen days after their initial plan was devised, Anurag's class had enrolled 181 new voters into the system—almost twenty times their target. The process, which started as a discussion that went awry, taught Anurag a few valuable lessons. His children were deeply resilient—more so than many of the adults he had met. When an adult would rudely turn them away, Anurag would feel the weight of that rejection. His children, on the other hand, would simply forget. Sure, a few of them would come to him in momentary hopelessness, but they would invariably continue their work the next day as if nothing had happened.

'If my fifth-graders can enrol 181 people in less than ten days,' imagine what we can do in two years?' Thinking aloud, Anurag soon realized that his kids had the potential to start solving many of the community's most intractable problems.

Gradually, he started seeing his role in the classroom as a cultivator of problem-solvers, rather than as a teacher. He couldn't run a classroom that he tightly controlled, standing in the front delivering lectures and then expect his kids to walk out with twenty-first-century skills.

'The traditional way of running the classroom is obsolete,' he wrote in a blog he maintained during the fellowship. 'My classroom needs to operate like a democracy—where the citizens, my students, have power, voice and rights. They need to know that they are in control of their destiny and their community.'

Making his children an integral part of the solution, Anurag knew, would require big changes. He had to relinquish control. He started by co-creating, with his students, a timetable from scratch. They needed to take ownership of their time in the classroom, a process that carried with it a number of struggles and lessons.

'To finish this syllabus, which you will be tested on by the school, I need seven periods of English.' Anurag was growing impatient with his kids, who had been debating the timetable for the last two hours.

'But we have to include dance. Five of us want it,' Aman interjected.

'And we need six periods of math. Last unit's test was hard,' said Muskaan.

'But what about music? Three of us asked for that,' Khalid was insistent. 'And computer!' he added before sitting back down.

'As in any democracy, we're going to have to reconcile our differences and find common ground,' Anurag reminded his kids as he tried to hide his restlessness. They eventually agreed to add computer and dance, keep mathematics, but scrap English entirely. It was a decision they would later regret after the first English test. While Anurag had the prescience to know it wouldn't end well, he felt it was important for his kids to experience, first-hand, the consequences of their actions. Those English lessons eventually found their way back into the next unit's timetable, which the kids agreed needed to be much more balanced.

They weren't just designing the curriculum, though; they were also starting to view Anurag as someone whom they could hold accountable.

'Your lesson today is boring, bhaiya. I don't think you prepared for it,' Aman interrupted Anurag fifteen minutes into his math lesson. He was surprised and shocked. He didn't know how to respond.

'What were you doing last night? Because I don't think you read the book.' Aman continued.

Beginning to blush, Anurag thought it best to be honest. 'You're right. I did not prepare. I was out with my friends. I'm sorry. I have broken my most fundamental commitment to you as your teacher,' Anurag told the class. The shift in power initially felt deeply uncomfortable. However, he was beginning to learn that his children could not only handle the added responsibility, but they also demonstrated a unique degree of forgiveness and gentleness while exercising it.

Over the months ahead, they continued practising an approach to governance that embodied the values of respect, honesty and accountability. They used every encounter—from a class representative not voicing student opinion to parents not helping with homework—as opportunities to learn and get better. That cycle of continuous improvement provoked personal reflection and ultimately prepared them for greater endeavours.

'Today, class, we're going to fulfil our commitment from last week. We're going to create our very own child rights charter.'

As soon as Anurag announced the day's objective, the class erupted into cheers. They had spent the past three periods reading and interpreting the United Nations Child Rights Charter, which Anurag hoped would lead to a series of discussions on its implications for slum-dwelling children in Seelampur. The class, however, decided that it was not right to simply adopt the charter; instead, they wanted to design their own.

They began making a list of the various rights that, according to them, were critical for every child in Seelampur to enjoy. Then, they would narrow down the list, draft a new charter and send it back to the UN for review. The discussion, which started humorously, grew insightful over time.

'The right to ice cream!' Khalid shouted out first.

'Okay, great. One condition: when you list out a right, you have to tell the class why you think it's essential for every child in Seelampur to have access to it,' Anurag chided the class, looking at Khalid sternly to bring a bit more gravity into the discussion.

'The right to meet our friends. Every child should be able to have friends,' Hifza interjected.

'The right to play with our friends in school. The streets of Seelampur are unsafe. If we can't play in school, where else can we play together?' Aman asked.

Anurag knew that Aman's comment might unearth a discussion that had been unfolding for months. After all, the tiny madrasa had no space for children to play together.

'The right to jump and play in puddles! My parents don't let me go out when it rains. They say it's too dirty or that I'll fall sick. It's just water!' Hussein said.

As the class giggled, Anurag began to worry if this would go anywhere. The discussion finally took a turn when Rehan weighed in: 'The right to shelter. Even when families have tough times, every child deserves a decent place to live.'

'If shelter is a right, then education also needs to be a right. Every child needs to learn,' Aman responded.

'Why does education need to be a right? Why does everyone need to study? What would happen if the kids of Seelampur don't study?' Anurag asked.

'That's true. Education isn't actually that good anyways,' Aalia said,

'Is my teaching that bad?' asked Anurag.

The class laughed.

'No, bhaiya, but the education my little sister gets next door is. They're learning nothing. And I know that majority of kids in Seelampur are getting the education that she is,' Aalia said.

'Actually, bhaiya, what is the education level in our country?' Aman asked.

Sensing an opportunity, Anurag wrote four bold letters on the board: 'ASER'.

He explained, 'Annual State of Education Report. This is one of India's biggest assessments. It's led by an organization called Pratham. They try to assess how much kids across the country actually know. They give a simple test to thousands of children, and then they publish that data.'

'What do they say?' Aman asked.

'Well, it tells us that more than 50 per cent of grade-five children in India can't read a text that is at a grade-two level. It tells us that two-thirds can't do basic subtraction and addition. It tells us that the children of India, on average, are years behind where they need to be. And it tells us that this problem is true not just for a few children, but for hundreds of millions of children across the country,' Anurag said.

'How many children, bhaiya? Hundreds?' Aalia asked.

'Tens of lakhs,' Anurag replied.

Over the next few minutes, the reactions in the room changed from surprise to outrage. They were horrified not because they didn't know that the state of education was bad; their Seelampur community affirmed that reality, every single day. But they had never realized that the problem was so pervasive—that it impacted a sizable majority of India's children. Television shows, movies and ads had led them to believe that the outside world was actually a much better place. They had assumed that their community was an outlier. The scale of the problem, more than anything else, disturbed them.

'Well, what are the learning levels of Seelampur?' Aman asked.

'I don't know. ASER doesn't cover Seelampur,' Anurag answered truthfully.

'Bhaiya, you gave up your career in engineering to teach us in Seelampur. And you don't even know the learning levels of our community?' While Muskaan's question was humorous, it didn't make the class laugh. They were genuinely surprised by his apparent ignorance.

'Haan, bhaiya. Aap ko humara hi nahi pata, aap duniya jahaan ki baatein kar rahe ho (Yes, bhaiya. You don't know our own community's learning levels and you're talking about India and the whole world,'Aman said.

'Hum pata laga lengey (We'll find out).' Muskaan decided.

'Yes, can't we just give the assessment to kids around us and find out for ourselves?' Rehan suggested.

'Bhaiya, you just teach us how to make people take the assessment. We'll do the rest,' Aman said.

The class was captivated by the idea and Anurag half-heartedly promised to come back with a plan. While he was impressed with their line of questioning, he didn't actually think they were being serious. As children often do, Anurag thought, his class would quickly forget and move on to a different topic.

But they kept asking.

And asking.

And asking.

A week later, they could think of nothing else. It became the first question they'd ask when he stepped into the classroom. Seeing their once-friendly morning greetings being replaced by incisive questioning and follow-ups, Anurag started researching. He chatted with friends who had studied survey methodology, read ASER's online reports to find out how they administered it and thought through the different skills his children would need to successfully administer the test and analyse the data.

His classroom, over the next two months, transformed into an ASER local office. To ensure his children didn't lose valuable class time, he tweaked their curriculum to teach them the skills needed to complete the project. Instead of reading textbooks, they started poring through ASER reports and using those to build their vocabulary. In mathematics, they were learning percentages and fractions. They figured out how to interpret histograms, pie charts and plots.

Anurag had never seen his kids so engaged. They were dissecting every piece of information they could find because they wanted to get the project right. They began debating the criteria needed to assess educational attainment. Inevitably, that led to questioning the fundamental purpose of education. Was it literacy? Was it critical thinking? Was it something more abstract like empathy and, if so, how would they measure that? Eventually, they concluded that using ASER's ready-made assessments would be not only the most valuable, but also the most efficient. Yet, even that decision was not as straightforward as they had hoped.

'We'll use the English assessment to measure literacy,' Khalid said.

'But that makes no sense. Just because someone doesn't speak English, does that mean they're not educated? We should measure literacy in Urdu or Hindi. After all, those are the languages you need to know to be a productive member of the community in Seelampur,' Aalia countered.

'I disagree. In today's times, knowing English is extremely important. For most jobs, you need to know English. Whether in Seelampur or anywhere in the world, I would say knowing English is critical to being educated,' Aman pushed back.

'I don't understand why we're having this argument. Why not do both English and Hindi assessments? Bas. Nahi toh hum puri raat yahaan behtengey aur "educated" ka definition tab bhi nahi milega (Otherwise, we'll be sitting here all night and even then won't be able to find the definition of "educated"),' Muskaan said.

'Hmm... Maybe even our data will help us learn something about what it means to be educated,' Khalid observed.

'I think I read somewhere that both Hindi and English are official languages of our country. Bhaiya, am I right?' Muskaan asked.

Anurag was standing on one side of the classroom, as he often did during class discussions. 'You're right, but—' he started to say as Khalid interjected.

'But we don't have the time and people to do all three—Hindi, English and math. I think we should skip math, maybe we can do it in a future round. But at least this way we'll get a holistic view of literacy in our community. Who here agrees?'

Twenty-one hands shot up in the air.

'Done. We'll test for Hindi and English,' Aalia announced.

This time, unlike the voter registration drive, Anurag didn't need to accompany his children. But before any of them could begin administering the assessment to their neighbours, they first had to successfully go through an assessment centre on survey methodology. They were evaluated on their interviewing skills, data collection and analysis skills and knowledge of the instruments used to measure English and Hindi literacy. Students who failed it were given the opportunity to retake it any number of times until they passed. Once they did, they were ready to join the group of students administering and implementing the surveys.

Eight weeks later, after data from more than 380 children across the community started pouring in, the kids plotted and analysed all of it. The results were just as shocking as the original ASER report.

'We have to do something about this! Now that we know how bad it is, we can't just let it be!' Khalid exclaimed.

'You tell me what we're going to do about it,' Anurag prodded.

'Maybe Anurag bhaiya can start taking classes with kids every afternoon,' Aalia suggested.

'And how many kids do you think I'll be able to teach as one person? I can't get to every child in Seelampur,' he replied.

'He's right. He can only teach so many. And any time he spends elsewhere is going to take away from time with our class,' Muskaan said,

'What if we started teaching kids?' Aalia asked. She glanced at the class, unsure of what she had just proposed. Most of the class readily agreed, but several objected, noting that it still wouldn't be enough.

'India is a democracy. There are adults who are responsible for our education. We need to hold them accountable. We need to write a letter to the government,' Aman said.

As Anurag—now a mere observer—listened to his students argue, he couldn't help but smile.

'And why do you think the government will respond to a class of fifth-graders?' Aalia shot back.

'You're right. We will write the letter. But we also need to do what they do. We need to hold a conference on the state of education in Seelampur!' Khalid declared.

The class continued brainstorming and evaluating solutions for days. The ideas they came up with were, by any measure, astounding.

The children began holding daily tutoring sessions after school, open to any child in Seelampur. They briefed Yogendra Yadav, then a leader of Aam Aadmi Party, on their findings. They designed, planned and coordinated one of Delhi's first student-led conferences called I-STEP (Inspiring Students, Teachers, Educators and Parents). They not only invited more than thirty stakeholders from across the city, but also managed to secure a spot for two chief guests in attendance: Atishi Marlena, who later became the advisor to the Deputy Chief Minister of Delhi; and

Rukmini Banerji, who headed the ASER assessment and, today, is the CEO of Pratham. Parents, teachers and students attended panels, engaged with speakers and discussed the findings from Seelampur. Rukmini was so impressed with their work that she invited them to a meeting at Pratham with the twenty staff members who were leading ASER's implementation.

'If they can do this in their community, why can't we inspire action across the country? Why can't we make ASER a tool that anyone can use? We put it in the hands of ordinary people, so they drive their educational progress,' Rukmini said with conviction.

'When we zoom out, we see that we don't have enough teachers in India today. That's the problem. What's the point of collecting the same data over and over again when we know what the problem is? We need teachers. How can we do anything without teachers?' a team member suggested.

As Rukmini began to respond, Aman stood up.

'I have a question for you, ma'am. Actually, it's for everyone here. My friend Amit asked me this. He's in Robin bhaiya's class,' he said, looking around the room. 'Can you tell me the name of Shakespeare's teacher? Actually, can anyone here tell me the name of Shakespeare's teacher?'

The group, unsurprisingly, was silent.

'I didn't think so. I'm not saying that teachers aren't important. But why don't we believe that maybe kids can do more for themselves than we allow them to do today?'

Rukmini looked at the silent crowd staring back at her in utter confusion. She knew that Aman's idea held tremendous power.

'These are twelve-year-olds. They're twelve!' Rukmini told the twenty-odd people in the room. 'We've seen through our ten years of running the ASER survey and the volunteers we work with that the first-hand experience of *feeling* the problem of low learning levels in our country is the first step towards action,' she continued. 'These kids have demonstrated to us what to *do* with that learning. Let's make it easy for people to do what these kids have done. Let's engage on a much larger scale with the communities and citizens in our country and help them bring about change.'

After that meeting, Rukmini launched Pratham's Lakhon Mein Ek campaign, which aimed to take this 'assessment leading to action' approach to 100,000 villages across India. It sought to involve residents in assessing the state of learning in their own communities. The ultimate goal: to invest citizens in the belief that educational institutions could be changed through voluntary action, much like Anurag's classroom had done. Since the programme's inception in October 2015, they've reached 165,795 villages and 374,138 volunteers and counting.

TEN

JHANSI KI RANI

Her presence was a blessing at the palace of Jhansi and
candles of celebration burned long
But as days passed the dark clouds of misfortune
overshadowed the royal palace.
She put aside her bangles and prepared for battle
For fate was unkind and made her a widow
Grief stricken she was, with no heir for her king,
The Bandelas and Harbolas sang once again of the courage
of the Queen of Jhansi,
How she fought like a man against the British intruders,
So was the Queen of Jhansi.

Jhansi ki Rani by Subhadra Kumari Chauhan
(excerpt from an English translation of the poem)[47]

'I want streamers, balloons, cake, whatever you can think of. I'm landing at 10.30 a.m. Not coming isn't an option, so don't even think about it. I better see every single one of you.' Soumya had just landed in Pune. He wanted his arrival to be a momentous occasion and, as a result, purposefully chose the only flight that landed late on a Sunday morning.

They were used to Soumya's theatrics. His sister, in fact, humoured him by blaring the *Swades* soundtrack on a set of portable speakers, which were now eliciting curious glances and murmurs from exiting passengers.

Building a better India, a pursuit at the heart of Soumya's decision to join Teach For India, was abstract and distant. Rectifying a country with 1.3 billion people seemed lofty.

Building a better Pune, however, was very real. He had spent the first eighteen years of his life in this city. He went to school at one of the city's best—the Bishop's School. He learned to play badminton there. Years later, he would spend his evenings on Fergusson Road, hanging out with college friends. As they drove home from the airport, every little thing—a new flyover here or his favourite night-time eatery there—seemed exciting. His inner drive—now purposeful and intentional—felt different. He wanted to give back to a city that had practically given him the world.

Staring at his laptop and a blank lesson plan, Soumya now knew that building a better country would start with the children awaiting him. He was only two weeks into his fellowship. He had read *Jhansi Ki Rani* more than a hundred times before. He had fond childhood memories of visiting the Jhansi Fort, along with his mother, every summer. As he'd hurriedly climb the fort, trying to stay in sync with his mother's footsteps, she'd recount the tale of the Indian Rebellion of 1857 and Rani Laxmibai's bravery.

Soumya wanted the Rani's story to, one day, become his own. Whenever he questioned his seemingly whimsical decision to leave the safety net of Lutron—a decision made no easier by the hordes of people advising against it—he would reopen the poem.

'If, at twenty-nine years of age, the Rani of Jhansi can give up everything and fight for our country, why can't I commit to building a better India?' Soumya reminded himself. 'She had an easy way out too. She could have accepted the British's offer. She could've taken the money. But she didn't.'

His 'British Raj' was, of course, India's deep-rooted inequity; it was the belief that freedom could transform India into a thriving meritocracy. He had returned fixated on the so-called 'American Dream', the idea that anyone and everyone should have the opportunity to succeed regardless of their background. In Soumya's mind, bringing that dream to India—and to his children—would be pivotal to the transformation he envisioned.

'You tell me how the caste system started. It had to come from somewhere, no?' Soumya was throwing questions at Section 6A, where he taught forty-five students in Kilbil High School.

'The Gods made it,' Sushant said.

'Brahmins came from Brahma's mouth. Kshatriya came from his arms,' Deepak expanded.

'And how do you know that?' asked Soumya.

'Everyone knows that,' Chaitrali confidently responded.

'Okay. If the Gods made our caste system, then why do so many people use it to discriminate?' Soumya asked.

The class was silent.

'Let's do this. Raise your hand if you've personally felt discriminated against because of your caste,' he asked.

He looked around as the students stared at each other. After a few seconds, forty hands were up.

'Would God put you through that? We're going to watch a clip from the movie *Swades*. It's one of my favourites, and it has a really important message,' Soumya said.

The class locked in as Mohan—played by Shah Rukh Khan—listens intently to the plight of Haridas. Having recently become a farmer, Haridas passionately recounts the injustices he faced at the hands of his surrounding community. Villagers refused to provide water, causing his crops to die. The ones that managed to survive, they refused to buy. According to the villagers, Haridas inherited his profession from the Gods; he had no right to change it.

'Do you think the villagers were justified in the way they treated Haridas?' Soumya asked.

'No, bhaiya. The villagers were wrong. He only became a farmer because he couldn't make money as a weaver. If everyone's using machines now, how could he make money? What choice did he have?' Sushant replied.

'Fantastic, Sushant. What about the caste system? Why is it that only Brahmins and Kshatriya can hold India's high-ranking jobs? Why can't Dalits? Is that fair?' Soumya asked. For the next sixty minutes, Soumya relentlessly challenged Section 6A. He was impressed by their ability to grapple with social hierarchy and its underlying dissonance. But he was also growing attuned to the accounts of personal discrimination it was bringing to the surface.

'I am a Dalit. And people in my community don't treat us well at all. They'll tell us we're less. They'll tell us we were born to be less.' As Deepak shared, Soumya could tell the class wasn't quite sure how to process his revelation. Truthfully, neither was he.

'My father tells me it's the caste we've been born into, that this is the price we have to pay. That, maybe, in the next life, we'll get a better turn. But why should I accept that?' Deepak continued.

After a few moments of silence, Jai interrupted: 'You shouldn't have to. And your ancestors shouldn't have had to. *My* ancestors, actually, shouldn't have treated yours that way.'

Soumya had intended to provoke a discussion that day. However, he was unprepared for what eventually unfolded: the class's five upper-caste students were visibly uncomfortable, donning expressions that verged on guilt. The rest of the class looked enraged. Soumya decided to give them a writing assignment to channel their feelings.

'What we do with our castes is, ultimately, within our control. It's in our hands. Take out your notebooks. Let's all make a commitment to change. I want you to write down two things you'll do differently, starting today.'

As Soumya walked around the classroom to read their responses, he was once again unprepared for what he saw.

I will not karry prejudis in my home I will talk my parents about this say to them god did not crate Caste System and it is emportent to change are mind set

'Gauri, they can't even spell! And half of them can't read!' Soumya knew he was venting to his now-wife—again—later that evening. But he admittedly didn't care.

'And they're in 6A. It's the strongest section academically. I mean they're twelve years old, Gauri. And they can't spell the words "important" or "create". They can barely read either. I had to basically walk them through the instructions word-by-word. The system has completely failed them by passing them every year, regardless of their learning levels. Even if they have great ideas, they don't have the tools—like reading and writing—to implement them or engage with them more deeply.'

He started running his hands frantically through his hair, a gesture that signalled he was stressed. Gauri had rarely seen him so defeated. Usually, he was the fearlessly optimistic one.

'But, Soumya, you knew what you were getting into when you signed up to teach these kids. Just don't think about where they are now. Think about the future. Think about the satisfaction in getting them to be India's next visionaries.'

'But how? How am I going to develop forty-five Nandan Nilekanis if they can't read and write? You can't build a nation if you can't read!'

Nandan Nilekani, a key founder of Infosys, epitomized Soumya's vision of the 'Indian Dream'. To him, Nilekani was the embodiment of hard work and commitment. As a teenager, Nilekani tirelessly laboured just to merit a spot in India's reputed IIT Bombay. As CEO of Infosys—a company he founded only a few years after graduation—he'd grown the enterprise six-fold in five years and, as a result, created hundreds of thousands of jobs. Nilekani is the quintessential 'nation builder'. He wrote an eye-opening book, *Imagining India*, that offered a pointed and compelling litany of solutions to India's countless problems. Shortly after, Manmohan Singh, the then prime minister, invited him to implement one of the book's signature ideas: the Aadhaar card. Building a class of forty-five Nandan Nilekanis, for Soumya, would have been an unqualified success.

'Nandan Nilekani was from a Brahmin, middle-class family, for God's sake. He went to Bishop Cotton in Bangalore—that's like one of the best schools in the city. Obviously your kids are going to be different. You need to be realistic,' Gauri pointed out.

'But don't you get it. That's exactly the point. In a meritocratic society, *anyone* can become a Nandan Nilekani. I'm not asking my kids to become outliers like Steve Jobs or Bill Gates. Both of them dropped out of school. They're unconventional. Nilekani is a product of the system, Gauri. His path is clear: you work hard, build strong fundamentals and go to a great school. Then you build India. That's the path I want my kids to follow. The problem is that their system—the one they live in—is completely different. It's not just different. It's broken.

'But it doesn't have to be broken. My kids have the same potential as Pune's middle or upper middle class. The students from a school like Bishop Cotton are thinking about college all the time; their parents ensure that they do. And they have the tools to get there. My kids and their parents don't. At least, not yet. But once they do, imagine what is possible.'

~

'6C, if you're not quiet, I can't teach. And if I can't teach, then you can't learn. It's not that difficult to understand.'

Soumya threw his hands up as dramatically as he could, and walked back to the front of the class. His classroom resembled a playground that day. Tulika and Jamal were throwing paper planes across the room. Chasing Sid, Chandni had just darted out the door. Laxman and Chetan had resumed bullying the new student. The rest of 6C continued to talk, laugh and do everything but heed his directions.

Soumya was exasperated. It was three months into his fellowship and his progress was mixed. He had been tirelessly planning and preparing for every class. Despite seeing progress, the differences between Sections 6A and 6C were noticeable and frustrating.

Soumya was disconcerted by the principal's decision, years

earlier, to segregate kids into differentiated performance-based sections. He had an endless list of grievances with the school, but nothing bothered him more. As a result of choosing to place the most 'struggling' students into one homogeneous block, the children of 6C had now fallen even further behind the other two sections. Frustrated, teachers had begun labelling 6C as the 'lower-order' group that simply 'didn't care'. They had even brought the previous Teach For India Fellow to her knees, where she sat outside the classroom and cried. That story was now folklore across Kilbil. When Soumya first started teaching, he was horrified by the teachers' derogatory accounts. He committed to holding himself to a higher standard. But now, he was facing the same set of kids, on the verge of his own breakdown. He wanted nothing more than to walk out. He was struggling to even *believe* that any amount of effort would turn this class around.

'Soumya?'

There was a knock at the classroom door. He turned to see Vasifa standing.

'Ms Bhalerao is calling you to her office.'

'Again? This is the third time this week. Vasifa—could you please take over?'

'Sure,' she smiled.

As soon as Vasifa walked in, much to Soumya's surprise, the rambunctious group went quiet. Vasifa was one of the school's youngest teachers, certainly not older than twenty-five—maybe twenty-six. She had a calm, gentle yet firm demeanour. All the kids and teachers loved and respected her. Now, Soumya was intrigued and eager to find out why.

Soumya's relationship with Headmistress Bhalerao, on the other hand, had been frayed since his first day. He was tired of her incessant requests, which almost always cut into instruction time. Walking towards her office, he wondered what grievances she would bring up this time.

'"Question 1: What is one of the values that Rani Laxmibai embodies that you have applied in your day-to-day life? Describe how you practised this value. Question 2: Read the newspaper article about Rosa Parks pasted below. Compare and contrast her with Rani Laxmibai. What are two similarities you see and what are two differences?" What is this? This is not a history exam paper!' Ms Bhalerao spoke in her characteristically caustic tone. And she was *not* happy.

'Ma'am—I have a plan and I am covering the textbook material as well. If my kids can answer these questions, I guarantee you they will be able to answer the typical exam paper. I even gave you—'

'Listen, Soumya. I have fifty teachers to manage. I don't have time to cater to each of your "creative" lessons. Do whatever "creative" nonsense you like. Give them a separate test for all I care. But the scheduled unit test cannot—will not—be this. It will be the same as what it is for all classes and as it has been for all these years. It. Will. Be. By. The. Book.'

'And, Soumya,' she gave him a piercing look as she continued. 'You don't hand me printouts of your test papers for review. You write them *by hand* in the journal—like everyone else. Rewrite this and submit it to me first thing tomorrow morning. And your handwriting better be clear! You may go now.'

After the bell rang and school ended, Soumya and Vasifa strolled towards the school's front.

'What is wrong with her?' Soumya asked, obviously frustrated.

He was tired of the seemingly endless challenges, now arising both within and outside his classroom. 'There's no professionalism in this school. Getting my kids to grade level is difficult enough. On top of that, Ms Bhalerao insists on wasting my time with her ridiculous demands. Like our hour-long staff meeting every day. Can't she just mail us that crap?'

'Haan toh. Ab kya? Bataoon mein ya aur rona hai (So? What now? Can I offer a solution now or do you want to cry about this some more)?' Vasifa interrupted, thinking pragmatically. Unlike Gauri, she had no patience for Soumya's rants.

'Soumya, here's the thing. You have high expectations from everyone around you—your colleagues and even your kids. Honestly, that's really impressive. But you have zero *empathy* for where they're coming from. I'm sure you're right, most of the time. There's a lot she can do better, a lot the school can do better. But the way you go about it matters just as much.'

'What are you talking about?'

'Ms Bhalerao has a staff of fifty teachers—*fifty!* And she manages all of them directly. Just think about that for a minute. On top of that, she has crazy amounts of stress from the school trustees. After all, this is the only English Medium School in the area. She's been working tirelessly for this school for twenty-five years. And she's balancing hundreds of random demands, every single day.'

'Like what?'

'Think about the fact that she's basically retained all her staff members. It's not like she has the corporate tools to do that. No salary increases and no promotions. Nothing.'

'Yes, but that doesn't mean she's doing it well. You can't tell me she's doing a good job in there.'

'I agree. But you've been here three months. You're trying to change things. Maybe you have some good ideas. But don't shove them in her face. Understand her. Build a relationship with her.'

Soumya grew pensive. He had never looked at it that way and, frankly, it had been a while since someone had challenged him that directly.

'Is that how you manage 6C?' Soumya asked, his voice getting lower.

'Yes, I guess so. You just have to get to know those kids. Tulika's mother is actually one of my favourite people. She runs a tailoring shop and made my brother's wedding jacket. And Jamal just tries to act tough. But I've helped raise that boy since he was a baby.'

'Siddharth, on the other hand, is a tough one,' she continued. 'His father is in jail and his mother has really struggled. It takes a bit of time to get through to him, but once you do, you realize he's actually quite sweet.'

As Soumya listened, he realized that Vasifa knew every single child in that class. 'How did you end up teaching at Kilbil?'

'I grew up around here. Right after I finished my B.Ed., I took the first job I could find. And that was here, at Kilbil.'

'And why did you want to teach?' Soumya asked.

'My mother's a teacher. When I was a child, I visited her class one day. It inspired me. She loves her job. She treats every day like a series of life-saving surgeries. I've learned pretty much everything I know from that woman.'

Over the next two hours, Soumya and Vasifa talked about her family and the monumental housework she had to complete every day, about the hours of preparation she put into every lesson and about the relationships she had carefully cultivated with each child and their families.

Soumya was mesmerized. He had walked into the fellowship with a plethora of notions he had grown to believe, most notably that teachers in low-income communities simply didn't care.

As he entered home that evening, Gauri caught him by surprise. 'Soumya. I have an idea!'

'That's great, but can we talk later? I've had an incredibly tough day.'

'No. Now. We have to talk now.' Gauri insisted. 'I've figured out how to give your kids the tools they need to express themselves— how they can change the world!'

'What? How?'

'I went through some of your students' work the other day. It's not that your kids can't write. It's that their vocabulary is really poor.'

'And?'

'Well, how did you and I learn vocabulary as kids?'

'We read a lot of books, I suppose?'

'Exactly. So, what if I came into class each evening, once I got off from work, and we read with the kids. Maybe we could move twice as fast?'

Over dinners that week, Soumya and Gauri devised the 'Building India Reading Club'. Over the next year, every child would commit to reading forty new books. By the end of two years, they hoped, every child would be reading at or above grade level.

Getting there proved to be arduous. They spent two hours, every day, after school. They built vocabulary lists, debriefed readings and practised written interpretation. Getting help from friends and previous employers, they raised enough funds to flood the classroom with 300 books, pegged at ascending levels to meet the class's diversity: Noddy (level 1), Famous Five (level 2) and Harry Potter (level 3).

The results were astounding. Not only did every single child read more than forty books that year, many of them also developed a sincere love for reading.

'He's not completing his homework, but he's also not outside playing. He just reads all the time,' Irfan's mother complained to Soumya in their end-of-year parent-teacher meeting.

'Asha reads even while making rotis. These kids are obsessed,' another parent complained.

Soumya couldn't help but smile. Asha was one of his students from the struggling classroom, 6C. He knew the lopsided balance had to change at some point, but the focus on literacy would eventually pay off.

'What's more, he's wasting other kids' time!' Irfan's mother continued.

'What do you mean?' Soumya asked.

Soumya did not expect the explanation that was to follow. By the end of it, he was deeply moved.

Using a nearby park, Irfan had recently started his own book club. A group of local children had watched him reading, every day, under the same tree. Eventually, curiosity blossomed into friendship and a shared, consistent intellectual pursuit. Some older gentlemen—dadajis (grandfathers), as Irfan would lovingly refer to them—joined the group as well. Sometimes, when Irfan didn't have enough books, they'd even bring newspapers for him to read aloud.

Suddenly, the recent uptick in Irfan's requests to borrow books started to make sense. Soumya was glad that he had trusted and obliged the child, despite usually being protective of the expensive library collection. But mostly, he was moved by the humility with which Irfan operated, not letting him or Gauri hear a whisper of his efforts to spread the light he had discovered.

Soumya reassured Irfan's mother and the other parents seated there.

'I can't tell you how happy this makes me. Trust me. If your children can read, I promise you they'll be able to access the world. And if they can access the world, I promise you they can and will change it. They'll be unstoppable.'

~

As things took a turn for the better in class, Soumya's relationship with Ms Bhalerao and the rest of the staff also improved. The conversation with Vasifa compelled him to better understand the other teachers. He began observing their lessons, chatting with them after school and even inviting them over for dinner. He learned about their likes, their dislikes, their families and their life experiences. After every conversation, he walked away more in awe, but also more disturbed.

'Vasifa makes a third of my fellowship stipend—a *third*. Gauri, that's 7,000 rupees a month! She's more experienced than I am. And my dedication pales in comparison to hers.

'Smita's been working at the school for twelve years. And she makes 14,000 rupees,' he continued. 'And get this—Ms Bhalerao— her salary is 25,000. She manages fifty people and runs an organization of 1,000 people. And she makes 25,000 rupees! Who else in today's world would do that?'

Soumya was troubled. He had inadvertently learned the salaries of the staff earlier that day. All he could think about on the drive home was how his cook made more money working in three houses than Vasifa did educating a hundred kids.

'And that's not all. Their pay is just one thing. Listen to what their day looks like. Smita ma'am—she wakes up at 5 a.m., cooks for four people, leaves home at seven, and arrives at school by 7.30 a.m. to take remedial classes for the students until eleven. She then attends an hour-long staff meeting, teaches from twelve to five and attends more meetings at 5.30 p.m. She finally gets home at 6.30 p.m., cooks dinner, helps her two teenage sons with their homework. Then, it's eat, sleep and repeat. All of this for the past twelve years and for what? 14,000 rupees!

'People who say the teachers are the problem don't know anything,' Soumya said. 'The system is broken, Gauri—that much is true. But it's not because of the teachers. It's *in spite* of them— in spite of their hard work and dedication.'

Until then, Soumya, like many, had always believed that the dismal state of education in India was primarily a product of an abundance of apathetic teachers. There were certainly some at Kilbil who were not sincere, but he soon discovered that most of his colleagues were dedicated and hardworking. After conversations with more than a dozen of them, he began to realize that building a better nation would require more than simply dismissing the current system. He would have to utilize it. His head was brimming with ideas and potential solutions.

'What if I could figure out how to better pay these teachers? What if we could make every school in India realize how valuable they are? About how we don't need better teachers—we just need to invest *more* in the teachers we already have. They need training. They need recognition. They need to be heard.'

He was restless with his discovery. Soumya spent the next three days after school devising a plan to test it out. Less than two weeks later, Soumya partnered with his colleague Prashant, also a Teach For India Fellow, to kick-start a teacher recognition programme. They started by enrolling every teacher at Kilbil. They even had a name: 'iTeach'. Every two weeks, Soumya and Prashant would host a series of workshops for teachers to attend. Teachers who successfully completed the 12-week programme would receive a 5,000-rupee award, a certificate and the opportunity to attend a private award ceremony that also hosted their headmaster and government officials.

To pay for the rewards, they not only cultivated a number of local donors but convinced the school to partially front the load. Since he taught in a private low-income school, though, they had to first get parents to agree to a 5 per cent tuition hike which would cover all the teacher-training costs. Many were initially hesitant. They could see the returns on tangible investments like computer labs and textbooks, but not a teacher training programme. Similar to most donors and governments in the world, they were sceptical of the results of investing in professional development for teachers. After several lengthy conversations—and likely a result of the relationships he had formed—Soumya managed to convince enough parents that it was a worthwhile investment.

The results were mixed. Only twelve weeks later, teachers were beginning to perform better. They received unanimously positive feedback. They also felt more celebrated and rewarded. Yet, they were still struggling to keep up with the school's onerous demands and structures. The needs of the iTeach training programme often clashed with the needs of the school administration. Choosing between a last-minute meeting, often called by the school's principal, and a three-hour iTeach training turned into a losing battle. Teachers were struggling to manage their workload, which ultimately resulted in less time for students. Funding was starting to become unsustainable, as valid financial hardships forced many parents to stop paying. Trying to retain them—which meant convincing hundreds of parents that the fee hike was valuable—was growing to be exhausting.

'Putting the right incentive structures in place *is* a great start. I know we're on to something. But it's not enough. It's not even close to being enough,' he told Gauri later that evening.

'I need to control their time. I need to control the structures. Professional development alone isn't going to fix this, when every other structure is broken. Honestly, I just wish I could run the whole damn school.'

PART THREE

Top: Soumya and students from iTeach engaged in a lively discussion.

Bottom: Tarun (third from left) and his team working towards ensuring children have access to a high-quality education through advocacy for RTE section 12(1)(c).

Top: Nalika being present and running a meditation circle with students.

Bottom: Nalika integrating her love for arts in the classroom.

Top: Anurag at an official Delhi Commission for Protection of Child Rights (DCPCR) meeting.

Bottom: Anurag behind a stack of government paperwork.

ELEVEN
THE MARCH TO FERGUSSON

'The remuneration is "to be determined and raised by the School Leader".'

Soumya was trying not to smile as he read out an email I had sent to all graduating fellows. Back then, as the City Director of our Pune site, I oversaw strategy and implementation for our regional programme.

'What does that even mean?' he asked, lifting his head slightly to meet my gaze. Genuinely intrigued, he hadn't touched his sizzler since we had sat down to dinner.

'It means that whoever takes this up will eventually become the CEO of the school.' I knew it sounded crazy, but it was the truth. I expected him to be frightened; it was the response I received from dozens of others. I was, therefore, more than a little surprised to see his smile grow larger as he continued reading aloud.

'"This year, the Pune Teach For India Team secured permissions to enter secondary government schools. Prior to this, the RTE only guaranteed us access to children until seventh standard." How the hell did you pull that one off?' he asked, incredulously.

'A lot of persistence,' I paused as I recollected all that had gotten us to this point. 'And, honestly, a lot of luck.'

Both of those statements were true. Before the Pune government issued that temporary resolution, we were on the brink of losing thousands of children we had served over the past eight years. A majority of them, I knew, were destined to drop out if we couldn't find a viable solution. India's RTE, passed in 2009, mandated schooling for children across the country.

The problem was that it only applied until the eighth standard. As a result, of the fifty-four English medium government schools in Pune, *none* had eighth-grade classrooms. After the age of fourteen, students in our schools had to choose from an impossible array of options:

(1) transfer to a Marathi or Urdu medium school and struggle academically,
(2) transfer to a private school if they could afford it, or
(3) drop out.

Exacerbating the issue was the poorly regulated nature of India's English-medium private schools. Knowing that students often had nowhere to go past the eighth standard, the number of Pune's 'affordable' private schools quickly mushroomed. Some of them charged preposterous rates, taking advantage of the stifled competition. Many provided a questionable quality of education. Naturally, those most adversely affected were the poorest children of Pune. They were the ones dropping out. That reality, perhaps more than anything else, weighed me down.

'We had made a commitment to those kids when they first entered a Teach For India classroom. We committed to getting them through school.' I could feel the emotion starting to well up again, something I couldn't help anymore. 'And if we can't get these schools started, it's game over for them.'

Soumya's smile quickly disappeared. Eight years ago, our team had personally signed the MoU that officially started an intervention for many of these children. Over the years, I had spent hundreds of hours and days in their classrooms, watching them grow up. If we couldn't secure access to secondary schools, I knew that their futures would be starkly different. For the vast majority dropping out, despite their years of effort and perseverance, they would join the hundreds of millions of Indians that simply can't participate in today's knowledge economy.

'But hold on—permission to *enter* secondary government

schools. But *there are none*. There are no secondary English medium government schools in Pune.' Soumya's rebuttal was true.

'Exactly. They've given us the approval to start them. But that's all,' I told him. 'That means there's no principal. No teachers. They won't even pay for textbooks. They've just given us a building. That's it.' While preposterous, it was the biggest success we had secured from the government till date.

Soumya's curiosity was unearthing the dilemma we had been battling for weeks. Running schools did not fall within the gamut of Teach For India's Fellowship model—a debate I had been having, and losing, with Shaheen for weeks. Even if we were to place fellows in secondary government classrooms, *someone* needed to be running the school. Realizing that, I had carefully crafted that mail a few days earlier. I knew that drafting a job description for an entrepreneur to start a network of schools was a bold move. But I knew it was possible and that I would have a pivotal role in getting it off the ground. Thus, I invested a significant amount of personal energy and commitment into finding the right person.

'Look, man, my classroom and kids have changed my life, arguably forever.' Soumya only had two months left till he completed his fellowship.

'And you and I both know that I can't go back to software,' he said, jokingly.

'I don't know if I would let you even if you wanted to.' I, on the other hand, was only half-joking.

'You wouldn't have to. I've seen too much. I can't just walk away now.'

It was a conclusion I had seen and heard hundreds of times. Over the past ten years, 70 per cent of our fellows have chosen to stay in education after their fellowship. The majority of them, when they joined, were clear that Teach For India would be no more than a two-year stint. Their classroom experiences, though, were transformative enough to trigger a seismic long-term shift in purpose.

Personally, I knew that shift all too well. I entered my fellowship in Washington DC more than twelve years ago thinking I would join medical school as soon as my two years were up. My classroom experience was fundamentally transformative. Teaching eighth grade in one of DC's roughest neighbourhoods— as tough and mind-boggling as that experience was—had simply exposed me to too much.

'And we both know that I'm an entrepreneur at heart,' Soumya added. He was right. He had the propensity to take risks, was a natural salesperson and loved uncertainty.

'Look, I wouldn't be talking to you if I didn't think that too. We need the right person to run these schools. I'm not saying it's going to be easy. But, it is going to be exciting.'

It was only a matter of moments before Soumya came down to earth. 'But, wait. What about the iTeach Fellowship? We've even got the funding, man!'

Of course. Prashant and Soumya's teacher training programme, which initially struggled, was now gaining momentum. They had refined the model and mitigated the challenges they had faced in the Kilbil pilot. No longer a teacher training 'service provider', they rebranded the programme as a fellowship. The newest version strived to recruit first-time teachers from B.Ed. colleges and subsequently train and place them in schools.

He had a great deal going on with iTeach, and I didn't want to take that away. However, I genuinely believed he would make an amazing school leader. Having been in his classroom just a few weeks ago, I knew he was a really strong teacher. He not only had the instructional expertise to lead a school, but also had the management experience from his time at Lutron to mobilize teams.

'What if you were to do both?' I asked. 'One of you could run the fellowship and the other could run the school.'

'That's ridiculous. It's one of your crazy ideas. I've heard so much about them,' he shot back, laughing nervously.

'Why couldn't you do both? Every effective teacher training programme needs a lab. In this case, your school becomes your lab.'

'That's going to kill me!' There was that smile again though, which I knew was masking his genuine consideration of the idea.

'Look, the school gives you an opportunity to run an end-to-end operation. You have control of everything that happens within that school. And you know that's the fundamental flaw of professional development programmes—you said it yourself. This is your chance. Look at it like this: the school becomes your lab for the fellowship programme. It'll be your centre of excellence.'

I could see Soumya getting excited and, honestly, I was too. Research shows that the school leader—just one person—can account for 25 per cent of the school's impact on student outcomes.[48] Over the years, I've watched this play out as hardworking teachers step into classrooms with the best of intent, only to find their efforts stymied by a hostile and unsupportive school environment. Our fellows confront a myriad of issues every day—from decrepit buildings and inadequate infrastructure to changing timetables and mercurial headmasters. Eventually, those issues spill over into classrooms. And when they do, our best teachers quickly find themselves disillusioned. While great teachers have the potential to create massive changes—as we've seen through the 4,000 fellows who have completed our programme—offering them a conducive school environment makes their potential for transformation exponentially more likely.

'You moved back because you wanted to build India. You wanted to build Pune. And if you're able to make this successful, I can't think of a better way to build the city. Think about it. What if, ten years from now, you could ensure that no child drops out again because they didn't have access to secondary school?'

I put down my food for a minute and looked intently at him, knowing that I had his undivided attention.

'What if you could do more than that? What if you could ensure that every low-income child in Pune got the opportunity to attend college? What if you could ensure Pune creates a thousand more Nandinis—kids who are not only proving the stats wrong but are also developing into leaders who will, we both know, change the world?'

For Soumya, and thousands of fellows and alumni across the country, Nandini was the ultimate symbol of hope. Many of them had heard her stories of struggle from Luhianagar. They were fascinated by her ability to overcome those challenges and gain acceptance into a prestigious college abroad; they were even more intrigued by her deep desire to make the world a better place. There would be no better way of building a stronger India than enabling a thousand Nandinis.

Soumya and I didn't say much for the rest of that evening. He was energized by the idea, but he was understandably nervous. Setting up schools to ensure that hundreds of low-income kids graduate and successfully enrol in college—a majority of who would be the first in their families to ever do so—would be no small feat.

~

'Thank you all for coming today. I know you've had to take time off from work just to be here with us.'

Soumya walked in confidently. He was prepared to address the fifty-odd parents gathered that hot summer day in May. It had been a month since he completed his fellowship, and so much had transpired during that time. He had incorporated iTeach Schools as an independent non-profit organization. He had made his first hire, Sweta Sarkar, also a Teach For India alumna. While undoubtedly proud milestones, Soumya saw them as mere formalities. Getting parents to enrol their students would be the critical first step. Soumya and Sweta had organized a parent meeting to build confidence.

'We've called you here this morning to share some really good news.' He was trying to ensure his voice reached them over the hall's cooler, which was half-broken and sputtering louder than an old car. 'We are starting a school for your children to attend. It will be free of charge. It will begin next month. We will ensure that your children graduate from the tenth standard.' As Soumya muttered the last few words, he knew they made him the most nervous. He had stayed up half the night wondering if he should publicly make that commitment, second-guessing if he would be able to actually deliver on it.

'How can that be possible? Just last year, they told us we were on our own. That we would have to find our own private school.' Deepak's father was incredulous.

'Yes, they told me the same thing. They said the government can't accept any responsibility after eighth. I've already started talking to private schools,' Anjali's mother said.

'We know they told you that. But the government has now given us permission to start two schools. And they've given us the infrastructure too,' Soumya responded.

'Bhai, this is an election year. Of course, they're telling you to start it. They're fooling you—and us. They won't keep that promise,' Deepak's father said.

The roomful of parents broke into chatter, resoundingly agreeing with Deepak's father.

'Sweta didi, he's right. They told us the same thing three years ago. My oldest son was ready to enrol. But, at the last minute, they told us it wouldn't be possible,' Anjali's mother said.

Soumya and Sweta, expecting a audience, had come prepared.

'No, it's real. We have the permission letter and the MoU,

stamped and approved by the government.' Sweta reassured them. She pulled out the letter from her purse and held it up.

'It's real.' Sweta could feel her hand shaking, ever so slightly, as she repeated those two words, this time much more slowly. Having taught for the past two years, she had addressed crowds, classrooms and halls filled with angry parents. She had never been this nervous though. And the room, now silent, was waiting for someone—anyone—to tell them she wasn't lying.

'So, are you saying I don't need to put my child in a private school?' Irfan's father asked.

'Are you saying you're going to get them to graduate tenth?' Chaitrali's mother chimed in.

'Yes, we will get them past tenth. We, in fact, intend to ensure that every student gets accepted into one of Pune's best colleges. That's our dream. And that's our commitment to you,' Sweta said.

Sensing his opportunity, Soumya moved into his favourite part of the presentation. 'Take a look at the screen. This is Fergusson College. Inside that grey brick building and behind that beautiful garden are classrooms where some of the city's finest have studied. I want you to close your eyes. I want you to imagine your child, three years from now, standing at that gate, waiting to walk into that classroom. What are you wearing? What is your child wearing? Are they carrying a backpack or a sling bag? And what colour is it?'

Soumya had done this exercise for his Kilbil classroom and found it powerful. He wanted parents to buy into their vision—to realize it was more than a whim.

'And what are you going to charge?' Irfan's father asked when he opened his eyes, bringing the group back to their current reality.

'Nothing. It's free.'

The parents began exchanging glances and murmurs. The vast majority of them had never made it to the tenth standard. Getting their children to do so would be a dream. And here were two ambitious twenty-somethings promising that they would do it at no cost at all. Understandably still unsure what to believe, they continued prodding.

'And who's going to run the schools? Who's going to teach?' Lalitha's father was shouting from the back of the room.

'Sweta and I will be running both schools. I'll run the Babu Jagjivan Ram School (BJR) here in Yerwada. Sweta will run Sant Gadge Maharaj School (SGM), our Kondhwa campus.' Soumya and Sweta felt the gaze of fifty parents sizing them up, as if to ascertain if they were both serious and capable.

'Listen, we know you're all sceptical. And you have reason to be. That's why we've made this entire presentation. Please just hear us out first. Then the decision is yours.'

For the next twenty minutes, Soumya walked them through their emerging model. Drawing inspiration from successful charter schools in the US, they had made some bold choices. They would run the school for 250 days, seventy days more than the typical school. They would run it for eight hours a day (compared to the five-hour days most schools utilize). They would differentiate instruction for struggling students and administer weekly tests to ensure that all students—some of whom were five years behind—would eventually be college-ready. With the government partnership taking care of a significant expense—buildings—they were betting on private-sector funding to ensure the school could remain free of charge.

As Soumya finished, Deepak's father stood up and looked directly at them. 'If you're serious, then this is one of the best things that could have happened. I had resigned to pulling Deepak out of school just last night.'

'Yes, if we won't have to spend half our monthly salary on tuition—then this is the best thing that could have happened, indeed,' Sushant's mother agreed.

'That means that my Irfan may actually graduate tenth!' Irfan's father exclaimed.

'And my Anjali may get into college!' Anjali's mother said.

Her proclamation got the group so excited, they erupted in applause. Their scepticism having dissolved, the parents were now jubilant. Deepak's father, however, broke the celebration for a brief moment of levity.

'You better be serious though. If you come back and tell us that the permissions aren't real, you'll have an angry mob of parents after you!' Deepak's father warned.

The room went silent again for a minute, before erupting into laughter and applause again. As Soumya sat at the front of the room, occasionally exchanging glances with Sweta, he took a moment to weigh the responsibility he was taking on. He was no longer accountable to teachers alone; now, he would be directly accountable to hundreds of students and parents as well. He knew that successfully getting their kids to graduate would require a mammoth effort over the next two years. He needed parents to share that weight. He stood up to get the room's attention and delivered the final part of their presentation.

'We're committed to doing this and we are very serious. But we need you to know that this is not going to be easy. It's likely going to be the hardest thing your child's ever done. And, honestly, it'll be the hardest thing we've ever done, too.'

Intent on belabouring the point and leaving little room for uncertainty, Soumya repeated his last line: 'It's going to be the hardest thing any of us have ever done.'

Sweta expanded, 'Sending your children to school for 250 days means a shorter Diwali, a shorter Ganapati, a shorter summer. Every Saturday will be a working one. For the next three years, it means your child likely won't have summer vacations— no time for trips back home or for weddings. Your children have had a Teach For India intervention for multiple years and, as a result, they are in a good place. But if they're going to get into the city's best colleges, they're still behind. So we're going to need every second of every day. You'll have to ensure they do their homework, because they will have homework daily. You'll also have to send them two tiffins, since the days will now be longer.'

She continued, 'This school will work if we work together—if you work with our teachers, and with us. We'll ask that you come to meetings regularly and that you communicate with us frequently.'

'Didi, bhaiya, you're telling us you're going to start this school. You're telling us you're not going to charge us. And you're telling us that you're going to get our kids to college,' Sushant's mother repeated.

She was now standing up too. She continued, 'If you're telling us all of that—and you are doing all of that—you can expect all the help you need from me. If that's going to take every minute over the next three years—and you're willing to work that much—then we'll make sure our kids are here. We'll make sure we do our bit.'

Anjali's mother added, 'Forget two tiffins, I'll send six tiffins—two for each of you as well.'

Once again the room broke into laughter.

Soumya and Sweta stayed back, for more than an hour, to chat with parents who still had questions. Some had already paid hefty deposits to private schools and wanted advice on how to get a refund. Others were still sceptical and wanted to read the MoU themselves. Once all the parents left, Soumya and Sweta walked out feeling an uneasy mixture of excitement, anxiety and relief.

~

Early Thursday morning, Soumya and I walked across the bumper-to-bumper traffic and through the rusted metal gates of Pune's Sant Gadge Maharaj School. As we entered, a small group of women were busily preparing dal and rice in a little shed to the left. The midday meal would be served to more than 750 children. The land in front of us was not only barren, it was also littered with empty bottles, plastic bags and broken glass. It served as the school's only playground. As we walked past the ground floor, both of us held our noses. The stench of stale urine was emanating from the boys' bathroom in the basement.

In the three months since its inception, Sweta and the teachers of SGM had been embroiled in a gruelling battle with local government officials. Because of competing demands from both Urdu and Marathi medium sections—all of who shared the building with Sweta's children—the government was no longer willing to offer the space they once so willingly promised. And because the construction of the school's new site had been stalled due to delinquent government payments, more than 750 children occupied a space otherwise designed to hold 500. Its crowded halls were filled with both garbage and children. There simply weren't enough classrooms.

'Trust me. It's going to get worse as we go up.' Soumya had repeated some version of that warning at least five times now. And he was right. As we entered the top floor, we paused to fully grasp the spectacle in front of us.

'Is that—?' I asked.

'What the hell?' Soumya cut in, aghast.

Two children, no older than thirteen, were defacing the school's 'wall of fame'. Angrily walking towards them, Soumya started yelling almost immediately.

'Kya kar rahe ho aap dono (What are you two doing)?'

'Yahaan pishaab kyun kar rahe ho (Why are you peeing here)?'

In seconds, both the boys darted down the stairs. Interrupted by the clamour, Sweta emerged, shaking her head.

'They're doing it again. They keep coming and they keep vandalizing everything,' she said calmly. Embarrassed to see me, she politely greeted me before echoing Soumya's sentiments: 'It's crazy, and it's going to get worse.'

As we turned the corner, we passed groups of children attempting to learn in the corridors. Teachers were holding up chalkboards, continuously interrupted by dozens of students running and playing.

'It's like we're at war. Kids from every other section keep running in and out of our classes. They're tearing down charts, peeing on walls and vandalizing everything. And now some of *our* kids are doing the same thing.' Sweta was clearly exhausted. She looked like she hadn't slept in days.

'And here's the main hall. This is the only actual space they've given us. They've also given us those two classrooms for the first four hours of the day, but that's it.'

Within the hall, as big as a school auditorium, were 180 children boxed off into imaginary classrooms. Having no walls, Sweta and her team used masking tape on the floor to delineate the separation of their classes. Each teacher was attempting to whisper so as not to disturb the class 'next door'. I paused and looked back at Soumya and Sweta, both of whom were clearly disturbed. It was far from the school they had envisioned less than ninety days ago. And it was far from the dream they sold at that memorable parent conference.

'We have funding. We have teachers. We have staff. We have kids,' Soumya said, still looking at the children chaotically running through the hall. 'But they screwed us on the space, man.'

Later that evening, Soumya decided to spend a few hours with the SGM team. Before heading back home, I suggested he hold an open space for people to share and express their feelings. It is something I've facilitated hundreds of times with teams over the years. That evening, though, went far different than planned.

'This is not what we signed up for!' Ankit shouted.

'We're exhausted. And we're in that hall, whispering then yelling, whispering then yelling for four hours a day, every day.'

'And the Urdu medium kids! They keep destroying everything—our posters, our boards, everything.'

'You're asking for eight hours of instruction, but we're doing the kids a disservice. Eight hours—any amount of hours—in that hall is a nightmare!'

'There's no way these kids are graduating if this keeps up.'

'When are we going to conduct science experiments? When are we going to teach them how to use computers? They need that for college.'

Soumya tried to step in, on multiple occasions, but team members cut him off each time. They were frustrated— understandably so. While they knew that it was a result of many things seemingly out of their control, they couldn't help but place part of the blame on the people incharge.

'You promised these kids and their parents that we'd get them to college. You said we had a bulletproof permission from the government. I want to believe in that and believe in both of you. But how can I? I can't keep yelling. My kids, I'm telling you, are learning nothing.' Monica was particularly upset. Her classroom had been moved four times in the last week—the corridor, the hall, the playground downstairs and then back into the corridor.

I met Soumya the next morning. Battered and weary, he hadn't slept much the night before. Uncertain of what to say—and also a little overwhelmed myself—I tried to sit and listen instead.

'Between the defacing and the yelling, I don't know which one bothers me more,' he started. 'I can see why they're upset, man. They have a right to be upset. We promised them space to teach. And we promised those kids a space to learn. We promised them the basics. Not a fancy computer room. Or air conditioning. Or a chemistry lab. Just a classroom. With a wall. And a door. That's it.'

Soumya ran his hands through his hair. 'Thankfully my school's infrastructure is fine. But how the hell did SGM end up in this mess? Sweta's strong and she'll hold that ship down. But this isn't fair to her either, man.'

As Soumya spoke, I realized that I had often preached about the struggles of starting a school. But I definitely didn't anticipate the challenges for space these two would face. Nevertheless, I tried to ease the situation and provide a little perspective.

'Soumya, you and Sweta are trying to make *history*. These

kids weren't meant to even graduate and you're trying to change that. You're trying to ensure they get the best education possible. We all know that the journey there wasn't going to be easy.

'Think about why they don't have space,' I added. 'No one expected them to even be in secondary school. The city expected those kids to either drop out or fend for themselves.'

'Have you and Sweta been talking?'

'No, why?'

'Nothing. She said the same thing.'

Soumya took a deep breath and charged two steps ahead. 'Don't worry. We're going to fix this. The truth is that I don't really have time to be overwhelmed. Because every minute I sit here, griping, those kids are there—not learning.'

Soumya's voice was getting both deeper and louder. 'We're going to fix the space, if I have to build that damn building myself. And we're going to fix instruction, if I have to spend every night researching pedagogy and introducing those systems myself.'

The tables around us were beginning to stare. He didn't seem to care though.

'Those kids will learn. They will graduate. They will get into college. And Sweta, the entire staff of SGM and I—we're going to pick ourselves back up because we have to. Because those kids need us to. There's too much at stake. We can't fail.'

~

I was walking through the corridors of Babu Jagjivan Ram School (BJR), the Yerwada campus of iTeach, less than two months after my initial encounter with SGM's chaos. Soumya had mentioned the Yerwada campus did not share the same challenges; still, I couldn't help but be a little anxious. As I studied the student work posted along the walls of the corridor, I heard a series of high-pitched yells and drumbeats from the classroom next door. More than thirty students were standing up and chanting in unison.

'We will.'

'We will march!'

'Where will we march?'

The teacher, Tanvi, stood at the front of the room and egged them on. A Teach For India Fellow, no older than twenty-five, she was clearly enjoying herself and fully caught in the moment.

'We will march to Fergusson! We will march to Pune's best colleges! We will march to the top five!' the kids responded, in chorus.

'And why will we march?' Tanvi shouted back.

'Because we belong there!'

'And why do we belong?' she asked them, screaming at the top of her lungs now.

'Because poverty won't dictate our destiny!'

'Because we are the future!'

'And what will it take?' she pressed on.

'We must show up!'

'We must work hard!'

'We must not give up!'

'We must fight—for our right—to belong!'

'That's right,' Tanvi abruptly lowered her voice and glanced across the classroom. She began to lower her hands, signalling for the kids to follow suit. Sweat dripping from their foreheads, they were more riled up than any ninth-grade classroom I had seen at 8.30 a.m. For a moment, I too felt energized. I later learned that the chant was their morning ritual.

'We are going to march. And we're going to march together,' Tanvi continued, now at a normal volume. 'But marching into college demands that we focus.' As Tanvi spoke, she walked over to the side of the room and stood by a giant white piece of laminated chart paper hanging on the wall. Scrawled across it were three numbers: '275'.

'That number may seem high, but it's going to fly by. I promise you that,' she told the class.

'If we can make it, in 275 days, we'll be walking across that graduation floor. If we can focus—and work relentlessly—we will get our grade-ten mark sheets. We will ace our tenth board exams. And then, we will begin our march. I promise you.'

As I stood there, my hands now trembling with energy, I couldn't help but notice the many colours and messages plastered across Tanvi's classroom. Pictures of colleges adorned the entrance door that kids walked through. Her walls were filled with images of leaders, such as Mahatma Gandhi, Jawaharlal Nehru, Subhas Chandra Bose, Sundar Pichai, Nandan Nilekani, Elon Musk, Nelson Mandela and even Teach For India's Shaheen Mistri. Below each image was a small caption that described the college they attended. But the most prominent was a message posted in the front of this and every classroom in the school: 'In August 2017, we will march into the top five colleges of Pune— into Fergusson College!'

Fergusson College is one of Pune's most prestigious higher education institutions. The school's founders, more than 150 years ago, established the university as a historic symbol in the fight against British imperialism. In their eyes, a modern education system was one of the country's best tools to realize Independence and build the foundations of a democracy. Since then, Fergusson has long been upheld as an institution open only to the city's best and brightest students. It has produced some of the city's wealthiest and most successful leaders, the majority of whom came from backgrounds diametrically opposite to the children chanting its name this morning.

Every moment of school for the children of iTeach is working backwards from the singular goal of getting themselves to and through college and, one day, building a better India. Fergusson, in their minds, is the symbolic realization of that goal. It's an acknowledgement that, if students can get into Fergusson, they can do anything.

Over the years, I've met dozens of sceptics and people who,

rightly so, question the value of promoting a vision of college-bound readiness for children from low-income backgrounds. They argue that India has many paths to success. They also claim that, as things stand today, colleges are far from being the beacons of higher education and liberation that we associate with institutions abroad. They contend that every child may not be 'college material.' Understanding Soumya's obsession with college, in that light, demands that we understand his beliefs about nation building.

'I agree that our higher education system is far from perfect,' Soumya told me, later that evening. 'And I also agree that there are many examples of entrepreneurs—very successful ones—who have never stepped foot into a college. But, for the vast majority of Indian youth today, the workforce demands that they have a college degree from a good institution. That is the signalling mechanism used by employers in the market to determine the aptitude of a candidate, however broken it may be. You simply can't get a high-paying job without it. It sucks, but it's true. You can't be taken seriously without it. And if you can't be taken seriously, there's no way you can build a nation. There's no way you can change a country, *especially* if you're already excluded from other kinds of social, economic and cultural capital.'

Soumya's pragmatism reflects the reality of our system today. While our institutions of higher education are in desperate need of repair, they are one of our primary paths to success for young generations. His goal of getting students to college is more than a privileged calling for them to enter a system designed for a few. Instead, it is rooted in the realization that getting children out of poverty—and enabling them to one day change the system—demands that they first have the knowledge, skills, mindset and credentials to succeed *within* it.

'I'm aware that not all of my children are going to graduate from college,' Soumya states nonchalantly. 'But I also believe that's not my choice to make. That's their choice. I don't have the right to tell kids that they should enter a vocational path or choose a "less complicated" route because they don't have the required skills right now.'

I realize that this was a topic that got Soumya riled up.

'Instead, when they get to that doorway of having to choose, I want to ensure that they're not limited by their backgrounds, their skills or their knowledge. If they choose not to enter college, I don't want it to be because they *can't*. I want it to be because they choose not to. That's the reality for every affluent Indian child out there. I want that to be the reality for my kids too, *despite* the fact that they're poor.'

I've heard hundreds of fellows and educators use the word 'choice' to describe their deepest aspirations for children. Their argument is simple: 'I want my children to choose the life path that is best for them.' Yet embedded within the very concept of choice is a loaded package of requirements. Students one day choosing their futures mean that they not only have the knowledge base, critical thinking skills and reflective capacity to make the best choices, it also means that they have the values and prescience to choose wisely. As Soumya notes, children from low-income backgrounds shouldn't be deprived of that choice simply because of their circumstances.

As I walked out of his school that evening, I started thinking about the low societal expectations Nandini and Nishi spoke about. It's an implicit despairing assumption on the potential of poor people. Those expectations are, in many ways, a function of what we've seen in the past: that most will live a life of penury and low opportunity. That was the realization that hit Nandini the hardest when she began interacting with her more affluent peers at the United World College. For them, the expectation was that they would attend college, do great things and be extraordinarily successful. It was antithetical to everything she had ever heard.

Nandini and Nishi's statements hint at a key question that underlies the college-bound debate and is more than applicable to the children of iTeach: if these were children from high-income backgrounds, would we even be asking whether college is the best option for them?

For Soumya, the answer was clear. And any debate, in his mind, was put to rest two years later—the day he watched 109 students receive their graduation diplomas. Despite seemingly insurmountable challenges, iTeach's first batch of students had proved the statistics wrong.

'Class of 2021, we expect the world from you.' Soumya deliberately chose to address the students by the year they would, one day, graduate college. He was delivering his parting speech for iTeach's first graduating batch of students, who now filled the auditorium of Pune's prestigious Symbiosis University—an institution that several of them would soon be attending.

'You have shown us—and this city—that this is possible. And because of the steps you've taken, you have now opened the door for hundreds of thousands of kids to do the same.' As he paused, his eyes starting to well up, he looked out at the darkened auditorium.

'Because of you, kids across this city will begin to believe that poverty never has to dictate destiny. They will believe that they are in control of their futures. Because of you, we are that much closer to building a better India.' Soumya paused again, this time to wait for the applause from parents, teachers and students to die down before continuing with his final line for the evening. 'You are now building a movement of children who are not only getting into the colleges of their choice, but who are going to change the face of this county. And that movement will soon be unstoppable.'

Sitting in the front row, that evening, I watched 109 students walk across the stage, one after another, and receive their diplomas. They were future doctors, engineers, activists, change-makers, authors, scientists and more. They were, hopefully, future nation-builders. And, as we would later learn, an astounding 96 per cent of them had gotten into colleges of their choice. In just a few months, they would begin their march into Fergusson and colleges across the city.

As each of them walked on stage, their parents and peers cheering loudly in the audience, I couldn't help but think about the untapped opportunity that was now available to them—opportunity that their parents never received. That opportunity was a direct product of the certificates—and the knowledge, skills and mindset—that they now held.

iTeach's vision over the next ten years is to create twenty schools across the city. Eventually, Soumya and his team want to ensure that 100 per cent of Pune's low-income children attend and graduate college.

TWELVE
WE'RE YOUR CHILDREN NOW

It was only two months into Nalika's new role as a Programme Manager (PM) with Teach For India. She knew she shouldn't be getting this frustrated so early. Managing a group of twenty adults was turning out to be vastly different than running a classroom of thirty-six fourth-graders.

She had loved everything about her classroom. It was, after all, the first place that had given her true purpose. It was also what, immediately after the Fellowship, compelled her to apply for the PM role. Despite her apprehensions, she wanted to help other TFI Fellows find their purpose, too.

Venil Ali, the City Director of the organization's Mumbai site, had reassured her a dozen times already. 'You've been great with kids. You're one of the strongest teachers I've ever seen. And you're going to be great with adults. Of course, give it time. It'll be a learning curve, but you'll figure it out.'

'But I get kids. I don't get adults. They're different,' Nalika replied.

'How exactly are they different? They're just bigger versions of little people, no?'

'These are highly capable adults we're talking about, Venil. They're not that much younger than me—and some of them are older! How am I even going to give them feedback?

'Why will they even listen to me?' Nalika continued. 'I know kids listen to me, but that's because they're so young and innocent. Why would an adult listen to me? I just feel like I'm setting myself up to fail.'

As Nalika continued, Venil patiently listened to her litany of questions. She was both humoured and fascinated by Nalika's deep sense of humility. For Nalika, it wasn't a lack of interest that bothered her. Her seemingly diffident personality, she worried, would prove disastrous in the face of unwieldy young teachers.

Adding to the confusion was her parents' unrelenting pressure. They were tepid about her decision to join the Fellowship, nevertheless they chose to offer her the space to experiment. Now, two years later, their patience had run thin.

'Are you sure you want to do this?' her mom had asked, dubiously.

'Yes, Mom. I'm sure. I wouldn't have applied if I weren't.' Nalika knew that was a lie, but insisted on a self-assured, confident front.

'You told us this would be no more than two years. And, Nalu, those two years are up.'

'Yes, I know but—'

Before she could finish her sentence, her mom had interjected: 'But what about academia? What about your dream of being a professor? Of studying at the world's best universities? What about your doctorate at Oxford? You've been dreaming of that life since you were a little girl. Have you just forgotten everything about the person you once were?'

'I know, Mom, but that's changed now. There's something more here. I don't know what it is, but it makes me feel alive. I need you to see that. I need you to trust me. It's like these kids have helped me find something I didn't know existed. They've helped me grow up, into a real person. And now I can't help but wonder if I can do more. What if I can now have an impact on twenty classrooms? What if I could change the lives of more than 500 children?' Nalika paused to give her mother a chance to absorb it all. 'Listen, Mom, I've got this. I'm not giving up that dream of academia. Don't worry. I'm just putting it on hold for a few years.'

'I just don't understand why. I don't understand why you can't do both. Be a professor who donates to social causes,' her mom had replied.

'Because, right now, both aren't important. This is important.'

By the end of that conversation, Nalika's hands had been trembling. The dialogue had undoubtedly shaken her. Her mother, after all, had been right thousands of times before. Growing up, Nalika had worked to emulate her mother's commitment to excellence and her perseverance; she, quite simply, adored her mother. Not seeing eye-to-eye with her biggest role model—a woman who had given so much to make her life possible—was tough. It only fuelled her apprehension. But the past two years had shifted something fundamentally at her core that, for the first time, Nalika felt both real and alive.

Distressed and nervous, Nalika had turned her computer back on and, a few moments later, officially sent in her acceptance. 'I hope this is the right decision,' she had muttered to herself before crawling into bed.

~

Vaishali ran through the door and glanced nervously at the almost empty room. 'I know I'm late. I'm so sorry. It was just—'

'It's okay. Just come in.'

Nalika was intently staring at her watch and tapping her right foot. It was fifteen minutes past five, and only half her Fellows had shown up. Worse, not a single one had called to say they would be late. She had spent hours the night before preparing for today's meeting. Having just completed their first month of school, she wanted to celebrate by gifting every Fellow a carefully written note and a personalized gift basket filled with energy drinks, fruit, doughnuts, stationery supplies and stickers.

'My headmaster was ridiculous today. He wouldn't let us leave.' Madhura had grown up in Mumbai and just graduated from Jai Hind College. This time, Nalika neither responded nor acknowledged her presence. It was now 5.25 p.m., and eight Fellows were still missing.

Nalika could feel her anger starting to boil over. She was genuinely perturbed. In her mind, it was unprofessional and unbecoming of teachers not to be exemplars of everything they expected from their students. At the same time, it was her first meeting of the year and she desperately wanted it to go well. Her Fellows had been struggling with the first three weeks of school and they were in need of a space—a celebration—to lift their spirits. Adding to the stress was the significance of today's workshop. Intended to teach them how to plan their quarterly units, it was one of the most foundational skills that first-time teachers needed to master. If they couldn't learn it today, they would likely only continue to struggle.

'It's half past five. You have got to be kidding me,' Nalika whispered to herself as she looked down at the box of uneaten doughnuts. Over the next ten minutes, the remaining Fellows briskly walked through the door, one by one. With each entrance—and each apology that followed—Nalika's irritation only grew. As the last Fellow entered, fifty minutes later, Nalika quietly contemplated how—and if—she should respond. What eventually came out surprised even her.

'I understand that many of you are new to the city. Many of you are rushing from school. And many of you have driven more than forty-five minutes to be here. It's monsoon season and it's raining cats and dogs outside.'

Nalika was twiddling her thumbs as she looked at the group of twenty new teachers, many drenched in rainwater. 'But this is just unacceptable.'

Nodding in acknowledgement, her Fellows weren't expecting what would come next.

'I'm cancelling today's meeting. We're not going to do this workshop today. If you don't value this space enough to be here on time, then the truth is that I can't really help you.'

Puzzled, her Fellows started to quietly exchange glances before jumping in.

'But we just told you it was pouring outside. You've been a Fellow,' Madhura protested.

'Getting around in this city is insane. You can't expect us to beat that,' Rahul reiterated.

They were all staring at Nalika in disbelief, waiting for her to respond.

'I understand that, but it's still not acceptable. If you had a meeting with Shaheen, or a job interview, none of you would be late. You wouldn't because you deeply respect them and that space. Please don't give me excuses about the weather. You just don't respect this space yet and you don't respect me.'

Her Fellows had never known this side of her before—and quite frankly, neither had Nalika. They were used to the shy and excessively polite girl who would only give constructive criticism, sandwiched between positive feedback.

After pausing a moment to catch her breath, Nalika continued.

'Parents, educators, staff members and dozens of others trust you to look after their kids. They trust you to be role models and are counting on you to change their lives. That responsibility is bigger than anything you've ever taken on before. It's bigger than your past jobs, it's bigger than your college projects, it's bigger than anything you've ever done. Your most basic responsibility to those kids is to be models of the behaviour you expect from them. And you can't even be on time for a professional development session nor have the courtesy to inform me that you will be late. Just think about that.'

She quickly grabbed the carefully wrapped notes and her supply bags. Without saying a word, she stood up, darted back down the stairs and ran outside. Standing alone in the middle of an alley in Mumbai's pouring rain, Nalika started sobbing.

She had countless reasons to be angry. The hours of preparation, the little notes, the celebration of their first month— all of that effort had just gone down the drain. Nalika nevertheless knew, deep down, that she had done the right thing. As a teacher, she knew that complacency was the biggest threat to greatness. In a system that is rife with dysfunction—and filled with parents and children who are overtly grateful for the smallest of things—it was too easy to simply walk into class, every day, and bring everything but your best. She knew that her Fellows were smart and capable enough to be competent teachers. Perhaps most importantly, she knew they had the potential to be great leaders. But to be on that trajectory, Nalika needed them to first experience greatness within their classrooms—to witness the type of transformation she had seen over the past two years. That endeavour, she knew, would require every inch of their energy and soul.

Her Fellows waited for another fifteen minutes, quietly hoping she would walk back in.

She didn't walk back in though. And they weren't late again.

~

In the first few months of her new role, Nalika would continue searching for the right balance between high expectations and empathy. Having been a consistently strong teacher herself, she had little tolerance for poor performance—a trait she often failed to fully understand. She also had a penchant for jumping head-first into problems. Seeing a class not going well, more often than not, would incite her to take over. As the months went on though, she not only learned to better understand her Fellows, but she also began to grasp the immense potential of allowing them to struggle.

Perhaps no one exemplified that shift more than Jesal.

Leaving behind a strong academic career, Jesal joined the Fellowship eagerly wanting to effect change. Her first few months into the Fellowship, however, were anything but easy. Exacerbating her struggles, Jesal's parents were less than enthusiastic about her decision to join Teach For India. Now that her life was immersed in daily failures, accompanied by endless nights of planning, their disapproval had only grown. They wanted her to quit.

Adding to the misery, Jesal grew alarmingly ill only three

months into the Fellowship. Suffering from dengue, she spent an entire week in the hospital. Her classroom performed poorly and her efforts seemed to make no difference at all—so much so that she quickly broached the possibility of resigning.

Initially, Nalika was shocked. After all, Nalika's Fellowship experience, eerily similar, provided a number of early stumbling blocks.

'What do I do? She was only sick for a week. And then this. I don't know about her parents. My guess is they're not supportive,' Nalika told her manager, Ikpreet, that evening.

'Why do you seem so annoyed, Nalika? The girl is sick.'

'Because I went through the same thing. I was puking blood in my first month. And I never missed a day,' she replied, somewhat proudly.

'Do you think she understands what's at stake? I mean, she decided to apply for the Fellowship. And she is here.'

Nalika paused. 'Yes, I guess. But not at the level that she needs to, in my opinion. If she did, she would not give up so easily. Ugh. I just don't know why adults are so damn hard to work with!'

'And you think it's your job to elicit that understanding?'

Sensing her annoyance, he tried to clarify. 'Go back to your Fellowship. How did your biggest realizations come about?'

She paused for a minute before answering, 'They were the moments I realized that my kids weren't getting what they needed, that I wasn't giving it the best I could have given them.'

'Right, you realized. She needs to understand that her kids are everything. She needs to feel what's at stake in her classroom. Your role is to simply create the enabling conditions for that, but the decision is her's to take. And maybe then she'll see that she can pull through this.'

The next morning, Nalika visited Jesal in the hospital. They spent the afternoon playing cards and talking about school. They shared stories of growing up with strict parents. They talked about life in Mumbai and they laughed about the time Nalika darted out of the workshop. Nalika even shared the story of Imran cutting Masira's hair. Later that afternoon, as Jesal fell asleep, Nalika sat by her bed. She started thinking about Jesal's Fellowship; it had only been a few months. She thought back to when she was two months into her own Fellowship.

'I can't thrust upon my Fellows all that I've learned over the last two years. I have to trust them to build their own journeys,' Nalika whispered to herself.

The next morning, Nalika returned to the hospital. She brought her lunch, along with several copies of letters from Jesal's students, professing how much they missed her. When she walked in, she didn't expect to see Jesal's parents.

Nalika could feel her palms sweating. Jesal's mother was sitting in front of her. She had never met Nalika before and seemed somewhat reluctant to talk.

'Good evening, Mrs Doshi.'

'Hello, beta.'

'I know you don't know me. But I feel compelled to speak with you... Your daughter is one of the most remarkable people I have ever met.'

'She is amazing, indeed. But I'll be honest with you—I'm not sure why she's decided to spend these two years doing what you guys do,' Mrs. Doshi replied.

'I'm aware that you're unconvinced, but—'

Before Nalika could finish her sentence, Jesal's mother interrupted. 'I'm sceptical because you have her off in this crazy classroom. Her health is deteriorating. She has no business spending her days in that dilapidated building with no ventilation.' Her mother voiced a litany of complaints and concerns about Jesal's school and the Fellowship—and the implications of all of it on her health.

As soon as she paused, Nalika quickly jumped in: 'I know this hasn't been the easiest time for Jesal. I know it's been really tough on her.

'And I know your daughter well enough to know that she has enormous potential,' Nalika continued. 'She can do some amazing things with these kids—if we just let her. It's still early in her Fellowship but I believe she has the potential to be one of the best teachers we've ever seen. She has the potential to change the lives of these thirty-six students.'

'And what makes you believe she can do all of that?' Mrs. Doshi asked pointedly. She was looking at Nalika with an uncertainty Nalika was all too familiar with. How could she take this young, small-built girl, with no experience seriously?

'Because I see that potential in all of our Fellows—though it's taken me some time to see it, I'll be honest. But I've seen the Fellows before her, before me, realize that potential. And I can see just how hard Jesal works towards her classroom. She will get to a point where she will see it herself and so will you.'

Nalika spent the next hour talking with Jesal's mother. She wanted her to see what she saw in Jesal, even if she wasn't entirely sure where her belief was coming from. As she got home that evening, worn out and exhausted from the marathon-like conversation, she jumped into bed and pulled out a green notebook. She was upset that Jesal was so demotivated. She was upset that Jesal's parents weren't helping. But, most of all, she was upset with herself for not seeing Jesal's potential sooner, for not believing in what she could do. Nalika thought back to her conversation with Ikpreet and the importance of her belief in the people she worked with as program manager. She flipped the pages and began writing.

My dearest Jesal,

My first impression of you was that you were this quietly brilliant, soft-spoken yet strong individual. I remember being so impressed...so grateful...so inspired when you said, 'Whatever is best for the kids.' Not many teachers operate with that in mind. :)

Jesal—I know the last couple of weeks have been tough, painful, disappointing, disheartening and just plain difficult. Don't lose hope. The strongest leaders are those who overcome defeat. Don't be afraid to be defeated. Know that you will rise up out of that defeat as a much, much stronger person.

The next couple of days are going to be a little uncertain. I know that's not always nice. But I need you to trust me, Jesal—and believe that I am on your team. I have your back. I always will. Stay strong, Jesal. You CAN do it. I believe in you. I really, really do.

Go be STRONG.
Much love,

Nalika.

Seven years ago, at Teach For India, I introduced a process designed to identify our strongest teachers across the Fellowship so that others can learn from them. We call it the 'Transformational Impact Journey (TIJ)'. Each year since its inception, I have facilitated a two-day debate and conversation amongst three dozen staff members and educators from our community to better identify the practices of our strongest teachers. Less than eighteen months after Nalika penned down that note, Jesal, the girl who once was on the verge of quitting, was selected as one of the TIJ finalists.

Over these seven years, we at Teach For India have learned volumes from our strongest Fellows. Every year, we have Fellows who redefine our very idea of education. They've shown us that poverty and destiny are not inevitably linked. We're learning that the ones breaking boundaries have a lot in common. They don't just want good things for kids. Instead, it is their singular mission to change their children's lives. No statistic, no matter how depressing or limiting, will dissuade them.

'Your kids have a 76 per cent likelihood of dropping out before tenth standard,' I told Jai Mishra, a 2013 Fellow and TIJ finalist. Jai's classroom had brought many of our staff members to tears.

'So what?' he replied.

'Jai, your kids come from one of Pune's poorest districts. That means that twenty five of them, statistically speaking, are likely to drop out in two years.' I was trying to be provocative, mostly out of curiosity.

'Well, those statistics can go to hell. My kids aren't a bunch of numbers. They're human beings. And they're going to prove this country—and you—wrong.' That was the first and last time I ever heard Jai curse.

Fellows like Jai and Jesal simply refuse to accept the very real limitations that accompany poverty. They do whatever it takes to unlock opportunities for their classrooms. They become obsessed with a vision of excellence that pushes them to truly understand every little thing their students need to break the cycle of poverty. And, once they do, they work tirelessly to make sure their students get it all. There is certainly a level of knowledge and skills involved—understanding pedagogy, behaviour management and much more. But what separates our 'good' teachers from our 'great' teachers is an obsessive, unwavering commitment to their children. And the transformation in their students speaks for itself.

Today, two years since Jesal's Fellowship ended, she continues to teach at her school. Just this year, one of her students was accepted to UWC—the same prestigious institution that Nandini attended. Six of her students are pursuing admissions at Sophia College, Nalika's alma mater.

~

A few years ago, I went to Teach For America's 25th Anniversary Summit, back in Washington DC, and had the privilege of attending a panel discussion led by Joel Klein. Responsible for implementing massive changes in New York's public school system as the District Chancellor, Klein is widely heralded for raising outcomes for children across the city.

Before the panel—which was filled with school leaders, politicians and organizational heads—commenced, he took a few minutes to frame the day's discussion.

'Never doubt that poverty is a complicating factor in all of our discussions. But I see that through a different lens.' Klein looked around at the audience of more than 500. The room was packed with educators, many of whom had spent their lives serving low-income children. They had spent years witnessing the US reform efforts oscillate—always showing small signs of progress, but often lacking the kind of wide-scale breakthroughs that would ultimately prove that all the poor children in a city, or a state, could receive an excellent education.

Klein recognized that reality, as he continued. 'The challenges that poverty presents in education make our commitment, our efforts and our work all the more compelling, even if they are all the more difficult. When you're fighting for children who experience the adversity that our kids do, you're fighting for more than quality schooling. You're fighting poverty. You're fighting injustice. You're fighting a system that's failed these kids for far too long.' As Klein spoke, the audience listened in rapt attention.

'For me, the answer to the question of what it will take to get to one day (when all children in the country have access to an excellent education) was provided long ago by Frederick Douglass, who said and I quote, "If there is no struggle, there is no progress. Those who profess to favour freedom and yet deprecate agitation are men who want crops without plowing up the ground; they want rain without thunder and lightning. They want the ocean without the awful roar of its many waters."

'It's all one giant struggle,' he emphasized again. 'But don't forget why we struggle. We don't struggle in vain. And we don't struggle for ourselves. We struggle for the children who have no choice but to struggle.'

I couldn't find a more apt word than 'struggle' to describe what educators across the world experience—particularly in their first year of teaching. For the multitude of teachers who enter the profession each year, the first year of teaching is one of the toughest experiences they'll ever encounter. And for Teach For India Fellows, the struggle is often unexpected. Most people outside the education sector come into teaching with a plethora of preconceived notions, most of which are built by an idyllic representation carried over from their childhood. We all remember many of our teachers as being poised and happy. We also remember their seemingly short work hours and their long summer vacations.

Over the years, I've watched hundreds of Fellows come into the classroom with that misinformed notion—only to be proven wrong. Having achieved outstanding results in college or led teams in large corporations, they believe that teaching will hardly be a challenging experience. Within days though, they've found themselves struggling to manage behaviour, growing frustrated with students who are unwilling to listen. They feel completely overwhelmed with the number of demands and constraints that they face.

I'll never forget my own struggles as a first-time teacher. Over the past twelve years, I have managed large teams, built curriculums, led operations for cities and worked on strategic plans designed to impact millions of Indian children. But none of that will ever compare to the mental, emotional and physical toll of teaching in a low-income classroom. Placed in a failing school in the heart of Washington DC, no amount of training in the world could have prepared me for what I experienced during my first year.

'Mr Rai, I know you're upset. But these are kids. These things happen.' My principal had been trying to calm me down for hours.

'It's more than me being upset. Why would they do that?'

I had spent hours the week before preparing my classroom to be an oasis for life science. I wanted my walls to breathe the diversity of living organisms. I had worked with local nurseries to donate plants, with the pet store to donate fish tanks and with college labs to offer science equipment. Earlier that day, before school started, someone broke into my classroom. They threw the plants out the window, poured bleach into the fish tank and broke the science equipment.

'I want those kids to pay a price. They have to learn. I want to punish them.'

'Mr Rai, calm down. You're upset. But you know that retribution isn't the answer. You've been preaching the opposite since you got here. We warned you that you would need thick skin to make it here. Remember that.'

'Yeah, but there's a limit to what I can take. To what kids can get away with.' I could feel the tears starting to well up.

A few weeks later, I found out that Daquan, an otherwise quiet child, was the one who had broken in. The principal offered me the choice to suspend him for three weeks, as per school guidelines. I wanted to visit his home first, though, and talk to his mother.

Later that evening, I marched towards Daquan's house. I wanted to tell his mother that his behaviour wasn't acceptable. I expected her to do something—anything. And then, I saw his house. As I walked through the front door, I saw Daquan's mother sitting in the dark room. They had lost their electricity three days before.

'Mr Rai, what are you going to tell me he's done this time? Go on. You're not the first teacher that's come here.'

'I'm sorry to bother you this evening, ma'am. I do need to talk to you about your son, though.' I was startled by the conditions surrounding me. I definitely wasn't angry any more.

'It's okay, Mr Rai. I want him to do well. And I'll punish him.

He just keeps getting in trouble. Tell me what he's done.'

We chatted for the next three hours. Daquan's father, I learned, had left when he was little. His mother was living off a monthly welfare check, which offered barely enough to pay rent, electricity and gas and put food on the table for Daquan and his two brothers. Though hesitant, I told her what he had done.

'I think you should suspend him. He deserves it. He needs to learn.'

'Yes, ma'am. The principal is recommending that as well. But I have an idea,' I said, not fully sure what I was proposing. 'What if we didn't suspend him? What if we kept him in school?'

Sitting next to me, Daquan gave me a look of surprise.

'What if, instead, we agreed that Daquan will spend the next three months with me, every day, after school? We'll spend time learning about science. He can also help me think through a new anti-vandalism campaign that I'd love to roll out across the school. And he can help me build a new garden outside the school.'

She loved the idea. The principal, initially reluctant, eventually acquiesced. Over the next few months, Daquan and I spent a lot of time together. We designed a school-wide 'hands are for helping, not for hurting' campaign. We even built a new garden. Through the process, I started to see Daquan's grades get better. He was more engaged in class and he started enjoying science.

I was proud of the turnaround. Then, fifteen days before my Fellowship ended, I received a call from Daquan's mother.

'Mr Rai, I've got some bad news. They picked Daquan up last night. He was caught stealing from the grocery store. He's in jail.'

I was devastated.

Exacerbating the struggles of first-time teachers are the abject poverty and unimaginable conditions our students face, every single day. Most of our Fellows at Teach For India confront a myriad of complex issues, like I did, that range from domestic violence, drug abuse, teenage pregnancy, poor nutrition and more. They deal with students who come to class with deep traumas from the violence they've witnessed only the night before. They deal with students who are malnourished and, because their access to healthcare is limited, often suffer from a bevy of otherwise preventable illnesses.

Each of these issues inevitably makes its way into the classroom. The circumstances demand that our Fellows not only respond, but that they work even harder to ensure their children can one day overcome them. They demand that we be resilient and continue to struggle even in the face of repeated failures. They demand, moreover, that we allow ourselves to get proximate— to be as close to their lives as humanly possible—to better understand the pain and suffering that our children undergo every day. While that effort is far from easy, it is necessary before we can understand how to truly become a part of the solution.

~

'What do you mean he's gone?' Nalika nervously asked.

'He's dead,' Bhavi replied. 'He died early this morning. They took him to the hospital. But they couldn't save him.'

Nalika held the phone, unable to say anything.

'Nalika, are you there?'

'Yeah, I'm here.'

'Listen, you should come to school. I think it would help the kids,' Bhavi said.

'Okay, I'll come first thing tomorrow.' Nalika hung up the phone.

Saahil was only thirteen years old when he passed away. He had been suffering from a high fever and chronic cough for weeks. Knowing that a trip to the hospital would be costly, Saahil had been insistent on treating it at home. He would regularly downplay his symptoms, so as to not alarm his parents, who continued to give him over-the-counter medicines. The night before he passed away, though, his fever gave way to violent fits of nausea and irregular breathing. Worried and distressed, his parents decided to rush him to the hospital. They didn't have enough money for a taxi. So, at two in the morning, they walked more than five kilometres with Saahil to the nearest hospital.

When they arrived, the doctors assured them that he would be okay. But, to be sure, they wanted to run a spate of tests and then make an official diagnosis. His parents waited for hours until the first set of tests began. Worried that he hadn't eaten all night, his father brought tea and biscuits for Saahil. As they waited, Saahil continued to be his calm and generous self. He refused to take the food and offered the tea and biscuits to his mother instead, knowing that she hadn't eaten either.

Three hours later, with no explanation, Saahil passed away.

When Nalika first received the news, she was distraught. Though she wasn't his class teacher, she had spent dozens of afternoons with him when he played one of the characters in the *Final Solutions* play. She was worried about his family and she was worried about the kids.

'I'm sure they're a wreck,' she told herself.

The next morning, Nalika rushed to the school. She cautiously walked towards the door of Saahil's classroom. On the way there, she had formulated thoughts and ideas to offer both perspective and condolence to the mourning class. Talking to them about death and sadness, she thought, would be essential for them to better understand that it is natural to grieve.

'Hi didi. Welcome back,' Suraj greeted her as she walked in. 'Do you want to help us?'

'What are you guys doing?' Nalika walked in and saw the class busy with giant sheets of chart paper.

'Well, we're making banners to commemorate what Saahil stood for. And we're going to hang them across the classroom, so we never forget.'

'And what did he stand for?' Nalika asked, a bit shocked to discover that they were several steps ahead of her.

'Happiness, didi,' Mariya answered.

'He was always smiling,' Ganesh said. His eyes were moist.

Nalika walked over to the various banners spread across the children's desks. There were more than thirty-five designs, each one belonging to a different child, that had drawings of Saahil in various colours and styles. Each of them had one consistent message, right in the middle: Saahil would have wanted us to smile.

Nalika took a few steps back. Her eyes beginning to well up; she felt chills running down her spine.

'What's wrong, didi?' Mariya asked.

'What made you decide to write that?' Nalika responded, evading her question.

'Saahil is...I mean, was, the happiest child in school. He always smiled, even when he was in trouble. So if we have to remember him by something, this is it,' Ahsan said.

'He would have wanted us to be happy. He would have wanted us to be smiling. Didi, he would have wanted us to be more focused on making others happy,' Faisal added. Nalika, her face now streaming with tears, didn't know what to say.

Which set of thirteen-year-olds process grief with this much grace? she thought to herself.

Later that afternoon, Nalika and the children visited Saahil's home. Grieving and distraught, his parents recounted stories of his teachers, his friends and even his favourite subjects.

'My child, even when he was dying, was trying to take care of me. He offered me his last cup of tea,' his mother said, fighting back tears. The class, now emotional and slightly overwhelmed, was silent. A few moments later, though, Suraj weighed back in.

'Aunty, you don't need to worry,' Suraj reassured her. 'I know we can't bring Saahil back for you. But now, we are all your sons and daughters. We are going to be here for you now.'

The rest of the students nodded in agreement.

Nalika walked out of Saahil's house holding a mixture of

emotions. She was distraught by the loss of a child she had grown to know and love. She was angry that the system hadn't been better equipped to help a patient with no money. Perhaps most of all, though, she was stunned by the reaction of his classmates.

Who processes grief like this? she asked herself again.

As soon as Nalika reached the office, she found Venil. 'These kids are more resilient than I'll ever be, than most adults will ever be. Our struggles are nothing compared to theirs. Yet, every morning, they're able to wake up and, even when they're staring down the barrel of the greatest struggle they'll ever encounter— of loss—they're still smiling about it.

'These kids aren't like this by accident, though, Venil,' she continued. 'They're like this because they've had a series of great teachers—of Fellows.'

'And they've had you.' Venil added with a smile. She loved Nalika for a lot of things, but mostly for her humility.

'I want to make sure that every child across Mumbai has what these kids have. I want to ensure that every low-income child in this city has access to the strongest teachers we can find.'

As Nalika continued talking, Venil unsuccessfully tried to interject at several points. Realizing that she needed the space to vent, she instead decided to patiently listen.

'I think I get it now,' Nalika concluded. 'I'm convinced that I need to make this a reality for every child in this city. And my role in that is to give this city a continuous supply of excellent teachers—of future leaders. That is my purpose,' Nalika said.

'That is powerful,' Venil finally chimed in. Before she could get any further, though, she was interrupted again.

'I want to make this city believe that something else is possible. I want them to believe that our kids deserve—and can expect—something radically different than what they get today.'

Today, Nalika co-leads the programme for Teach For India's Mumbai operations. She is responsible for the development of more than 200 fellows, impacting 10,000 children across the city. The significance of this is only really understood when we consider the impact of teachers on student performance. A study published by McKinsey in 2007 comparing the top ten performing school systems in the world—Alberta (Canada), Australia, Belgium, Finland, Hong Kong, Japan, the Netherlands, New Zealand, Ontario (Canada), Singapore and South Korea—found that all of them universally focused on improving instruction.[49] These systems did three things consistently well: attracting the right people to the teaching profession, developing them into effective instructors and putting processes and structures in place to ensure that every child receives excellent instruction.

THIRTEEN

THE CARDS OF PRIVILEGE

'This is utterly unbelievable.'

Tarun was mesmerized. He couldn't take his eyes off the bright green grass outside the Harvard Kennedy School cafeteria. As he watched from the inside, through the large French windows, he saw a row of quintessential New England red-brick buildings. He was amazed at the harmony between their old-school facades and their modern wood and glass interiors. He reflected on the rich history—spanning hundreds of years—that existed between the two. He thought about the many great minds that had studied there before him. He remembered the legendary tales that filled his Happy Harvard lessons, ones that evoked the names of Gates, Gore and Kennedy. His kids had bombarded him with questions, asking him how he could love an institution he had never seen.

Studying at Harvard, Tarun once believed, would always remain nothing more than a dream. Receiving the prestigious Fulbright and Joint Japan/World Bank scholarships, which paid for the entirety of his tuition and cost of living, was even more improbable. To everyone, these were mere fantasies that could never have materialized thanks to his seemingly whimsical decisions. After he dropped out of his IIT coaching classes, his friends had told him that he was headed for a life of mediocrity. Deciding to join Teach For India, they assured him, would only add penury and misery. For Tarun, though, those decisions weren't whimsical at all. They were a function of a moral compass that wouldn't stop turning. And so, here he was, pursuing his master's at the Harvard Kennedy School of Government on a full scholarship.

'I'm not supposed to be here,' Tarun whispered. His new

surroundings—as improbable as they were—could not have been more different from the tin sheds and mouldy walls of the National Children's Academy. Forgoing a high-paying salary and comfortable job at HUL was tough; in fact, it had consequences that were real and lasting. But, maybe those decisions had a purpose that was higher than even he realized.

'Perhaps this is the universe's way of rewarding me for those risks,' Tarun told me. 'I owe this debt of gratitude to my students and their parents. I am standing on their shoulders. I'll never forget the experiences and the love that their families have given me.' Tarun promised to keep that memory firmly rooted in his mind over the next two years. In that moment, tears streamed down his face. They crystallized his second talisman: his thirty-three kids and their families.

Tarun had ended his TFI Fellowship with a deep connection to and understanding of the ground realities of being poor in India. He wanted to supplement that by learning how policy could be used to solve the systemic issues of educational inequity at a large scale.

The classes at Harvard were exciting and tough. He was attending lectures on the promises and perils of globalization and writing position papers on economic policy in developing countries. His evenings were filled with countless discussions and debates on the role of government in uplifting the poor. Tarun was, undoubtedly, intellectually fulfilled. He continued, however, to deeply miss his kids. He craved the emotional connection and physical challenges his classroom had afforded. Campus life did offer small ways to reconnect with that purpose. On weekends, Tarun would volunteer at Ramakrishna Mission and spend his time tutoring a visually impaired Palestinian activist. When he needed time to tune off, he would simply flip through TV channels, watching hours of cable news—a practice that would reignite purpose in the most unexpected of ways.

Tarun spent one Friday evening in the summer of 2011

mindlessly flipping through channels when he saw Barack Obama onscreen. The then-American president was standing next to an African American woman who looked like she was in her fifties. They were both staring at a painting of a little girl walking down a paved path surrounded by federal agents. Intrigued, Tarun looked closer.

'Wait, I know that painting,' Tarun whispered. 'That's Ruby Bridges.'

Created in 1964 by Norman Rockwell, the painting depicted one of the most memorable victories for the American civil rights movement. Ten years before the incident depicted in the painting, the United States Supreme Court handed down a landmark ruling, Brown vs. Board of Education, which effectively declared the segregation of students in schools across the country as unconstitutional. The law attempted to eliminate decades of practices that were rooted in a history tainted by racism. As a result, it took more than six years to even start implementing it.

Ruby Bridges was the first African American student to enter William Frantz Elementary, an all-white school in the state of Louisiana. White citizens from the neighbourhood were so outraged by the decision that state officials eventually concluded police escorts were needed to ensure her safety. Not only did most parents withdraw their children from William Frantz, almost every teacher quit. For over a year, Ruby—a first-grader back then—was taught alone by the only teacher who agreed to stay: Barbara Henry.

Rockwell's painting, *The Problem We All Live With*, depicted Ruby's first day of school, surrounded by federal agents and police officers. Controversial at the time, it has now famously grown into a symbol of a movement that paved the way for future education reforms. Choosing to temporarily host the painting outside the White House Oval Office, President Obama invited the fifty-seven-year-old Ruby Bridges to celebrate the fiftieth anniversary of her much-lauded entrance.

'I think it's fair to say that, if it weren't for you guys, I wouldn't be here today,' Obama told Ruby that day.

Tarun was transfixed by the notion of America's first black president celebrating a landmark event, which took place more than fifty years ago, as being pivotal to his very existence. As he watched them both talk about the painting—and what that day meant for future black citizens—Tarun started thinking about his Happy Harvard community. He had left his classroom worrying that many of his children would never truly be accepted across Indian society, no matter how well they did in school. It would not be because of the colour of their skin, but potentially because of their caste, class, religion or financial situation—all of which they held little control over.

Ruby's example transfixed Tarun that evening. Ruby, after all, was only a child. But her courageous decision—supplemented by the widespread media coverage it garnered—fuelled a nationwide dialogue. It gave way to a movement that ultimately improved the quality of life of African Americans. She became a civil rights icon. As Tarun watched Obama and Bridges talk that evening, he wondered what it would mean for India to have an equally powerful example.

~

After his first year of graduate school at Harvard, Tarun found a summer opportunity that would bring him back to his hometown of Andhra Pradesh. Karthik Muralidharan, a renowned Indian economist and professor at the University of California, offered Tarun the opportunity to work with him on a research project on the Right to Education (RTE). It would ultimately become his graduation thesis. One of the law's key provisions is Section 12(1) (c). Cognizant that government schools don't have the capacity to serve all of India's population, Section 12(1) (c) mandates that private schools across India reserve 25 per cent of their seats for children from disadvantaged backgrounds. In essence, that means that there are approximately 20 lakh private school seats open for poor children to attend, free of charge.

The project in Andhra Pradesh allowed Tarun to study the law's implementation by analysing a sample of more than 2,000 children. For Tarun, the project was the perfect opportunity to marry the intellectual rigour he was receiving at Harvard with the purpose and calling he felt in India. In the summer of 2012, he spent months better understanding the law's multiple provisions, interviewing children and families who, through it, had gained access to schools. He was also visiting private schools across the state to gauge their receptiveness.

His findings were overwhelming. Thirty per cent of children who heard about the scholarship never explored or accepted it. An additional 35 per cent, who initially accepted it, dropped out less than two years later. Taken together, that left a mere one-third of children who would continue attending their new private school for more than five years. With regard to the children who never accepted the scholarship, their reasons were actually quite rational: they couldn't travel the far distances to access the schools; they were worried about assimilating with children from different social backgrounds; or they couldn't afford the costs of books and uniforms which they would inevitably have to pay for, even with the scholarship.

The cases of the 35 per cent who dropped out, though, unearthed some disturbing trends. Tarun discovered that many of these children were being beaten and publicly shamed, mostly because of their caste, economic status or religion. School administrators would often ostracize children as soon as they entered, marking their collars, making them sit in the back benches and referring to them as the 'RTE kids'. Many of these children, Tarun discovered, were so scarred by the blatant discrimination that they refused to attend anymore. The findings proved to be surprisingly unsettling and deeply personal. Back in Boston a few weeks later, he expressed his angst on a call with

Professor Muralidharan.

'One of the parents told me that they've created a separate class for the "RTE kids" and the school cleaner teaches this class. Another mother said her son was not allowed to participate in any extracurricular activities like swimming or singing because the school claims he has to pay an extra fee for those. Another parent complained that her son was not being given any homework. She asked me: "Are children only children if they come from rich homes?" Throughout my interviews with these parents all I could think about was that these could have been my kids. That they easily could have been Treza or Akanksha. It could have been Aditya.'

'It is disturbing, Tarun. But now we need to do something about it, don't we?' Karthik advised.

'Yes, I need to get back to India and I need to fix this. I need to be on the ground with these kids.'

'Maybe so. But what will you do on the ground? And how many people will you reach? Listen, I would advise you to think about the long run, Tarun. Think about what you can do for India over the next twenty years. Your biggest contribution to the country could very well be through your intellect, which is one of the strongest I've seen. Think about what you could do with a doctorate. You could influence policy, positions and laws that shape the education system for decades to come. You could ensure that the next version of India's RTE takes care of all of this— at scale—and is exponentially better.' Pofessor Muralidharan's argument was not only deeply compelling, but also firmly rooted in a holistic vision for India's future.

Later that evening, still feeling torn, Tarun lamented to his close friends, Ismail Ahmed and Li Wei.

'This isn't making sense. I know it's not making sense. I'm just going to end up publishing paper after paper. And if, fifty years later, the same things are happening to these children, I'm not going to be able to live with myself. I'm not saying there's no role that policymaking and research plays in the solution. I'm just saying that that's not *my* role in it. It *cannot* be my role in it.'

'But getting your doctorate would be a really exciting—' Ismail started to say.

Before he could finish, Tarun jumped in again. 'No! I refuse to get lost in the glory of tenured professorship, in statistical stars and exciting tables of data!'

Sensing that his friends were perhaps taking a bit of umbrage at his comments, Tarun nevertheless continued.

'Maybe, at some point in life, I'll come back to the field of academia. And then, maybe this will appear a lot more exciting. But right now, I belong back on the ground, with my kids,' Tarun paused for a moment and started thinking about Treza, Akanksha and the parent-teacher meeting where he had made the two read and explain a text—something he had never managed to completely forget. The angry comments the girls had endured had always bothered Tarun, not only because they were unfair, but also because he knew it had been his fault.

'Right now, I have to respond to the stories. I can't sit by and allow this to happen.'

'I get what you're saying, Tarun. I just think that this law does have its limitations. It'll ensure the kids get that scholarship and get access to a better education. But it's not going to guarantee their success,' Li told him.

'It's more than that. Ismail, think about you and Fadia.' Ismail had been dating Fadia for less than six months. He had grown up in Lahore, Pakistan, and she was from Lucknow. 'You would both be excoriated if you were to get married and go back to either of your countries.'

Ismail let out a chuckle at Tarun's digression.

'You would be! All jokes aside, you know it's true,' Tarun reiterated.

'Okay, so where are you going with this?' Ismail asked.

'Why should you be? In the US, you're both simply known as

"South Asians". Your grandparents are from Lucknow, for God's sake. If Partition hadn't happened, who knows, maybe you would have gone to the same high school. We're fighting such narrow identities—gender, class, religion. They're all so damn narrow!'

Tarun rarely cursed and, when he did, it usually accompanied a passionate rant. 'There are two sections of society in India where you won't find discrimination. One of them is with children. They don't understand these false boundaries until they become teenagers. The second is with the privileged. They have the luxury of receiving an education that breaks those boundaries. Think of the power of the diverse classrooms at Harvard. And then think of what we could do if we could create that diversity in Indian classrooms as early as the first grade.'

Ismail and Li went silent. They hadn't thought about the law as being an instrument to facilitate equity and foster understanding. They had merely seen it as a tool to help a seemingly resource-strapped government.

'Guys, 12(1) (c) is India's chance to fix the rampant discrimination that plagues the country today. It's a chance to break every single boundary possible.'

In the months that followed, Tarun's agitation rapidly began translating into a flurry of ideas. After classes, he would find himself scribbling down half-baked thoughts on napkins and leftover paper scraps. Around the same time, he began collaborating with a group of five Indian friends that were all in US graduate schools across MIT, Harvard and Yale. They shared an interest and desire to work towards India's development. After a few informal meetings in coffee shops and local restaurants, they agreed to explore how they could work together when they returned to India. Each of them would pitch an idea, and they would go with the best one.

Tarun pitched first.

'I want you to close your eyes, for a few minutes, and I want you to imagine.' Tarun could see their smirks in response to his clichéd opening, but that didn't deter him.

After waiting until all eyes were closed, he continued. 'You all know about the RTE. But you should also know that the same law stipulates that 25 per cent of seats in private-aided schools be reserved for the underprivileged. That means there are two million private school seats open to India's poorest children, every single year. I want you to visualize those two million seats.

'Right now, we have 1 per cent—only 20,000—of those seats being filled. *One per cent.* There are many reasons for this, but the primary one is simply a lack of awareness and mobilization. The poor and marginalized in our country don't know their rights and how to take advantage of them. And the systems don't make it any easier for them to do so.

'Now imagine if we were able to help them fill just 50 per cent of those seats. If we were able to fill one million of those seats in the next five years. One million seats given to India's poor. We've given one million children constitutional rights they never knew they had. And we've made it happen across every state in India.' Tarun paused to let the group soak in the power of his last image.

'But don't stop there. Think about what will happen to the children sitting in the classrooms with them. These one million children make up only 25 per cent of their classrooms. Think about the three million private school children—the 75 per cent—who will interact with them. Their stereotypes and biases will be completely shattered. For those four million kids, it's a fundamentally different school experience,' Tarun paused again. He could feel his hands tremble in excitement. 'And, the crazy thing is that it doesn't even stop there. Think about their parents, the school leaders, teachers—and all the people who interact with these students. Their prejudices and biases are challenged as well.

'Now, imagine what we could do after five more years. Imagine us adding one million children every single year from year six to year ten. When you add it all up, in ten years we've impacted more than 100 million people in India. More than 100 million people will believe in a more equitable India. More than 100 million people will have their stereotypes shattered. More than 100 million people will believe that India's poor deserve the same rights that the rich have today.

'Now, open your eyes. I know society isn't going to change in ten years. And I'm not naive enough to think that all six million admissions will be success stories. But what if we could make one million of them become real bright spots—children who made it all the way through, whose lives are transformed? What if we had one million stories to tell?' Tarun asked.

The group was enthralled. They were speechless. He took a deep breath in preparation for his biggest revelation.

'And imagine, if out of those one million stories, one of them was the story of a poor, Dalit Muslim girl from a rural village who goes on to inspire our future prime minister, fifty years from now. Imagine the next prime minister being someone who bears all the markers of disadvantage but is able to rise in spite of them. Imagine our very own Ruby Bridges who goes on to inspire our very own Barack Obama.' As Tarun finished, the group erupted in applause.

'I'm not pitching after you, dude. I'm just going to jump on-board!' Kavikrut responded.

'I've got goosebumps. You've got a venture here that could literally transform India, Tarun,' Aarti added. 'But what are you going to call it?'

Tarun thought for a few minutes before responding. He was slightly nervous. He had never seen himself as an entrepreneur, but he knew the idea had power. And he knew it had the potential to fundamentally change the narratives he had witnessed back in Andhra Pradesh.

'Indus Equity,' Tarun replied.

'Tarun, what's most exciting about this work is you're choosing to *do* something about it,' Kavikrut said. 'You're making a commitment to *act*. And I think your name needs to reflect that. What about Indus Action?'

'Love it. That's it. We're going to commit to changing these stories through Indus Action.'

~

The first few months back in India were tough for Tarun. Indus Action had been established. They had immediately raised an initial round of funding. None of the team members, however, could commit full-time, and they were beginning to realize that progress would demand an intensive all-hands-on-deck approach. That's when Tarun decided to hire a small four-member team to run their operations. They were spending dozens of hours, every week, meeting government officials and doing focus groups in communities. Because the application process for admission under RTE was manual, eligible families not only had to individually complete one application per school, but they also had to submit them in person, a process they found quite daunting. Often schools were resentful towards the law's principles. They not only vehemently disagreed with the need for reservation, but were having to spend many hours invigilating lotteries to fairly sift through the high volume of applicants.

For Tarun and his team, that meant dedicating time going door-to-door, advocating families to take advantage of this opportunity for their children, accompanying parents on school visits and even arguing with local school leaders. They were intent on mobilizing parents to apply for the scholarship, but also keen on ensuring schools officially accepted them. In the first two years, the inefficiencies were evident in their results. They had ensured 15,500 low-income families applied for the scholarship. Out of those applications, though, only 5 per cent converted into admissions. In other words, there were only 600 admissions.

Parents began to grow irate.

'The lottery is fixed! They don't want us,' one parent alleged. Tarun had no evidence to support those claims, but this was not the first parent to share such a grievance. He knew something had to change. A few weeks later, he ended up making a pivotal hire: Anurag Kundu.

Tarun and Anurag first met at Teach For India. Tarun had stayed overnight with one of Anurag's students in Seelampur after he moved back to Delhi. He was eager to learn more about Delhi's communities and, as many of our Fellows and alumni often do, decided to immerse himself in one. Anurag was in his first year of Fellowship at the time. Tarun was immediately impressed by the voter registration projects Anurag's ten-year-olds were leading. As both of them were passionate about politics and policy, they would often spend hours debating the chaotic landscape that was Delhi's local government. Inspired by the themes of equity and justice that underpinned the mission of Indus Action, Anurag volunteered with the organization and eventually joined Tarun's team after completing his Fellowship.

Only a few days into Anurag's tenure, during one of their intense conversations, Tarun and Anurag concluded that advocating for the Delhi government to move the application process online would be paramount.

'Our intensive ground efforts are working. But the truth is we're not going to reach a large scale like this. It's just inefficient. We're spending all our time filling out private school RTE applications and delivering them to schools. We have to leverage technology,' said Tarun.

'Well, we can't just go up to the government and tell them to move the application online. Doesn't matter how good the idea is. The government just doesn't work that way,' Anurag said.

'Yeah, I know, I know. We need to approach this more strategically,' Tarun replied.

'We need to create a situation where the government has no option but to implement such a system. In the last year, Tarun, we've filed 1,500 grievances on behalf of families. I'm sure that's increased their burden of work. Some of those grievances are being addressed, but the majority are being dismissed. I think we can build more pressure from the bottom-up. Let's follow up on every grievance. If it's dismissed, let's ask for the justification. That's our right.'

'Hmm, sure, give it a try. Do you have any contacts in the government?'

'I can have a word with Atishi Marlena and, if required, Manish Sisodia.' Manish Sisodia was the deputy chief minister at the time and Atishi Marlena his advisor.

'Also,' Anurag continued, 'let's author a report on the RTE implementation and publish it, try to get the media's attention. Basically, we need to use all the levers in the system. We need to create pressure from the ground and from the top. It will be grinding work. But I'm confident it will bear fruit.'

Eventually, Anurag's prediction proved to be true. Amplifying the current painful scenario to create enough push for an online enrolment process was slow and painstaking work. Some tactics worked, while others were not as effective. Yet, at the right time, when the government was ready—in fact, eagerly looking—for a solution to fix the issues and ease their workload, Indus Action stepped up with a solution.

'Think about the parents that are submitting these applications,' Tarun pleaded to a room full of government officials. They had finally got the attention of all the right stakeholders.

'Every interested parent has to visit ten different schools to submit ten applications. These are people that are working in the unorganized sector, in jobs that aren't very forgiving. Think about the loss of income that that's creating. Think about the time they're wasting.' As Apoorva, a member of the Indus Action team spoke, she could feel the cold indifference of each official. Most of them were not even making eye contact with her.

'On top of that, think about the fact that these parents, on every visit, are literally fighting with school officials for their rights. Their experiences are, by and large, quite negative,' Tarun added.

'The system is meant to take time. This is their kids' education. If they can't commit a few hours to getting their children into one of the city's best private schools—free of charge—then maybe they don't deserve to attend,' an official replied.

'And moving this online is going to be technically too complex. It's going to open us up to litigation, left and right, from parents and schools across the city. As it is, these schools all hate this law!' another official added.

The room wasn't budging. Tarun wasn't disheartened. In fact, he struggled to hide a slight smile. Anurag had predicted this. While preparing for the presentation, he had pushed the team to pitch the idea keeping the benefit to the government front and centre. The plight of the parents and families drove Tarun's team to action, but the government needed the remedy to make systemic sense.

'What if you saw this from your point of view?' Tarun continued. 'The government of Delhi is committed to making Section 12(1) (c) a success. Am I right?'

'Of course. That's why we've mandated lotteries for thousands of schools across the city,' the official curtly replied.

'And the government of Delhi is committed to reforming the public education system. That's your mandate, correct?' Tarun asked again.

Growing agitated, they shot back. 'What are you trying to say, son?'

'Well, then think about what that means. You have 2,500 schools across this city. Every school is required to hold two lotteries, invigilated by the two most senior people there— the principal and vice principal,' Tarun replied. 'That's 10,000 collective person days from the two most important people in 2,500 schools across the city during the start of the school year, which is arguably the most important time of the year for them as well.'

As he looked across the room, Tarun could feel the mood shifting.

'No wonder schools hate this law. It's taking them forever to implement it!' one official chimed in.

'If you're serious about school reform—*really* serious about it—then back it up with action,' Tarun continued. 'You have the opportunity to free up 10,000 days from school leaders across this city. Think about what that could do for reform.'

Tarun paused. He had clearly struck a chord, and he knew it. 'Think about how much goodwill you'd earn from these schools.'

Less than ninety days later, in collaboration with Indus Action, the government migrated their entire application system to an online portal. Applications, which once took ten days to submit, could now be completed within ten minutes. Parents could apply to dozens of schools with just one click. The seat allocation, which used to be a manual, opaque process facilitated by school leaders, would now be conducted via an online algorithm.

The results were astounding.

In 2016, the Delhi Government received 70,000 applications for 28,000 seats. Indus Action facilitated 6,000 new admissions that year compared to 600 the year before. To keep up with the growth, in addition to the online migration, Tarun began conceptualizing the Shiksha Sahyogi (Supporter of Education) programme. As part of the programme, Indus Action selected and trained entrepreneurial women in low-income communities looking for opportunities to earn a living. These were most often mothers who themselves benefitted from Indus Action's work, and whose kids were now in private schools. Through the programme's training, they became on-the-ground advocates working with Indus Action for Section 12(1) (c). Together, these women spread awareness amongst parents in their communities, supported them in filling out the online applications and managed Indus Action's 24-hour helpline.

Having found a model that was beginning to work, Tarun recognized the opportunity and quickly began expanding. They began working with other state governments to move their lotteries online. They hired entrepreneurs to lead local operations in cities they couldn't reach. Utilizing a newly minted 'campaign-in-a-box toolkit' in 2017, they spread the impact of Indus Action across Bengaluru, Lucknow, Raipur and Pune to facilitate a total of 23,000 applications across India.

The growth was promising. It was guaranteeing thousands of low-income children access into India's best and most privileged schools. As Tarun had already learned from his research project with Karthik Muralidharan though, making Section 12(1) (c) work would demand much more than access alone. Instead, success would require not only ensuring that schools began accepting the law, but that the people within those schools—and our wider society—start growing more inclusive of our less privileged neighbours.

~

'What do you mean they wouldn't let Deepak stay?' Tarun asked, incredulously. He was speaking with Saleem, one of their partner entrepreneurs based in Lucknow, about Deepak, a child who had been recently admitted to one of the city's private schools.

'They made his mother pick him up from school. It's completely unacceptable!' Saleem replied. 'Deepak had an accident in school this morning. He couldn't help himself.'

'What do you mean an accident? What happened? Is he okay?'

'Umm... He relieved himself in the classroom. He's only five. He couldn't help it. It was an accident.'

'And then?' Tarun asked.

'The school refused to clean it up. They made his mother

come to the school, walk into the classroom while the teacher was taking a lesson, pick up the stool in front of all the kids and then take Deepak home.'

'Oh my God!' Horrified, Tarun didn't know what else to say.

'And now they're refusing to let him go back. They've suspended him for two days.' His mother doesn't even want to send him back. She tells me, "Would they have behaved like this with their regular admission children and parents?"'

'She's absolutely right. Look, get someone from our office to go there tomorrow morning.'

The next morning, Tarun's staff talked with the school and, after much arguing, convinced them to reverse the suspension. The damage, however, had been done. Tarun knew that Deepak would continue to face discriminatory comments from his classmates as soon as he returned. He thought back to the things he had learned from the kids in Andhra Pradesh during his internship. He thought about the violence, bullying and pain they encountered. He wondered how many more of the children placed in these schools through Indus Action were experiencing something similar.

'Should we be putting these kids through this experiment?' Anurag asked that afternoon.

'We think we're doing something good. And we're trying to give them greater opportunity. But that process inevitably includes subjecting them to the biases and prejudices of people across the country,' Tarun replied. His tone made it clear that he was feeling utterly defeated.

'And that's only magnified by today's political environment,' Anurag added. 'I know. It's tough. I don't know what's happening to our country today. You know the father of one of my students at Bab-ul Uloom called me the other day. He was unsure of sending his son on a field trip with the new Teach For India Fellow because the Fellow is a Hindu.'

'But you're a Hindu too. And they were fine with that when

you were their teacher?' Tarun asked perplexed.

'That's exactly what I said. And you know what his reaction was? 'Haan, par aap alag Hindu hai aur woh alag Hindu hai (Yes, but you're a different type of Hindu).' Basically he didn't really have an answer.'

'Or he had the time and opportunity to get to know *you*—as a person—and then your religion didn't matter anymore.'

'Yes, precisely. Regardless, that's not the point,' Anurag said. 'Look, I've been there. And I know that these kids are facing the brunt of a lot of angry people. I was that child, actually,' Anurag said. His parents had worked hard, despite not having the money, to ensure he attended a private school growing up.

'Yes, but not all of these children will succeed like you did.'

'True, but if some of them do, then that's a victory, isn't it?' Anurag quipped.

'It's not just that school leader or this one instance that's bothering me, Anurag. Everybody seems to hate this law. The government officials were right. Schools are starting to retaliate against it, and in such horrid ways, like what happened with Deepak. The government is losing its will, but it is also not in the clear. It is not even reimbursing these schools in time, so of course the schools are pushing back. I just don't know why *everyone* is so against making this work.'

'Actually, I know why,' Tarun continued. 'They're against it because it makes them uncomfortable. Diversity makes them uncomfortable. Honestly, they're afraid that these kids are going to take something of theirs.'

'We simply have to give it time,' he concluded. 'They'll soon realize. They'll grow into it,' he added.

'I believe they will. I wouldn't be able to do this work otherwise,' Anurag thought out loud. 'But what happens in the meantime? We're just putting these kids directly in the line of fire.'

~

Through Indus Action, Tarun endeavours to ensure ten lakh Indian children from low-income backgrounds access the benefits of Section 12(1) (c) over the next five years. In doing so, they will gain admission into one of India's many private schools. Dozens of cases of discrimination and prejudice have forced Tarun and his organization to confront the many needs that must accompany access. Once these children enter their new classrooms, school communities must ultimately accept them as well.

'What do you think it's going to take for this acceptance to happen?' I ask Tarun. We've been sitting in his office and talking for the past three hours.

'People need to see the stories of success. Right now, the media is flooding us with stories of what's not working—like Deepak's story. Private schools are exercising every ounce of available energy and power to amplify the stories of failure. Making this law a success, however, demands that people hear the stories that are working. We have to change the political and social narrative of what's possible. Once we do that, Section 12(1) (c) will be here to stay.' His belief in stories isn't new; it's been an integral part of his vision since his original Indus pitch in Boston.

At Teach For India, we've similarly seen the immense power that examples can hold. Internally, we call them 'proof points'. Graduating from tenth standard and being vocal about gay rights in Govandi, Asif is an example of what's possible. Being the only child in Luhianagar to attend college abroad and break the cycle of poverty, Nandini is an example of what's possible. These children have provided glimmers of hope to hundreds and thousands of others within their communities.

In the next ten years, Tarun wants to create one million such 'proof points'.

Tarun is acutely aware of the general discrimination and biases that constitute the opposition to Section 12(1) (c). According to the 2015 Equity Watch Report, there has been a 19.4 per cent increase from the previous year in crimes against Dalits and a

47.5 per cent increase in rapes against Dalit women in the past decade. In the face of such atrocities, justice is also served based on caste. Only 2 per cent of perpetrators were charged in rape cases against Dalits versus the national conviction rate of 25 per cent.[50] Similar themes play out in the form of discrimination in education. Like poverty and inequity, eradicating them won't be easy. It demands that we fully understand the fears and forces driving them. That, however, is the power that these examples and stories hold. In isolation, Ruby Bridges could have been one person's success story, and nothing more. Her example did much more than that, though. It inspired people to believe that desegregation was possible. It forced the American consciousness to recognize the irrationality underlying their fears. It made way for a young, African American boy getting a good education and believing that he too could be the president of the United States.

For Tarun, the Indian Ruby Bridges will arise when people begin to realize that Deepak deserves nothing less than Devashish, his more affluent neighbour. They both, in fact, deserve the opportunity to receive an excellent education. Recognizing that we are far from ensuring all of India's children have a brighter future isn't pessimistic, it's accurate. But we must simultaneously understand that the path to realizing that vision has to begin with belief. People need to believe not just in the power and imperative of a more equitable society, but in its feasibility. Once we change beliefs, we begin to change the conversation from 'this country will never change' to 'how do we change it?'. And that, in turn, is a precursor to a new, more just, reality.

Tarun recognizes that in addition to creating examples, the painstaking advocacy work fuelled by programmes like Shiksha Sahyogi must continue in parallel. After all, the headmistress's refusal to clean up after Deepak is more than a lack of belief. It's deeply rooted in a sense of privilege and power.

The headmistress of that school doesn't understand that, compared to Deepak, she is extremely privileged. And it is her privilege that allows her to even have the power to refuse him,' Tarun tells me. 'That, more than anything else, is what Teach For India did for me. It helped me better understand that we're all part of the problem. I can't escape the fact that I'm a Hindu upper-caste male who could afford a private school education. Part of my success, sure, is because my parents worked hard. But a large part of it is because I was lucky enough to have the right religion, the right caste and even the right gender. While I can't escape it, I can understand how not to *perpetuate* it.'

Tarun's comments reminded me of the countless stories I've heard over the years. They're sentiments that were echoed in Manoj Kumar's insistence that laziness was the real culprit underlying the ill fortunes of Jahangirpuri, in Pankaj's adamant insistence that the government's inaction was rooted in apathy for the poor and in Nishi's recognition that society expects low-income communities to merely perform worse. Within each of these stories—as with the headmistress's refusal to accept Deepak into her school—is the belief that the poor have merely created their own problems.

Perhaps building a more equitable—and a more just India—starts by recognizing that India's disparities are also the product of luck and privilege that, today, benefit only a few. It behoves us to look inward and examine how our own beliefs and actions perpetuate other people's poverty. Tarun's reflections on his journey perfectly summarize that recognition.

'If you compare my identity to that of a Dalit Muslim girl from rural India, you quickly realize that I have all the cards of privilege. It's impossible to argue that my fortune isn't a product of at least some luck. Instead, it's the opposite. I am actually part of the problem. Somewhere, in my history, my ancestors have likely oppressed the ancestors of that Dalit Muslim girl. And, though I'm not responsible for that oppression myself, it's hard to argue that I'm not benefitting from it now.'

Whenever I've chatted with folks about privilege, over the

years, it's usually resulted in feelings of angst and guilt. Thinking about the actions of our ancestors, decades before many of us were born, can arguably be a bottomless pit. While each of us must wrestle with that guilt and make sense of it, the first step is to acknowledge that what the most disadvantaged children of this country experience is due to more than a lack of hard work. What they experience is the result of a system that was designed to oppress them. It's analogous to apartheid that oppressed the Black, Coloured and South Asian populations in South Africa. It is those same systems that perpetuated the legacies of slavery in the United States long after it was legally abolished, into lasting institutions of segregation and laws that promoted disparity. It's the same systems that relocated half of Mumbai's slums into poorly planned resettlements in the heart of Govandi.

America has indeed progressed since the days of Ruby Bridges. Their progress is spurred by a collection of examples that fuelled belief in a better day, coupled with advocacy to awaken the country's consciousness. For Tarun, getting kids accepted into private schools holds immense power that, crazily enough, is even bigger than the transformation it promises their individual lives. Similarly, the Shiksha Sahyogi programme is not just about filling out more 12(1) (c) applications or making women in these communities financially independent. Its true power lies in enabling parents to build a collective voice to fight back, to build awareness and capacity in communities to mobilize others to demand their rights, when organizations like Indus Action cease to exist tomorrow. In refusing to merely be grateful for what they have—in fighting back against every case of discrimination—these empowered parents are awakening the consciousness of India's schools.

In a country where hundreds of millions live in poverty, perhaps what India needs most is its consciousness awakened.

FOURTEEN
THE DELIVERANCE OF JUSTICE

'I'm not giving you more than thirty,' Anurag said resolutely.

'What are you saying?' the autorickshaw driver retorted, as he gauged his potential customer.

'I take this route every single day. And I never pay more than thirty.'

'You're ripping us off, every single day, brother.'

'Maybe I am. But that's the official rate.'

'Well, the official rate is ripping us off. And it's 8 a.m. It's one of the busiest times of the day.'

'That's not my problem, is it?'

'Fine. Just sit.'

Feeling a twinge of guilt, Anurag climbed into the backseat of the autorickshaw. He was running thirty minutes behind. Haggling over ten rupees, he knew, was far from purposeful. He had left the house both flustered and annoyed. Taking it out on the autorickshaw driver, who likely needed that additional ten rupees much more than he did, was not what he intended.

Trying to redeem himself, he made small talk with the driver. They talked about the weather, each other's families and even politics.

'What do you think of Arvind Kejriwal?' Anurag asked the driver.

'That's the Aam Aadmi Party. Everyone's saying they're different. But they're all just a bunch of politicians, aren't they? Everyone in the government's the same. They definitely won't care about the poor.'

For months, Anurag had been fascinated by the rise of Arvind Kejriwal in 2014. He would read about his campaign and subsequently talk to anyone who would listen about Kejriwal's work. Riding an anti-corruption and populist mantle, the Aam Aadmi Party (AAP) had steadily, albeit surprisingly, gained momentum in Delhi. On his forty-ninth day of service as Delhi's chief minister, Kejriwal abruptly resigned after failing to secure enough votes for Jan Lokpal, an anti-corruption bill that formed the heart of the party's sudden rise to power. His resignation prompted widespread criticism across the city; many pointed to it as a sign of the party's inexperience and ineffectiveness. For Anurag, though, it was a sign of integrity.

Fortuitously, Anurag was introduced to Anup Kalbalia, a lead engineer at CodeChef. Anup would eventually be his bridge to AAP. They met while piloting a coding curriculum at Anurag's Fellowship school. Based in Mumbai, Anup had recently moved to Delhi to volunteer with AAP. Anup's commitment moved Anurag. He had given his children dozens of lessons on democracy, intended to instil values of empowerment and responsibility for civic change. Anurag quickly realized, however, that those lessons would prove hollow if he didn't heed his own advice.

Three weeks later, Anurag began campaigning for AAP as well. The volunteers he met eclipsed his level of passion and fortitude: a father still grieving from the loss of a son, an expectant mother who insisted on campaigning seven months into her pregnancy, an executive who had left his job, essentially putting his life on hold—like Anup—in service of a larger mission. Though AAP had little evidence of proven leadership in public office, Anurag was drawn to their commitment for change, to their ideals. And so, he began initiating conversations with anyone who would listen: autorickshaw drivers, street vendors, friends and even random strangers. Every Saturday, after school, he would spread the word on street corners, parks and metro stations.

After a few weeks of non-stop volunteering, Anurag was hungry for more. He begged Anup to find a way to arrange a meeting with Manish Sisodia, one of the party's leaders.

Eventually, through an assistant who worked for Manish Sisodia, Anurag secured a ten-minute early morning meeting. A former news producer, Sisodia was a key architect of the Jan Lokpal bill that Anurag was extremely fascinated by.

'Mr Sisodia, I'll only take a few minutes of your time and I'll get right to the point.' Anurag had showed up outside of his house, as instructed, promptly at 6 a.m. It was a cold day in February, and Manish was on his customary morning walk.

'Son, catch your breath first. Have you had breakfast? Would you like some chai?' Manish asked.

'No, sir. Thank you.'

'Okay, great. Walk with me. What can I do for you?'

'I've always believed in the power of government, sir. In my opinion, our public institutions are a direct representation of our nation's ideals. I know people are cynical, but I believe we can make them work. I believe we can return them to the ideals of Nehru and Ambedkar. I believe we have to.'

'I do too, son. So, tell me what I can do for you.'

Anurag realized he was rambling.

'I want to work for AAP, sir. I'm willing to do anything. But I want to help this party win. There's too much at stake here in Delhi. Be it education, health—' Before Anurag could finish, Sisodia interrupted.

'What kind of work are you looking for?'

'I know how to read, write and do research. I can help draft policies. I know a lot about education. And I'm willing to do anything.' Anurag knew he sounded desperate.

'And how do you know a lot about education?'

'Well, I've been teaching in a low-income classroom here in Seelampur. And while it hasn't been long, it's exposed me to our country's ground realities in ways nothing else could have.'

'Son, that's the tragic thing about our country. Everybody wants to work on policy, but nobody wants to be on the ground. You've *started* working on the ground, but that's not nearly enough. All of these bureaucrats who are making decisions for the country have little to no direct experience. And those who are on the ground—well, no one involves them or values their insights. If you want to become a policymaker, spend the next five years working on the ground and then come back to me.'

Anurag was undeterred. 'I'll commit to being on the ground. I'll do it. But I want to be on the ground with AAP. I want to change the way our government works.'

'Call Rajmohan Gandhi. I'll give you his number. Do whatever he needs you to do. That will put you on the ground,' Sisodia replied before walking to his car.

The grandson of Mahatma Gandhi, Rajmohan Gandhi had been a research professor at the University of Illinois before joining the Aam Aadmi Party. Having spent more than fifty years advocating against corruption and inequity, he was similarly intrigued by the rising party. At the time, he was contesting from the East Delhi constituency. As a volunteer working under Rajmohan, Anurag spent the next several months doing everything from planting posters and writing press briefs to coordinating social media campaigns and serving volunteers food and water. Though his job description was far from defined, Anurag couldn't have cared less.

The 2014 elections were less than three weeks away, and Anurag was spending every minute of his spare time campaigning. He was exhausted and fatigued. And he was beginning to understand the messy—and sometimes dangerous—aspects of a hotly contested election. After the Delhi elections, together with Anup and a small cadre of campaign volunteers, he planned a ten-day trip to campaign in Banaras. On their way, they encountered the most disquieting kind of opposition.

'Get out! Get out!' a saffron mob shouted. They were chanting in Hindi and waving bats. Three dozen opposition protesters quickly surrounded the car, which they had recognized because of the AAP symbols and Kejriwal's photo painted on it. After a few moments, they began smashing their windshields. Intent on driving through and avoiding conflict, the driver quickly—but unsuccessfully—moved to lock the car doors. The protesters began beating him. A few grabbed Anurag by the collar and tried to yank him out of the car. They even broke into the back of the vehicle, grabbed the posters and other campaign materials and destroyed them. After a brief yet frightening tussle, the driver managed to make a sharp left turn.

The experience left Anurag both scarred and sceptical— testing the very ideals that underpinned his obsession with politics. 'Why beat us? Why threaten us? Why can't two parties run peacefully? Aren't we a democracy?'

It was perhaps an omen for things to come. Eight days later, after a bitter and long campaign, AAP resoundingly lost the elections. Anurag was dejected. The campaign had exposed him to the dark side of politics—to discrimination, bias, scapegoating and more. He was beginning to wonder if democratic change was even possible.

Anurag's obsession with democracy, which officially started in college, has several provenances. For years, he had dedicated his afternoons to reading Gandhi, Ambedkar, Nehru, Abdul Kalam and Amartya Sen. Their musings taught him the power of a nation built on unwavering ideals. On the other hand, though, Anurag's childhood battles with inequity—combined with the deep disparities he witnessed as a Teach For India Fellow in Seelampur—often underscored the country's collective failure to deliver those very ideals. He discovered, moreover, that India's social contract was broken.

The dichotomy forced him to start seeing every instance of inequity—the struggles his children encountered, the failing state of his school, the achievement gap in Seelampur, his parents' financial hardships—as a product of failed policy and, ultimately, a consequence of injustice.

~

'Government schools are in bad shape solely because vested interests have crept in.' Arvind Kejriwal was addressing a crowd of 400 students, educators, parents and practitioners at Teach For India's InspirED Conference, less than two months before the 2015 elections. TFI had invited representatives from multiple political parties to talk about the key issues underlying India's dismal state of education.

Kejriwal spoke for twenty minutes, outlining a litany of problems along with potential solutions and regulations. 'We are not against schools being run by private organizations; in fact, some of them are good schools. But some of them are run by big businessmen and politicians who have destroyed government schools so that their own schools can run, and so that they can have a large number of students enrolled in their schools in order to earn more and more money.'

I sat in the audience with Nandini, who had travelled with me to attend the conference. I watched as Anurag and his team stood on the sidelines. They were glued to their phones, tweeting to ensure coverage of Kejriwal's speech. Meanwhile, Kejriwal continued to lay out what would become the founding principles of the party's stance on education.

'Forty-eight thousand crore [480 billion] rupees of black money is given as donations to private schools all over the country. Forty-eight *thousand* crores!' he exclaimed. 'Our teachers have been made clerks by the government. They are engaged in all sorts of work that isn't teaching: writing attendance records, preparing reports and election duty.

'If elected, in five years, we will do everything possible to improve the condition of the government schools. Even rich people will start voluntarily sending their children to government schools.' As Kejriwal delivered his final promise, the crowd erupted in applause.

Anurag repeatedly downplays his contributions by referring to himself as a 'thoroughly ordinary volunteer'. The way I perceive it, he was a key contributor to the party's official Education Manifesto, elements of which Kejriwal was sharing with the audience that day. Two months after that speech AAP would go on to resoundingly win the 2015 elections. In their third attempt to gain power, they surpassed everyone's expectations and won sixty-seven out of seventy seats in Delhi. Anurag was jubilant. Filled with emotion, he spent the entire day oscillating between crying and celebrating on the city streets with several Aam Aadmi volunteers he had begun to call family. Though it's a time that he now refers to as 'the greatest day of his life', he nevertheless felt the expectations that the election carried with it.

'We have to deliver. We have no choice. The margin by which we've won proves the enormity of people's expectations. If we don't deliver, they are not going to be forgiving.' Anurag was confiding in a fellow volunteer, who didn't appreciate his sober reaction only two hours after the results had come in.

A few days later, Anurag was one of the people picked to join the Education Task Force responsible for putting together a roadmap for education reform. Less than three weeks later, however, his appointment was blocked. Staying true to his commitment, Anurag offered to work pro bono two days a week, while simultaneously accepting an offer as a community engagement and advocacy leader, with Tarun at Indus Action.

~

In the same year, 2015, but in a different part of the world, another famous political leader delivered a powerful message. Responding to one of America's many mass shootings, where a white man walked into an African American church in South Carolina and ruthlessly fired into the crowd, Obama delivered a moving eulogy for the congregation's preacher. Obama told the emotional audience that creating a more just world would demand that we start by looking inwards.

'Let us not allow ourselves to slip into a comfortable silence again. Because that's so often what we do to avoid uncomfortable truths about the prejudices that still infect our society, to settle for symbolic gestures without following up with the hard work of more lasting change. That's how we lose our way again.' His eyes tearing up, Obama continued to talk about what the fallen reverend would have wanted the crowd to understand—and to fight for. 'Justice grows out of the recognition of ourselves in each other. That my liberty depends on you being free too. That history can't be a sword to justify injustice. Or a shield against progress. It must be a manual for how to avoid repeating the mistakes of the past. How to break the cycle. A roadway for a better world.'

Changing the systems perpetuating injustice means we begin by unpacking our own sense of privilege and prejudice. As a society, it means we begin to recognize, and eventually discard, the feelings of hate and discomfort that accompany differences in caste, religion, gender and economics—divisions that have long torn the civil fabric of India apart. Going down that painful road demands that we confront the fears that prevent us from sharing meals and tables with autorickshaw drivers and slum dwellers. Those same fears are the very feelings that are preventing people like Pankaj and the children of Govandi from getting a seat at the table. And, perhaps more than anything, it means that we start to replace those fears with feelings of love and acceptance, that we start to teach our children to do the same. For Anurag, that's the role that education must play. It's also the driving force behind his relentless pursuit of working in government.

'I know learning outcomes are important,' Anurag tells me. 'But, to be perfectly honest, I don't give a damn if children are solving fractions if they can't simultaneously learn how to live peacefully with each other and avoid slitting each other's throats.' His belief in the power of social justice has not only led him to grow disillusioned with today's schools, but to also believe that their very purpose must change.

'Our schools must adapt and understand the need of the hour. Today, we see our very democracy being threatened. We see girls being raped across the country, people killing each other because of religion and caste. Yet, pick a school across India, and you'll find less than 1 per cent of them talking about that. Instead, they're talking about fractions.' An engineer by training, his aversion to fractions may be a bit misplaced. His loss of faith in India's education system is fuelled by an increasing belief that our schools are growing obsolete.

'Children are too young to discriminate, to oppress, to murder, to assault. They're too young and they're too innocent. If we can teach them to embody the values of a more just world— along with the skills needed to get there—then we have a real chance at the type of generational change the world needs but has rarely seen. The government, I believe, is the only institution that has the power to do that at a large scale.'

Too often, we find ourselves giving up on our public institutions. Our loss of faith is understandable. Entrusted with delivering on the ideals of equity and justice, today's institutions are instead beleaguered by accounts of corruption, ineptitude and nepotism. For our country's most vulnerable citizens, those accounts also include apathy.

I'll never forget my mother's reaction to my decision to move to India.

'Do you think you're a saviour? You're an idiot, in my opinion.' She was yelling. 'I grew up in that country. You're not talking about thirty-five children anymore. Picture a country that's filled with 1.3 billion people. Picture a country whose government is more corrupt than anything you've ever experienced.

'How the hell are you—one person—going to change that?' My mother's lack of belief was also understandable. She, like many of India's citizens, spent her childhood watching dysfunction and post-Partition strife unfold right outside her doorstep. And I, too, have often dismissed India's government institutions as simply being anachronistic. That very cynicism, a sentiment shared by millions, is what makes Anurag's commitment so powerful. He has the audacity to believe in the power of change, even in an institution that has—for more than a century—proven itself to be unwieldy.

As a teacher in Washington DC, I witnessed first-hand the power of audacity to yield change. The decrepit state school I had been placed in was under a local government that had been failing children for far too long. The District of Columbia Public Schools was beset by four decades of declining student enrolment. Since the 1960s, the government had lost more than 100,000 students to private schools. Parents, by and large, were losing faith in the ability of institutions to deliver. And they had every reason to. According to the National Assessment of Educational Progress, a standard American benchmark used to gauge student learning, the district had the country's lowest student achievement scores.[51] Graduation rates were steadily declining. The achievement gap between the city's rich and poor—between white and black Americans—was at an all-time high.

People were frustrated.

Anxiety and disbelief eventually translated into electoral results. In November of 2006, citizens elected a reform-minded young mayor, Adrian Fenty, who ran on a campaign which focused primarily on fixing the broken public education system. One of his first hires was a Teach For America alumna named Michelle Rhee, who he tapped to lead and transform the school system. Within her first two years in office, during my Fellowship, Rhee made a number of controversial, wide-scale moves. She fired more than 250 public school teachers and shut down twenty of the city's failing schools. She also restructured Sousa Middle School, where I spent my two years; our headmaster was eventually fired. Picking a series of unpopular battles with local teachers' unions, Rhee soon renegotiated a teacher evaluation and salary system that offered educators a choice: if you give up tenure and agree to have your performance evaluated using student learning, the government would offer you a 40 per cent pay raise.

The changes—which yielded a number of rapid results—carried a high political cost. Rhee's moves were highly controversial. Two years later, Adrian Fenty lost his re-election battle. Rhee resigned after only two years in office—she was the district's sixth chancellor in ten years.

Her successor, however, was also a Teach For America alumna. Kaya Henderson, who had worked with Rhee for decades, continued many of the reforms started under Rhee. She just managed to do so with a softer touch. Kaya made community engagement one of her most pressing priorities. She began hosting town halls, listening to parents' concerns and soliciting inputs from across the aisle. Kaya served as the district's chancellor for the next six years. During her tenure, reading proficiency increased by 16 per cent, graduation rates went up and enrolment declines were finally arrested. For the first time, public schools were seeing an increase in enrolment.

Collectively, Rhee and Henderson's success has been widely hailed across the country. President Obama even used parts of their initiatives to inform educational policies for other states to follow. At the heart of their drive was the audacity to believe, the courage to stand up for change and the willingness to engage with a public institution that many had signed off on.

~

Within the first six months of the AAP's rise to power, Anurag spent four days every week with Indus Action, running community awareness programmes, publishing reports on the state of 12(1) (c) and—as we already saw—leading the government push to ensure the admission process migrated to an online portal. During the rest of the week, he worked tirelessly as a member of the Delhi government's Education Task Force.

In those first few months, he began chipping away at broken systems. He co-led the design of regulation that restructured the powers attributed to school management committees. He reviewed the teacher recruitment processes practised by the Delhi government and co-authored, with five others, a bill—which would later be passed—that changed the city's private school regulatory framework. It worked to ensure that Delhi's private schools could no longer charge exorbitant fees to the city's most vulnerable students and, once made into law, would eventually impact more than 1,600,000 children across the city of Delhi.

Balancing Indus Action along with the Delhi government's Education Task Force proved to be arduous and taxing. His work with the government, which was compounded by the need for rapid transitions and fast-paced deadlines, often demanded sleepless nights. Indus Action, under Tarun's leadership, was also expanding rapidly to meet the demands imposed by Section 12(1) (c). Sixteen months into his tenure, in August 2016, Anurag made the difficult decision of picking one. He left his post at Indus Action. Unsure whether or not the government would officially bring him onto their payroll this time, he nevertheless committed to joining them full-time.

'You put in your papers at Indus Action already? Are you crazy?' Vignesh, his flatmate and a Teach For India alumnus, asked.

'Maybe I am,' Anurag shot back defensively.

'You were making a change at Indus Action. You were impacting tens of thousands of children. You work with the Delhi government, and you don't even know what you'll be doing. Your work changes every week based on what's political priority. You don't even know if you're going to have a salaried job!' Vignesh was genuinely worried about his flatmate.

'It's not even about impact anymore, Vignesh. It's about our ability to deliver on promises made to the people of this city. Even though I played a small role, I helped craft those promises. That responsibility is mine too. I can't ignore it. A democracy's primary responsibility in today's society is to deliver social justice,' Anurag said. A year had passed since the elections in 2015, but the weight of responsibility he felt after his party's victory still hadn't left him. His inability to dedicate himself fully was gnawing at his conscience. He didn't care that he didn't have a confirmed title or a source of income. He only felt an overwhelming sense of relief.

'And what will you place on your visiting card? "Government do-it-all"?' Vignesh joked.

'I don't know,' Anurag paused to think about that for a moment. 'It was a defining moment for our democracy when people chose to trust a bunch of honest and crazy people. It was a defining moment for our democracy when thousands—no lakhs—of ordinary people came together to fight for the India of their dreams. I cannot be petty at a time like this. I know the future is uncertain, and it will be tough. But I want to focus on the work. We will see what happens.'

'Calm down, you don't have to get all sentimental. It was just a light-hearted joke.'

'No, no, I'm serious, Vignesh.' Anurag could feel his voice starting to rise. 'I don't want to be defined by my role. I just want to do whatever is needed to make us more just. I want to solve the problems that are preventing us from being a just society. And right now, the biggest problem—and opportunity—standing in the way of that happens to be education. Tomorrow, something else will likely need to be fixed and I'll happily dedicate myself to that.'

'Just think about your security, that's all I'm saying. Make sure they pay you.'

'Even if they don't pay me, I don't care. They can continue to block my appointment orders. But they can't stop me from working—from actually *doing something*. I'm going to do whatever it takes to bring social justice to this country.' It is Anurag's very ideals—the belief that fully realizing Ambedkar's vision of a just society is the single greatest effort he can undertake—that fuel his relentless commitment towards equity. Doing less than 'whatever it takes', in Anurag's mind, would be an abdication of responsibility.

Anurag continued working for the government of Delhi for the next twelve months without a salary. Despite being offered a position, his appointment was blocked again. In his own words, it was an 'exercise in both gratitude and humility'. He quit taking Ubers and autorickshaws and started using the Delhi metro. Friends and supporters—like Vignesh—chipped in. For the next twelve months, Anurag lived off those donations to ensure that he could keep his commitment to the people of Delhi. His work progressed beautifully. Eventually, in August 2017, his third appointment finally came through. Now a salaried employee, Anurag is a member of the Delhi Commission for Protection of Child Rights (DCPCR). DCPCR is a statutory watchdog that ensures the enforcement of education-related rights like RTE's Section 12(1) (c). The appointment makes Anurag a high-ranking official, equivalent in rank to the education secretary of any state in India, a position usually held by IAS officers. He is responsible for the monitoring and implementation of the Right to Education across 6,000 Delhi schools that, collectively, impact more than 4.5 million children.

Anurag is currently leading a project to implement a revamped school evaluation model for Delhi's 6,000 schools. With a budget of 15 crores (150 million), he's endeavouring to ensure a more holistic evaluation model gets implemented— one that assesses schools based on what children should be learning to succeed in today's society. For Anurag, designing and implementing that model would be his biggest, and most gratifying, success to date. It would be a giant step towards his vision for a more just India.

Sitting with Anurag in his government office one Wednesday afternoon, I couldn't help but think about his potential to dramatically reshape opportunity for the children of Jahangirpuri, and more broadly, the children of Delhi. He has the potential— and the power—to ensure that children like Arbaaz and Yasmin no longer face the discrimination and abuse that have long threatened their futures. He has the ability to one day reshape the educational experience for the thousands of children that, simply put, have lost any hope for a reimagined future.

When I told Anurag that, and asked him how he was handling the weight of his role, his reply was telling.

'This is my constitutional oath. I took that oath for the people of this city, for the people of India. That's what every single day boils down to: am I going to wake up today and fulfil my constitutional oath? If I can do that, I think I can ensure that the kids of Delhi are getting the justice they need and deserve,' he said, before pausing again. 'It really is as simple as that.'

CONCLUSION
GREY SUNSHINE

The month of May is my favourite time of the year. It's the month we welcome Teach For India's incoming batch of starry-eyed Fellows. Every May, I make my way to our summer institute, where Fellows spend their first five weeks immersed in a residential training programme. There I get to meet hundreds of young men and women who have travelled across the country and the world. They've often left secure jobs and defied parents. They've replaced their carefully crafted plans with a search for something greater. It's the search for sunshine amidst greyness.

I still remember meeting Tarun, ten years ago, when he walked through the front doors of our first summer institute. He was passionate and eager. Having just left Hindustan Unilever—a guaranteed path to long-term security—he was also scared.

'I want to be part of something bigger,' he had told me. 'I want to find purpose. I want to find my next talisman.'

His sentiments are echoed, every year, in the thousands of Fellows that follow. Their resolve is peppered with similar notes of uncertainty and anxiety:

'How did your parents react? Mine won't even talk to me. I would make the same decision, though, a thousand times over.'

'When do I get to meet my kids? I hope they accept me. Whatever happens, I'm going to shower them with love.'

'Do you ever think about going back to the US? Life is so different here, but my kids will make all of this worth it.'

'Will I get a job after the Fellowship? My family is worried.'

Since Teach For India first started, 4,000 young people have completed the Fellowship. They've collectively served more than 38,000 of India's children. Through their service, they've worked tirelessly to ensure that students leave our classrooms on a fundamentally different life trajectory. At Teach For India, we believe that transforming the lives in an individual classroom is the first step towards long-term leadership. In our classrooms, students have shown twice the improvement in math and seven times higher gains in English as compared to classrooms without Teach For India Fellows. An incredible 94 per cent of our tenth standard students graduated successfully from school, with 22.7 per cent getting distinction (above 75 per cent) and 31.3 per cent securing first class (above 90 per cent).

Our Fellows' efforts are not just limited to academics. In the pursuit to give their students the tools to escape the vicious cycle of poverty, Fellows have established community centres, mobilized parents, started sports tournaments, hosted musicals, built libraries and reinvested parts of their own income into their classrooms—all while serving as full-time teachers. They've worked to surround their children with the supporting ecosystem necessary to climb out of poverty.

I've had the privilege of watching many of their children grow up—of walking through Asif's classroom doors when he was only eight years old and of seeing Nandini when she was a young teenager. Having benefitted from a relay of strong Fellows, Asif and hundreds of our students are now studying in some of the country's best colleges. Most notably, many of them are *leading* initiatives to empower their communities for the better.

Nandini, who now studies at Franklin & Marshall College, is currently writing and directing a play about tribal India, where she hopes to highlight issues surrounding rural inhabitants. Last summer, she brought ten college friends—from England, India, Netherlands and France—back to her Luhianagar community to work on a project called 'Bridging the Gap'. They spent three weeks deeply immersed in three low-income schools, where they taught students English, public speaking, dance and drama. Intent on helping her more affluent peers grow more conscious of their privilege, she hosted them in her modest home in the slums of Pune.

Asif is now enrolled at the Rizvi College of Arts, Science and Commerce in Mumbai. He loves his classes and is excited about navigating his future possibilities, which have expanded to include not only fashion design but also a newfound interest in psychology and even a career as a teacher. Despite a hectic academic schedule, he makes time to volunteer in a Teach For India classroom. When I asked him why he would now consider teaching, he instantly responded: 'because of "One Day", bhaiya.' He was referring to Teach For India's vision: one day all children will attain an excellent education. In that moment, I realized that I may have been speaking to a future Teach For India Fellow.

Hundreds of our students like Asif and Nandini are finding ways to impact their surroundings. They're mobilizing children and adults to design simple solutions—sanitation projects, water cleanliness drives, tutoring centres, school enrolment campaigns—to make their surroundings a little better. In the process, they're joining a growing movement committed to eliminating educational inequity. These children have beaten the odds—a statistical number that adamantly declares 76 per cent of them *will* drop out.[52] They've become examples of hope. Their stories have instilled a sense of belief that the crippling effects of poverty and injustice don't have to determine their destiny; that security, knowledge, and networks aren't things only reserved for the privileged and that our country's most vulnerable children can be the authors of their journeys, too.

Their stories, however, simply aren't enough.

If the past ten years have taught me anything, it is this: working with poverty and injustice is grey and complex.

Take Yasmin's story, for example. Growing up in Jahangirpuri, she had a 2 per cent chance of making it to college and fulfilling her aspiration of becoming a teacher. For five consecutive years, Fellows wrangled with her parents and siblings, searching for ways to ensure that that dream becomes a reality.

A few weeks before writing this, Yasmin dropped out of school. Enrolled in a madrasa, she's resigned to her change in circumstance: 'This is my life now. This is reality. I'll make the most out of it and I'll move on,' she tells me.

Or take Pradnya's story. A thirteen-year-old growing up in Pune's slums and taught by a Teach For India Fellow, Pradnya was one of the most lovable students in class. Her teachers were drawn to her generosity of spirit. Every day, she brought extra lunch for classmates. She helped friends who were struggling with homework. She was smart, hard-working and determined.

One Sunday afternoon, Pradnya got into a fiery argument with her mother. After a few heated exchanges, her mother slapped Pradnya across the face. Five minutes later, without saying a word, her mother went to the local market. The encounter left Pradnya enraged. She ran behind the house and picked up a can of gasoline. Dousing herself in the flammable liquid, Pradnya impulsively lit the match.

My staff and I rushed to the hospital that evening, only to find Pradnya dead less than twenty-four hours later.

Or take the District of Columbia Public Schools, where I once taught. Over the last twelve years, policymakers and government officials have poured in millions of dollars. They've brought together some of the country's best minds. Under the leadership of Kaya and Michelle, graduation rates increased, student achievement improved and enrolment numbers stopped declining. But, the city's poor students continued to perform worse than their more affluent peers.

Accompanying every glimmer of sunshine are ten shades of greyness.

Improving literacy and mathematical proficiency is tough. Providing students an education that is transformative— one that fundamentally alters their life trajectories—is much tougher. Figuring out how to make that happen—how to change institutions that perpetuate oppression and injustice—for all 320 million Indian children... Well, that's the toughest.

Too often, I hear policymakers and experts debating which intervention will rectify the situation. Do children in India need a revamped curriculum? Or do they need excellent teachers? Should we work to strengthen the government system? Or should we create a new set of schools? Should we prioritize technological solutions? Or should we invest in better principals? Should we focus on India's many unregulated private schools? Or should we fix our dismal state of higher education?

Choosing between those is nothing more than guesswork. The truth is that our institutions are broken. And while that doesn't mean we need to accept the greyness, it does mean that the search for silver bullets is likely to be futile. If we're going to ensure that all of India's children receive the education they need and deserve, we're going to have to address *all* of these issues. Alleviating India's educational crisis, as a result, demands that we brace ourselves for the long haul.

So how, then, do we get the sun to shine for all of India's children? I believe, more than anything else, that we need to focus our energy on five things:

1. Believe in our country's potential

I believe that we need *India* to believe in the potential of our children. We would be remiss to argue that we haven't found glimmers of sunshine that are real and lasting. Our Fellows and students have together demonstrated that transformation is possible. Less than 9 per cent of our Fellows, when they walked through our front doors, were even thinking about a career in education. The vast majority were intent on returning to their original career paths. They were searching for purpose and fulfilment and, as a result, were willing to give two years of service to building India. But that was it.

Today, 75 per cent of them continue to work in education. Through their work, we have thousands of examples at all levels of the system showing us that transformation is possible. Our alumni are founding schools, running teacher training institutes, staying in classrooms and fighting on the ground for community-level change. Working directly with children, they're contributing to our collective goal: ensuring that Indian children receive an excellent education.

And that's only a fraction of what our alumni are doing. Others are impacting national and local policy, advocating for student rights, designing curriculum, creating cutting-edge technology and educating parents and families on how to create safe learning environments at home. They've started thirty-five enterprises that are working with low-income children. Some have joined well-known private sector organizations to effectively mobilize funds and much-needed resources towards social change. Collectively, these alumni are reaching millions of children through their efforts. They're proving that, while the classroom may be the first step, it is leadership that stays *within* the system that will fundamentally change it. While we have yet to fully transform India's social landscape, we have undoubtedly fuelled this country with examples that, together, are proving that poverty does not equal destiny.

The average Indian citizen, however, still doesn't believe that poor children can succeed. They are confused when they encounter stories like those of Nandini and Asif. Throughout this book, it's possible you found yourself sceptical at times too, and understandably so. We are all inundated, daily, with a barrage of messages telling us that economic circumstance dictates life outcomes.

We have to take charge of that narrative and change the conversation. We have to stop wondering *if* it's possible and open our eyes to see the countless examples that exist, proving that it is possible. We have to start talking about *how* to make those examples multiply. We are undeniably facing a crisis of epic proportions. Solving it, however, demands that we have the audacity to believe in a new reality. We must, as a country, dare to hope.

2. Nurture leadership that is brave

Second, I believe that we need leadership with the courage to rediscover India's light. Tarun, Anurag, Nalika and Soumya demonstrated this in heaps through their individual journeys. We need brave leadership like theirs and those of the 4,000 alumni, working at every level of the system—leadership that refuses to accept India's current reality.

We need leaders like Eshwar.

Eshwar grew up in a small town 90 kilometres outside of Bengaluru. The son of a farmer, he was the first in his family to graduate school and attend college. His parents were ecstatic and hopeful.

In his third year of college, Eshwar drove a friend to an IBM assessment centre and, in the process, found himself in an unexpected situation.

'Just come and take the placement test,' his friend said.

'I haven't even signed up,' Eshwar replied dismissively.

'Don't worry about that. Just take the test. Who knows—what if we could both end up working at IBM together?'

Eshwar convinced the administrators to let him take the assessment. He spent the next six years of his life at IBM, getting promoted four times along the way. The newfound security enabled him and his family to take risks that were once unthinkable. He took out loans to pay for his sister's wedding. He bought his parents a house. His father quit farming.

After a few years, though, Eshwar began questioning his surroundings. He knew that his time at IBM, while intellectually fulfilling and financially secure, was incomplete. A few months later, without telling any of his friends or family, Eshwar resigned and applied at Teach For India. The conversation with his father, several weeks later, was painful.

'Dad, I know we've got the EMI. And I know you're depending on me. If you tell me to, I'll say no. But I want you to know that, for the first time in my life, I've found purpose. I've found happiness.'

He wasn't sure what to expect in response. At Teach For India, he would be making a small fraction of his IBM salary. And the implications were huge. He would no longer have the means to offer much financial support to his parents. He expected them to yell at him. The response that eventually came though, after a few minutes of agonizing silence, was astounding.

'Listen, son. This is a surprise, to be honest. The past few years have been good for us. But, your happiness matters more. If serving India's children is what's going to make you happy, we don't want to argue with that.' Two weeks later, his parents sold their house. His father went back to work.

Eshwar spent the next two years teaching in one of Hyderabad's low-income government schools. He turned his classroom into an oasis of creativity. Every day, for one hour, his children would spend time innovating and designing real-world solutions to community problems. They created solar-powered lamps to study at night and manual devices to enable laundry without electricity. Eshwar quickly concluded that his children were natural problem-solvers; their school, however, was stymieing their creativity.

Today, five years later, Eshwar runs an organization called InquiLab. Their mission is to transform India's schools into havens that will promote innovation. They serve 3,500 low-income children across the city of Hyderabad. And to this day, Eshwar sends 50 per cent of his salary, every month, back home to his parents.

Changing broken institutions is going to demand leadership

that is courageous and, when needed, willing to disrupt the status quo for the greater good.

3. Embrace our children as partners

Nandini and Asif, along with thousands of other children we've met along the way, have shown us the immense power and hope that our children possess. Changing India necessitates that we not only see our students as assets, but that we fully embrace them as *equal partners* in leading change. That thought, for the majority of people, is quite radical. Admittedly, I've taken my time to fully embrace it as well.

Stories like Nandini's and Asif's have, however, forced me to recognize that seeing our children as mere recipients of an educational process is, by definition, embracing an anachronistic view of today's world. The more time I spend with children—within our communities and classrooms—the more I'm convinced that we actually have much *more* to learn from them.

Neida Khurshid is a 2015 Teach For India Alumnus (and now staff member) working towards this vision. She leads the student leadership team in Ahmedabad. In her work, Neida aims to shift people's mindsets about what students are capable of. The students she works with lead sizable projects of their own. They run learning circles in communities and peer mentorship groups, with limited and targeted support provided by Neida. She demonstrates the strength of her belief when she says, 'I don't understand why student leadership is even a specific term. Students should be synonymous with leaders, and inherently considered as partners in education. With the right guidance in some areas, students can be positioned not as consumers of education, but producers of their own learning experiences.'

India's children are the direct recipients of its inequity. They understand the depths and implications of the educational crisis far better than any scholar or practitioner; because they've experienced it, they understand their context. Yet, they're too often powerless and voiceless, largely because of their age and their penury. Solving this crisis isn't going to happen through a recycling of old, detached ideas. We need our children—the recipients of these solutions—to be co-creators along with us. We need them to lead the change, along with us.

4. Commit to a mobilized and ignited collective

Fourth, I believe that any hope of transformational progress demands that we work together. There are more than two million NGOs in India today—that's one organization for every 600 citizens. While many of those organizations are doing work that is laudable and rooted in progress, the vast majority are taking a piecemeal approach to change. Transformation that is sustainable can't happen as long as well-intentioned change-makers in Delhi *only* provide low-income children with healthcare while similar entities in Pune *only* provide access to sports. The truth is that the individual child needs both of those, along with a host of other interventions, to truly be successful. In order to do that, we need to be actively seeking out opportunities to work together.

Santosh More and his Bengaluru-based organization, Mantra4Change, embody this principle to the fullest. Their approach to change is rooted in open-sourcing collaboration. While many organizations prefer to work in silos, Mantra4Change's school transformation model hinges on partnerships with existing organizations. It can be challenging to work with others, resolve differences between people and approaches, but when done in the right way it leads to better outcomes for the ultimate beneficiaries: children.

'At Mantra, we worry about the scaling of *ideas* instead of scaling the organization,' Santosh shares with me. 'It's why we're so willing to work closely with other NGOs. Transforming lives is tough and it means we have to share our resources with anyone who approaches us. We're publicizing our models for anyone that wants them—for school transformation, community empowerment—so they can contextualize their goals. They, as a result, give back their findings to the body of knowledge we started. And through the process, they make our models better.

'Tomorrow, if a gram panchayat wants to run a school transformation project, they shouldn't need Mantra4Change to do it. They should be able to leverage the work we've done and lead the project themselves. At the end of the day, if we want to strive for educational equity and social equality, we have to accept that one organization cannot do it alone. Even the government can't do it alone.'

Spending a day in the Mantra4Change office with Santosh, I didn't need more evidence to witness that spirit of collaboration come alive. As soon as I walked in, I met a team member from Loop Education Foundation, a startup founded by Saahil Sood, another TFI alumnus. As a participant of Edumentum (an incubator run by Mantra4Change for early stage organizations working to effect change), he travelled to Bengaluru just to glean wisdom from Santosh. Over the course of the day, I learned that the breadth of their collaborations spans industries and organizations.

'When we started with a needs assessment framework for school transformation, we realized our implementation had to be supported by an academic backing. We needed someone to critique what we were doing and so we approached the professors at Azim Premji University (APU). The academicians at APU are people who have a wealth of knowledge. Instead of lamenting about the disconnect between academia and those on the ground, we decided to bridge that gap and bring depth to our work.'

In the well-intentioned attempt to ensure every child receives *some* support, we've perhaps forgotten our end goal: transformation. Offering children independent piecemeal changes—a healthcare programme here or a curriculum revamp there—will lead to growth that is merely incremental. Changing lives, however, demands something far greater. We have to start ensuring that our stakeholders, including government officials, parents, NGOs and children, are working *together* to deliver each child an ecosystem of support that is transformative.

5. Mobilize exponentially more people

Finally, I believe that we need more people. Our most promising young minds today are choosing every career path but education. As a result, we're left with a sector that's experienced one of the world's greatest brain drains.

Teach For India has expanded significantly since our inception. We are now operating in seven cities: Mumbai, Pune, Delhi, Bengaluru, Chennai, Hyderabad and Ahmedabad. Having said that, 4,000 leaders trying to effect change for a country with 1.3 billion people is far from enough. Conventional wisdom suggests that the alternative solution is to look for interventions that are easily scalable. And so people look for the next piece of technology or a newly drafted policy. But, by definition, 'wicked' problems do not have straightforward solutions. Silver bullets just don't work. I've often daydreamed about Teach For India's exit strategy—about a day when the organization is no longer needed because we know that our children's futures won't be dictated by circumstance. I dream about a day when the median gap in years of schooling between the rich and the poor is zero, not 8.7 years.[53] I dream about a day when more than 54 per cent can understand the written instructions on a sample ORS packet.[54] I dream about a day when we no longer have to worry about continuing the 'relay': placing a new set of Fellows every two years in our classrooms. Perhaps that day will come when India's rising youth find a job in education as enticing as a high-paying corporate position. We need the people of India to see what we see: solving an educational crisis that threatens the country's very existence is undoubtedly the most vexing challenge our generation will face. Successfully tackling it will unleash not just the potential of the system, but will lead to transformation for the very individuals striving to lead change—as it has done for Soumya, Nalika, Tarun and Anurag.

More than seventy years ago, Gandhi and Nehru built a movement of freedom fighters who ushered in a new era for India. These were revolutionaries who were committed to unleashing India's new wave of torchbearers. They ensured that India's people—tens of thousands—stood up with them. And they did so because they grasped the urgency of the moment. Together, they envisioned an age of prosperity that would deliver on promises of justice and equity.

Seventy years later, their steps have ushered in progress that is undeniable and laudable. But that progress has hit its limits, and it has only reached a fraction of India's citizens. Based on current trends, India is projected to achieve universal primary education in 2050 and universal upper secondary education only in 2085.[55] These projections say nothing about the quality of education children will actually receive. The greyness that chequers today's sunshine is the product of years of oppression and injustice; of institutions that are obsolete and unable to cope; of leadership that, while well-intentioned, was unable to deliver for India's poor. The need for more people to revolutionize our education sector, and in turn our country, couldn't be more apparent.

If 4,000 Teach For India Fellows and their students can create a giant wave of 'proof points', imagine what 40,000 could do? Or what an army of 400,000 could do?

Transforming a broken system will take more than a few thousand examples. It needs a movement of torchbearers working together for transformational change. It demands a generation of people committed to reigniting India's grey skies. And with every young Indian citizen that stands up and commits to a new tomorrow—that refuses to accept greyness—we get closer to a country that is more just and more equitable. We get closer to ensuring that India's brightest days are yet to come.

EPILOGUE

SHAHEEN MISTRI

I remember sitting in a large, dark auditorium, starry-eyed, as Muhammad Yunus began to speak. With a twinkle in his eye, he spoke of a day when his grandchildren would find poverty only in a museum. At first, I was confused. A museum of poverty? Then, slowly, lured by the gentle conviction in his voice, I allowed myself to envision the world he saw: a world where poverty exists only behind glass exhibits, video footage and time-stained photographs. A world where you'd take your grandchildren to visit each year as a powerful reminder that the painful memories of the past no longer haunt us.

In that moment, I had goosebumps. We can end poverty, I thought. We can end poverty for all of our citizens.

In my mind, I started visualizing the museum as Yunus spoke. It's a museum of educational inequity. I call it the Museum of Grey Sunshine. I can see myself standing in a long queue to buy my ticket before walking by exhibits depicting things that I've actually seen in my three decades of serving children. While its displays won't be relics of the past—we're not there yet—perhaps it could serve as a powerful reminder of what our world holds today.

My hope is that you can visualize it too.

First, there's a grand foyer. It is there that you experience how kids travel to school. You jump on a fast-moving treadmill to endure the five kilometres that many of India's children walk, every day, just to reach school. On the other side of the foyer, you ride in a chauffeur-driven Honda City, which will show you how other children reach in just twenty minutes. You can even climb on a camel to get to a school in a makeshift tent or take a simulated ride in an overcrowded Kerala boat-school.

Once you enter the museum, you'll encounter a big, bold sign which says 'Classrooms of Oppression'. In the first room, secondary school students are seated on benches so cramped they're forced to hold on to their backpacks all day. They mindlessly copy answers from the board. Their teacher diligently corrects every answer to show their 'right' answers to the education officer who will soon visit. The second exhibit transports you into a second-standard classroom where a seven-year-old is excitedly raising her hand, almost jumping out of her seat to answer. She speaks, makes a mistake, and is mocked.

'Can't you *ever* get anything right?'

In that moment, you see her face becoming a little smaller. She does not want to try any more. She has lost the will to learn.

The third room makes both you and I gasp with horror: a teacher marching up and down her classroom with a cane, using it liberally to keep control of the tightly packed class of ninety-three students. The rooms go on and on; they're all versions of spaces that take a child's natural eagerness to learn, and slowly and systematically, stamps it out.

The section's last room has no teacher. Chaos prevails. Half the children run to a nearby classroom, the only one where a teacher is present and children are learning. They crowd at the door, pushing to peek inside, knowing that that is the only learning they'll get.

We continue down the dark hallway beyond the 'Classrooms of Oppression'. We're asked to sit on a hardwood bench. A rod in front of us locks us in place. As we move through the darkness, headlines light up:

'Fourteen-year-old Sunitha jumps off a building due to examination stress'
'Depression in school children on the increase'
'Mother thrown out of school when she asks why her

twelve-year-old son Vijay can't read'

'Only half of India's grade-five students can read a grade-two text'

'Twelve-year-old Aditi runs away from home to escape marriage'

The bench halts and turns, slowly, before moving faster and faster. As it spins, I hear the pained voices of teachers, parents and students, overlapping each other.

'Can't you ever do anything right?'

'Leave me alone!'

'Do what I say!'

'I hate science!'

'Find something else to be interested in. You aren't good at math!'

'Can I ask a question?'

'Stupid child!'

'Why do I have to do so much administrative work as a teacher?'

'Please help me!'

'How do you expect me to teach 135 children?'

'I can't do it!'

'How can I raise a family when my salary is 3,000 rupees per month?'

The darkness seems to grow. The same chills I once felt as a child in a haunted house run down my spine now. The ride comes to an abrupt halt and the safety rod lifts. Shaking from the ride, I stand up and attempt to ignore the voices still swirling in my head.

We're soon guided to sit on the floor of a large, carpeted circular room. It's the 'Hall of Truth'. Within seconds, the stage in front of the room fills with actors dressed as trees. The room is filled with the sound of machines tearing them down. After a few minutes, we are interrupted by a jarringly loud bell, at which the second performance begins. This one is about rape. We hear the sounds of a screaming woman. Then the school bell rings again, and another performance starts. Reams of plastic bags fall from the ceiling, landing on us while the sound of waves fills our ears. You look at me and at the people in the audience before shaking the plastic bags off. My head starts to hurt with the incessant cacophony: falling trees, a woman's screams, an ocean churning to rid itself of plastic. But the bells and performances continue. Bell, maternal mortality. Bell, malnutrition. Bell, refugee crisis. Bell, unclean drinking water. Bell, terror. As each new performance starts, it joins the previous performance. It's deafeningly loud. My head starts to throb now. And then, as quickly as it started, the performers disappear, and on a screen in front of us, a question appears:

What you see is the truth.
What is the purpose of education?

Unnerved, we find cushions lying around and rest our heads for a while, looking up at the question while the crowd scurries out of the dome-shaped room. I feel hopeless. We are responsible for so many of these issues, I think. We created that world.

This contemporary museum may indeed be a figment of my imagination. However, it draws attention to the truth, to the fact that at this very moment inequity plagues India's children. I still walk into too many classrooms and see kids copying mindlessly. I still hear the whack of a slap across a child's head, or the threat of a bamboo cane being waved around. I've seen a child run away to join a group of eunuchs after his family shunned his homosexuality and I know that millions of children are fearful that their identities won't be accepted. I watch too many children agonize at their apparent uselessness, when the student next to them scores a 97 per cent compared with their 85 per cent.

I see learning slip, slip, slip
And with this, children fall
Their colours fading from the bright neon of fun and
sunshine
To the dull grey of helplessness and mediocrity.

And I know that in these moments, our children have hated school, and life, a little bit more.

As I continue to listen to Mohammad Yunus, he reinforces what I have seen up-close: we are raising kids ill-equipped to even function in our existing world. The need for education is far graver than ever; it's the need to equip kids to change the very world that they live in. That is the purpose of education. That is what education has the power and responsibility to do. After all, if we've created the world that we live in, then we have the ability to design and create a radically better one.

Now, for just a moment, come back into the Museum of Grey Sunshine with me.

We catch a glimpse of a yellow light, right outside the door to the next exhibit. Leaving the 'Hall of Truth' behind, we're now bathed in golden sunshine. The room feels warm. We sit down and close our eyes to soak it in. When we open our eyes, the number '1' is projected, mid-air, in front of us. Curious, we look around. Through the yellow sunshine, more numbers appear.

Like a casino, they flash. They keep increasing, faster than we can count. 7, 26, 389, 2,937, 10,001, 55,679, 369,884, 503,388, 7,300,410, 28,933,342. This continues for several minutes, and we smile to ourselves, intrigued. Finally, there is a shrill bell and the numbers stop at the jackpot: 320,000,000 Indian children.

That's it, you see. The 32 crore children of India are not our problem. They're our hope. They're our hope. They're our hope. Our children are our country's greatest hope.

We get up, reluctant to leave the comfort of the sunshine after rooms of grey. The delightful sound of children's laughter comes from beyond, and we eagerly chase it. The 'Hall of Light' breaks into a series of warm, yellow rooms. In a secondary school classroom, children are excitedly chatting about the state of education—and how *they* can fix it. They'd recently read the RTE and surveyed their community. I shake off a sense of déjà vu. Now, they're generating prototypes of solutions that will ensure every child receives an excellent education. They're planning student-led conferences, where they'll soon present their prototypes to senior government officials.

Eager to see more, we enter the next room. Again, I can't shake off the feeling that I've been in this second standard classroom before.

'Mistakes are how we learn' is written in cheerful pink on a wall. The letters sit amidst a blast of colourful photographs of children. I smile at the captions describing each of them: 'I'm very fast in math'; 'I want to be a doctor because too many poor people don't have good healthcare'; 'I am courageous.'

The eight-year-olds in this class are seated in a circle, discussing love. 'Love means not fighting with my little brother.' 'Love is when people make fun of my friend and I tell her I will always be with her.' 'Love is the only thing that will change the world.'

The kids in these classrooms are safe. Along with their teachers, they are crafting dreams. They're growing to understand their strengths, practising values and taking ownership of not only their own education but also that of their peers.

We continue on.

I enter a room with ninety-three students. The children are sitting in stations of six, each one led by a student and each learning something different. The student facilitators anchor their stations with a learning style that best suits the group. There is joyful chatter in the room, fall-off-your-seat engagement and a palpable passion for learning. *These ninety-three kids are actually teaching each other.* The sense of déjà vu from having seen such exemplary classrooms before overwhelms me. These classrooms recognize a fundamental truth: each individual has something to give and something to receive. The teacher is both offering to help and *asking* for help. This feels like the future of education.

We pass the last room in the 'Hall of Light', wondering why the kindergarten class is empty. The front wall is adorned with a large arrow, pointing up to a young child's scribble, 'Be careful of our nest. We're looking after baby birds here.' I look up and smile at the baby pigeons, safe in the classroom nest. The seats have been pushed back into a large circle. In the centre is an elaborate, twenty-foot-long structure made of wooden blocks. We walk closer and see a carefully constructed space station. They've thought of every detail, labelled each section, created escalators and space suits. These children are learning advanced engineering at the age of five—all through play. On the door is another sign, 'We'll be back this afternoon. Our class is out learning from the world!'

I don't want these rooms to end. They are the rooms where teachers and students weave dreams not just for the future, but for today.

Before long, we reach the museum's closing stretch and find a room called 'The Hug'. Intrigued, we enter. Visitors are sitting in a circle. A child facilitates the discussion with passion and energy, sharing her understanding of a hug, its power to comfort and connect. She then demonstrates a ten-second hug, looking into the eyes of her partner and letting her purest wishes for him flow through the hug. She invites all of us to do the same as she plays happy, upbeat music. We watch as people tentatively walk towards each other. I lock eyes with an old lady with thick glasses. With all the love I can muster in my heart, I walk over to her and give her a warm, tight hug. We stay like that for more than ten seconds; two strangers, motivated by a student to remember that ultimately, we're all deeply and intricately connected.

We arrive at the final section: 'The Space of the Collective'.

I'm seated in a large auditorium, facing a black stage. The hall is packed, similar to the hall I sat in when I heard Muhammad Yunus speak of the Museum of Poverty. Children, from all ages and backgrounds, are speaking and singing. They perform spoken word poetry, speaking of how they've been discriminated against as girls. They grace the stage with exquisite dance formations depicting what a reimagined education could look like. They rise up and share powerful stories of the things that they want to stop in the world—violence, inequality, poverty. They fill the aisles with their joy and hope, appealing to us to see them as partners who have the voice and conviction to change the world for the better.

I leave the museum in quiet contemplation. I marvel that there will be a time when we look back at a past where we allowed and perpetuated violence, apathy, humiliation and a deadening of the mind, heart and soul in our schools. I am convinced that there will be a time when no Indian child studies in one of the rooms that I walked through before I entered the 'Hall of Light'. I am confident that with years of committed action and with hope, the status quo will be shifted.

I yearn to visit the Museum of Grey Sunshine one day to be reminded that we've turned the Classrooms of Oppression into Classrooms of Light. I yearn for the day the grey disappears.

ACKNOWLEDGEMENTS

I have always been a big believer in the power of storytelling. I have seen the impact stories can have on the minds and hearts of those reading or listening. The journey of writing this book is the first time, however, I experienced the immense power that storytelling holds for the *storyteller*.

When I started writing this, I set out with a somewhat simple goal: to tell the story of Teach For India's journey through the stories of our Fellows, alumni, and students. It is through their stories—through the communities and schools in which they have served—that our journey has unfolded. In the process, though, I have been inspired. I have been moved. At times, I have even been horrified. But perhaps most of all, the stories of our children and alumni—the ones doing this work every single day—have shaken my soul in ways that I'll never quite adequately convey. They have changed me.

Many people have contributed to that journey—and thus to the completion of this book—in different ways, and I am grateful for their efforts.

I am grateful to all the children—particularly Yasmin, Adil and Nandini. I am grateful to you and your parents, friends and neighbours who welcomed me with open arms into your homes and communities. You shared your experiences, your honest ambitions and your deepest fears. I can't tell you how much that meant.

I am grateful to the 3,000 alumni who are the torchbearers of Teach For India. I am grateful to the young men and women among you who spent countless hours with me, recounting your stories of transformation and struggle.

I am grateful to Shaheen and the more than 300 staff

members at Teach For India who have dedicated their lives to building this organization and this movement.

I am grateful to the people who I may not even know but who are champions for this book and this work, helping us spread the light far and wide.

I feel incredibly privileged even to tell this story—to have spent thirteen years serving and learning. I am grateful to the dozens of people who have enabled that—Raj, Dorothy Kitchings, Keith and many more.

I am grateful to the many people who reviewed this book and offered copious amounts of constructive feedback. And most of all, I'm grateful to Anamta Farook, our editor and coordinator, who guided this book to completion.

And, finally, I am grateful to the people who are relentlessly working and searching for the sunshine amidst the greyness. Thank you.

ENDNOTES

1 'India no longer home to the largest number of poor: Study', *Times of India*, 27 June 2018.

2 'Gross enrolment ratio-secondary School from 2006 to 2010', *Open Government Data (OGD) Platform India* <https://data.gov.in/catalog/gross-enrolment-ratio-ger-0> [accessed: 9 August 2018].

3 'All India survey on higher education (2015-16)', New Delhi: Ministry of Human Resource Development, Department of Higher Education, 2016 <http://mhrd.gov.in/sites/upload_files/mhrd/files/statistics/AISHE2015-16.pdf> [accessed: 9 August 2018].

4 Ibid.

5 Ibid.

6 'Welcome to ITI, Jahangirpuri', *Govt. of NCTof Delhi* http://delhi.gov.in/wps/wcm/connect/doit_jahangirpuri_iti/ITI_Jahangirpuri/Home/ [accessed: 9 August 2018].

7 'Education in India: NSS 71st round (January-June 2014)', New Delhi: Ministry of Statistics and Programme Implementation, 2016 <http://mospi.nic.in/sites/default/files/publication_reports/nss_rep_575.pdf> [accessed: 17 March 2018].

8 Vaclav Havel, 'Hope', *Trauma Ministry* <http://www.traumaministry.org/resources/havel-on-hope> [accessed: 9 August 2018].

9 'Inside Asia's largest dumping ground', *CNN*, 5 February 2006 <https://edition.cnn.com/2016/02/05/asia/gallery/mumbai-deonar-garbage-dump/index.html> [accessed: 27 March 2019}.

10 Nergish Sunavala, '57% children stunted in Mumbai's Govandi slum: Survey', *Times of India*, 17 January 2017.

11 Ibid.

12 'Annual Report 2014-15', Apnalaya.

13 'M-Ward Initiative' TISS <http://platinum.tiss.edu/m-ward-initiative/> [accessed: 16 March 2018],

14 Smruti Koppikar, 'Give us homes, give us schools, give us gardens, say residents of Mumbai's poorest slums', *Scroll.in*, 18 February 2017 < https://scroll.in/article/829642/give-us-homes-give-us-schools-give-us-gardens-say-residents-of-mumbais-poorest-slums> {accessed: 27 March 2019].

15 Sunavala, '57% children stunted in Mumbai's Govandi slum: Survey'.

16 Inferred using percentage of children aged 0-14 in total Indian population (Census 2011).

17 'School enrollment, primary (% net)', World Bank <https://data. worldbank.org/indicator/SE.PRM.NENR?locations=IN> [accessed: 27 March 2019].

18 'Annual Status for Education Report (ASER)', New Delhi: ASER Centre, 18 January 2017 < http://img.asercentre.org/docs/Publications/ASER%20 Reports/ASER%202016/aser_2016.pdf> [accessed: 27 March 2019].

19 'Gross enrollment ratio, secondary school, both sexes (%)', United Nations Educational, Scientific, and Cultural Organization (UNESCO) Institute for Statistics <https://data.worldbank.org/indicator/SE.SEC. ENRR?locations=IN> [accessed: 13 March 2018].

20 'Educational statistics at a glance', New Delhi: Ministry of Human Resource Development (MHRD) <http://mhrd.gov.in/sites/upload_files/ mhrd/files/statistics/ESG2016_0.pdf> [accessed: 13 March 2018].

21 Ibid.

22 Ibid.

23 TNN, '32.5% population of city lives in slums,' *Times of India*, 19 January 2011.

24 Ibid.

25 Radheshyam Jadhav, 'Pune growing into city of slums, *Times of India*, 18 December 2007.

26 Nabil Khattab, 'Students' aspirations, expectations and school achievement: what really matters?,' *British Educational Research Journal*, Vol. 41, No. 5, October 2015, pp. 731–48 <https://doi.org/10.1002/ berj.3171> [accessed: 13 March 2018].

27 'Infographic: India's poverty profile infographic', World Bank, 27 May 2016   <http://www.worldbank.org/en/news/infographic/2016/05/27/ india-s-poverty-profile> [accessed: 13 March 2018].

28 'Census of India 2011: Houses, household amenities and assets—figures at a glance', Office of the Registrar General & Census Commissioner, India   <http://censusindia.gov.in/2011census/hlo/Data_sheet/India/ Figures_Glance.pdf> [accessed: 13 March 2018].

29 Gemma Corrigan and Attilio Di Battista, '19 charts that explain India's economic challenge,' World Economic Forum, 5 November 2015 <https://www.weforum.org/agenda/2015/11/19-charts-that-explain- indias-economic-challenge/> [accessed: 13 March 2018].

30 'Census of India 2011: Houses, household amenities and assets—figures at a glance'.

31 'Poverty headcount ratio at $1.90 a day (2011 PPP) (% of population)', World Bank, Development Research Group <https://data.worldbank. org/indicator/SI.POV.DDAY?locations=IN> [accessed: 13 March 2018].

32 'School enrollment, primary (% net)', United Nations Educational, Scientific, and Cultural Organization (UNESCO) Institute for Statistics <https://data.worldbank.org/indicator/SE.PRM.NENR?locations=IN>

[accessed: 13 March 2018].

33 'India country profile', United Nations Educational, Scientific, and Cultural Organization (UNESCO) <https://en.unesco.org/countries/india> [accessed 13 March 2018].

34 Hemali Chhapia, 'Indian students rank 2nd last in global test', *Times of India*, 15 January 2012.

35 Corrigan and Battista, '19 charts that explain India's economic challenge'.

36 'Annual Status of Education Report (Rural) 2017', ASER Centre, 16 January 2018 <http://img.asercentre.org/docs/Publications/ASER%20Reports/ASER%202017/aser2017fullreportfinal.pdf> [accessed: 13 March 2018].

37 Assume eight years as minimally mandated by the RTE (or twelve plus three, i.e. fifteen years if they attend a higher education institution) out of an average of sixty-seven years (average life expectancy in India.

38 'India Skills Report 2017', United Nations Development Programme <http://www.in.undp.org/content/india/en/home/library/poverty/india-skills-report-2017.html> [accessed: 13 March 2018].

39 Yogesh Kumari, 'Over 1 lakh schools in India have just 1 teacher', *Times of India*, 9 August 2016.

40 Radheshyam Jadhav, 'Teachers appoint proxies in govt schools says World Bank study', *Times of India*, 24 April 2018.

41 Nazmul Chaudhury, Jeffrey Hammer, Michael Kremer, Karthik Muralidharan and F. Halsey Rogers, 'Missing in action: teacher and health worker absence in developing countries', *Journal of Economic Perspectives*, Vol. 20, No. 1, Winter 2006, pp. 91–116 <http://siteresources.worldbank.org/INTPUBSERV/Resources/477250-1187034401048/ChaudhuryandothersMIA.pdf> [accessed: 13 March 2018].

42 'India school education vision 2030', Central Square Foundation, December 2014 <http://www.centralsquarefoundation.org/wp-content/uploads/2015/08/India-School-Education-Vision-2030.pdf> [accessed: 13 March 2018].

43 'Singapore: teacher and principal quality', Center on International Education Benchmarking <http://ncee.org/what-we-do/center-on-international-education-benchmarking/top-performing-countries/singapore-overview-2/singapore-teacher-and-principal-quality/> [accessed: 1 May 2017].

44 'Global teacher status index 2018', Varkey Foundation <https://www.varkeyfoundation.org/what-we-do/policy-research/global-teacher-status-index/> [accessed: 1 May 2017].

45 'Higher education in India: Vision 2030', Ernst & Young <http://www.ey.com/Publication/vwLUAssets/Higher-education-in-India-Vision-2030/$FILE/EY-Higher-education-in-India-Vision-2030.pdf> [accessed: 1 May 2017].

46 Eric A. Hanushek and Ludger Woessmann, 'Universal basic skills:

what countries stand to gain', OECD, 13 May 2015 <http://dx.doi.org/10.1787/9789264234833-en> (accessed: 28 March 2019].

47 Subhadra Kumari Chauhan, 'The Queen of Jhansi', Po*em Hunter* <https://www.poemhunter.com/poem/the-queen-of-jhansi/> [accessed: 28 March 2019].

48 Robert J. Marzano, Timothy Waters and Brian A. McNulty, *School Leadership that Works: From Research to Results*, Virginia: Association for Supervision and Curriculum Development and Colourado: Mid-continent Research for Education and Learning, 2005.

49 'How the world's best-performing school systems come out on top', McKinsey & Company, September 2007 <https://www.mckinsey.com/~/media/mckinsey/industries/social%20sector/our%20insights/how%20the%20worlds%20best%20performing%20school%20systems%20come%20out%20on%20top/how_the_world_s_best-performing_school_systems_come_out_on_top.ashx> [accessed: 1 May 2017].

50 Nalori Dhammei Chakma, *Access to Justice for Dalits in India*, Equity Watch, New Delhi: NCDHR, 2015 <https://idsn.org/wp-content/uploads/2015/12/Access-to-Justice-Equity-Watch-2015-report-NCDHR.pdf > [accessed: 1 May 2017].

51 'The Nation's report card: Mathematics 2017', National Assessment of Educational Progress at Grades 4 and 8, p. 16 < https://nces.ed.gov/nationsreportcard/pdf/main2007/2007494.pdf> [accessed: 1 May 2017].

52 Sunavala, '57% children stunted in Mumbai's Govandi slum: Survey'.

53 Corrigan and Battista, '19 charts that explain India's economic challenge'.

54 'Annual status of Education Report (Rural) 2017', ASER Centre, 16 January 2018 <http://img.asercentre.org/docs/Publications/ASER%20Reports/ASER%202017/aser2017fullreportfinal.pdf> [accessed: 1 May 2017].

55 PTI, 'India will be late by 50 years in achieving education goals: UNESCO', *Indian Express*, 5 September 2016.